WISH DOWN THE MOON

Linda Sole titles available from
Severn House Large Print

Amy
Bridget
A Bright New Day
Give me Tomorrow
Kathy
A Rose in Winter

WISH DOWN THE MOON

Linda Sole

Severn House Large Print
London & New York

This first large print edition published in Great Britain 2006 by
SEVERN HOUSE LARGE PRINT BOOKS LTD of
9-15 High Street, Sutton, Surrey, SM1 1DF.
First world regular print edition published 2005 by
Severn House Publishers, London and New York.
This first large print edition published in the USA 2007 by
SEVERN HOUSE PUBLISHERS INC., of
595 Madison Avenue, New York, NY 10022.

British Library Cataloguing in Publication Data

Sole, Linda
  Wish down the moon. - Large print ed. - (The country house)
  1. World War, 1939-1945 - Women - Fiction 2. Large type
  books
  I. Title
  823.9'14 [F]

ISBN-13: 9780727875693
ISBN-10: 0727875698

Printed and bound in Great Britain by
MPG Books Ltd, Bodmin, Cornwall.

One

'Oh, Arthur,' Georgie Bridges said as the bedroom door closed behind their family doctor. 'Why wouldn't you take his advice? If you need tests, surely it would be best to let Benton admit you into hospital for a few days?'

'If my number is up that's it, old girl,' he replied with a grimace. 'I don't particularly want to be pulled about by every Tom, Dick and Harry only to be told, in the end, that there's nothing they can do for me. Besides, this thing runs in the family. We Bridges don't often make old bones.'

A blackbird was trilling outside the window. It had been a beautiful day, but the bedroom was stuffy and smelled of sickness. Arthur had refused to let her open the windows despite the heat.

'Don't, Arthur, please,' Georgie begged and felt the pain nag at her breast as he gave her one of his gentle smiles. Everyone loved Arthur because he was a dear, but he could be stubborn when he chose. 'I hate it when you talk of dying. You're not old.' He was only in his mid fifties but he chose to think of himself as much older and nothing she said

5

would change him.

'I should have snuffed it during the war. I've been living on borrowed time ever since, Georgie – but I've been happy with you and I've no real regrets.'

'You might think about me!'

'As it happens, I am,' he said and gave her an odd look. 'I know you'll grieve for a while, Georgie, but I'm a bit on the ancient side for you and I got you on the rebound. I've always known that. It may all turn out for the best. It's not right that you should be tied to an invalid for the rest of your life. You could find someone else, start over...'

'Oh, Arthur...' Georgie shook her head. Her chest felt as if it were being squeezed and she had to bite her lip to keep back the words he would not want to hear. It was impossible to deny what they both knew was true, of course. She'd been in love with another man and he'd been married. Ben was still married, though Georgie knew that he was unhappy and spent most of his time working in London on his writing, which had become more successful over the years. Benedict Tarleton had had two plays performed and published three books of short stories, besides managing a weekly column for a national newspaper. 'You know that was over long ago. In fact it never really got started.'

'I know you've been faithful to me,' Arthur told her and smiled again. 'You've given me as much of you as you could and I've been content – but you've never been in love with

6

me, old girl. I never expected that and I don't blame you, but it's a fact. When I've gone I want you to get out there and make a life for yourself. You're too young to stay mouldering in the country forever.'

'I'm not mouldering and I like living here. I've been happy with you, though you might not believe it.'

The expression in Arthur's eyes told her that she'd hurt him over the years without meaning to – but she hadn't realized until now. God knows, she'd tried to be a good wife, tried to make his life comfortable, but something had always been missing, and of course he'd known that.

'Will you eat some supper if I send a tray up?'

'Perhaps a sandwich and a glass of warm milk with brandy. Don't trouble yourself, Georgie. I'll ring for Mrs Townsend when I'm ready.'

'Don't shut me out, Arthur – not now.'

She went out and closed the door softly, going downstairs. The tears were very close but she held them back. It was too late for weeping, too late for anything really. Doctor Benton's expression had told her that there wasn't much hope for Arthur, and she felt as if the bottom was dropping out of her world.

She went into the sitting room, picked up a newspaper and tried to concentrate, but the news was so depressing with all the troubles in Europe. Her eyes pricked as she fought against her tears. Arthur seemed to have

7

turned against her, almost as though he was blaming her because his illness had caught up with him too soon.

The church clock was chiming the hour as Georgie heard the stairs creaking and went out into the hall to greet her guest. Everything creaked in this old but much loved house and it was impossible for anyone to come down without announcing their arrival.

'What a charming dress,' she said as the young woman reached the bottom. 'Where did you find that, Beth?'

The hall smelled faintly of flowers, some of it from a bowl of pot-pourri on the well-polished oak hutch placed against the wall just outside Georgie's front parlour, the rest from a large vase of sweet peas that she had picked from her garden earlier.

'Hetty sent it for me from Paris,' Beth Rawlings replied and crossed the hall to kiss her cheek, not from habit or duty but affection. She was rather worried about her friend at the moment; she knew Georgie was struggling to keep her spirits up in the face of her husband's latest illness. 'Isn't it lovely?' She did a little twirl to show off the movement of the beautifully cut dress as it clung lovingly to her slender figure, flaring out at the hem. 'Hetty sometimes designs things for that fashion house, as you know, and Madame Arnoud lets her buy things for next to nothing. This dress was left over from last season but that doesn't bother me in the least.'

They could hear the drone of a light aircraft

8

from the airfield some two miles distant. It seemed to circle overhead for a few minutes and then the noise faded away. Both were aware of a slight tension in the other but neither referred to the noise, which was becoming more frequent of late. It seemed to bring home the threat of the war everyone said was inevitable.

'I should just think not,' Georgie said of the dress. 'I would love to be able to buy something like that myself.'

'If you tell Annabel she might be able to fix it up for you. She visited her sister last year, as you know, because she thought Hetty might want to come home now that she has left Henri, but of course she wouldn't. Annabel isn't thinking of going out again herself at the moment, not as things are, but Hetty said in her last letter that she might come home for a visit with us.'

At seventeen Hetty Tarleton had run away to Paris to live with Henri Claremont, who was a successful artist but a rather selfish man, some years her senior. Pleas from both her brother Ben and her sister had met deaf ears these past nine years. Hetty was settled in Paris and enjoying her life too much to think of giving it up.

'It might be a good idea if she came sooner rather than later,' Georgie said anxiously. 'If this wretched war is on the cards, as everyone says it must be, she could be in serious trouble. But I don't suppose it's any good Annabel telling her that, of course. Hetty was

9

always headstrong. Annabel suspected at the start that Henri would prove unreliable but she couldn't change things. Hetty was in love and Annabel had her own problems at the time.'

They had gravitated into the small but comfortable sitting room. Its furniture was perhaps a little shabby but well tended and familiar, the scents of lavender and beeswax mixing with the fragrance of the pine logs piled in the grate and the copper box next to it. Papers and books lay on various tables, a sherry decanter and glasses took pride of place on the sideboard, and Georgie's knitting was on her chair. Arthur preferred hand-knitted socks to any that could be bought in the shops.

'I know that Hetty can be very stubborn...' Shadows clouded Beth's eyes for a moment as she recalled that some of the problems Annabel had been dealing with at the time of Hetty's elopement were because of her. 'Annabel was afraid that Hetty would be unhappy and I think she was for some months before she finally made up her mind to leave Henri, but although she came home for a few days she wouldn't stay.'

Beth was quite a tall girl, slim and graceful with dark hair and rather serious grey eyes. Her manner sometimes made her seem older than her nineteen years, perhaps because of events that had happened in the past. The old scandal of Alice Rawlings' violent murder had been forgotten by most, but Georgie thought that Beth had been more affected by her mother's death than people realized.

She had been fortunate to have her grandmother, but perhaps more importantly Annabel had taken her into her own family. There were no formal adoption papers but to all intents and purposes Beth was Paul and Annabel Keifer's daughter and as much loved as their own two children, Paula and David.

'When I last heard from Hetty she seemed content enough,' Georgie said thoughtfully. 'But, like everyone else, she's worried that there might be a war.'

'Paul says it's inevitable,' Beth said and wrinkled her smooth brow.

'Yes, Arthur thinks the same. After the last war everyone thought it couldn't happen again, but I'm afraid it will.' Georgie sighed and poured them both a sherry. She took a sip of the golden liquid, her forehead creased by an almost permanent frown of anxiety.

At twenty-eight, she was an attractive woman, though her clothes were a little staid and chosen to match her lifestyle, which was that of a country housewife. However, her hair was cut into a stylish bob and her complexion was creamy, her eyes a soft brown that reflected her feelings only too well.

Beth knew instinctively that the sigh was as much for Arthur's precarious state of health as any worries her friend might have about the probable war with the Germans.

'How is Arthur this evening?' she asked. 'What did the doctor say when he came earlier?'

'Nothing very much,' Georgie admitted. 'Arthur's chest is weak and he gets bouts of chronic bronchitis and that's really all there is to it...' But deep down inside she knew that Arthur was failing and it couldn't be long now.

'Is Arthur coming down for dinner?' Beth asked, interrupting her thoughts.

'No, not tonight,' Georgie said and forced herself to smile. She took another sip of her sherry and glanced at herself in the mirror over the fireplace. She knew she was an attractive woman, not beautiful; she had never been conventionally pretty, but as a young woman she had been full of life and fun. She had become more serious over the years, recently because of her husband's failing health, and for other reasons that she preferred not to remember. 'I'm sorry as it's your last evening with us but I know Arthur would be pleased if you would pop in later and have a word. He has been ordered to stay where he is for a few days, and for once he's doing as he's told.'

'Of course I'll go in and see him,' Beth promised. Arthur was a dear man and she was fond of him. 'Does Geoffrey know his father isn't well?'

'Arthur doesn't want him to know,' Georgie said. 'He's away with a friend from his school at the moment, but he'll come home for a couple of days before he goes back to boarding school. Besides, he can't do anything to help, and Arthur is unable to do any of the things they used to enjoy together. They are both keen cricket fans, you know. Arthur played for the local team on Sundays until this year...'

'It's such a shame,' Beth said. 'Arthur isn't old really, is he?'

'He's fifty-five,' Georgie replied. 'I am twenty-eight this month. I suppose the gap was too wide, but it's been a good marriage in many ways.'

She would miss him terribly if the worst happened, Georgie thought and blinked back the tears that threatened. Perhaps she wasn't in love with him, but she did love him very much. No one could help loving Arthur.

She wandered over to the sitting-room window to gaze out at the garden, which was always a riot of colour in the summer. She was a keen gardener and she had found solace working in her flower beds when she was first married, when forbidden thoughts of Ben had come to her all too often. But she had conquered her regret, fought her way to a kind of happiness – and now it looked as if her secure life was going to be ripped away.

Georgie raised her head proudly. She wasn't going to give way to self-pity. No sense in that. She had chosen her life, chosen Arthur as her husband, no one had forced her. She hadn't regretted it despite small disappointments over the years and she wouldn't start now. Turning, she smiled at Beth who was watching her with those big, serious, grey eyes.

'So, what are you going to do with yourself now that you've finished college?'

'I've only been to tech,' Beth said. 'All I'm trained for is secretarial work so I suppose that's what I'll do – unless there is a war, of course. I think I shall apply to join one of the women's services then.'

'Didn't Annabel say she would like you to work as a receptionist at the hotel with her?'

'Yes...' Beth looked doubtful. 'Don't you think that's a bit too easy, Georgie? Annabel has looked after me since I was nine and I think it's time I stood on my own feet, don't you?'

'Obviously you do,' Georgie said. 'I think Annabel might be disappointed, but it's your life. I think you should talk to her about it though, make her understand that you want some independence.'

'I know it sounds ungrateful, but I can't lean on her forever. Besides, if there is a war I could be more useful elsewhere – don't you think?'

'I think we should have our meal,' Georgie said and put down her empty sherry glass. 'My advice is to decide what you want to do with your life, Beth, and then talk to Annabel. If you simply announce your intention to go off somewhere she might be hurt and you wouldn't want that, would you?'

'You know I wouldn't,' Beth agreed. 'Annabel has been like a mother to me and I love

14

her, but...'

'She is a little overpowering sometimes,' Georgie finished for her and laughed. 'She takes after her mother, though she would be horrified if anyone said that, and she isn't a bit like Lady Tarleton in most ways. She isn't selfish or thoughtless but she is a successful business woman and she does rather take charge sometimes.'

'That's exactly it,' Beth said and smiled fondly. 'Annabel is so good at running things that she organizes us all – Paul too sometimes. He laughs at her and does exactly what he wants of course, but I feel obliged.'

'Annabel would hate it if she realized,' Georgie said thoughtfully. 'She doesn't mean to try and run your life, Beth. She probably still thinks you're a little girl and is trying to make everything easy for you.'

'Yes, I think that is the exact problem,' Beth agreed. 'She is only being kind and protective, but sometimes I feel smothered. And I can't say anything because I'm afraid of hurting her.'

'Something of a dilemma,' Georgie said with a smile. 'Well, I think you should very gently tell Annabel that you want to spread your wings a bit. I shouldn't be surprised if she understands more than you imagine. And now we really must have our meal or Mrs Townsend will be on the warpath!'

'War imminent! Children evacuated from London!'

15

Beth shivered as she heard the strident tones of the newspaper boy standing outside the railway station. She'd had to change trains in London and having an hour to spare had gone for a quick shopping trip. Now she saw that the station was crowded. A party of young children were being herded by a harassed looking woman, who was obviously in charge of getting them to their destination in the country. Though most of the travellers appeared to be young men; several of them dressed in army uniforms. Some were saying goodbye to family or girlfriends; others were obviously together and in a boisterous mood.

As she watched them jostling and shoving each other in a good-natured manner, she wondered if one or two had been drinking a little too much. Or perhaps it was a mixture of excitement and nerves. One of them noticed her glance their way and a loud wolf whistle made her turn her head aside, her cheeks pink.

It wasn't the first time she'd been whistled at, but being a reserved girl, except with her close friends, she didn't particularly care for it and decided to make sure she entered a different carriage to the one picked by the party of boisterous young men.

When the train arrived, Beth chose a carriage already occupied by a woman and her son and another young man, who was dressed in the uniform of an army officer. He didn't look at her as she sat down and Beth settled herself to read a magazine she had bought.

However, the train had a corridor rather than being individual closed carriages and she heard the laughter of the noisy young men as they made their way along the train, but thankfully by-passed her carriage.

'Terrible news, isn't it?' the woman sitting opposite said to Beth, obliging her to lower her magazine. 'All those children being evacuated. I shouldn't want my Marcus to be shipped off to strangers like that. I'm taking him to my sister's and I'm going to stay put until all this nonsense is over.'

'I think that's a good idea,' Beth said. 'But I think you may be in for a long visit.'

'Oh, don't say that!' the woman exclaimed. 'My husband says once they get to grips with the Germans it will all be over in a matter of months. He joined up a couple of days ago, but he's sure he'll be home for Christmas. That's what Daddy said, isn't it, Marcus?'

'I want to go and fight the Germans,' the lad said giving her a mutinous look. 'Don't want to stay with Auntie Peggy.'

'You'll like it when you get there. It's nice in the country.' She nodded at Beth. 'Ask that young lady – it's nice in the country, isn't it?'

'I like it,' Beth replied, eyeing the sullen lad doubtfully. 'You'll enjoy exploring and climbing trees I dare say.'

His mother looked horrified. 'For goodness sake, don't put ideas in his head. Climbing trees is much too dangerous.'

'Want to go to the toilet,' Marcus said. 'And I feel sick.'

'You went before we came,' his harassed mother said and frowned at him. 'I suppose I'd better take you.' She looked at Beth. 'Would you mind keeping an eye on my parcels? I don't want to cart them all the way to the toilet and back.'

'Yes, of course,' Beth said and smiled as the lady went out.

She glanced at the man in army uniform sitting opposite and he grinned at her. 'I wouldn't be in her shoes,' he said. 'That young chap has been spoiled if you ask me.'

'Yes, I think he has,' Beth agreed and looked down at her magazine. She was just beginning to get interested in one of the articles when the door was thrust back and three of the noisy young men from the platform entered.

'Don't mind if we sit here, do you, darlin'?' one of them asked with a cheeky grin.

'Two of the seats are taken,' Beth said, 'but there are two available.'

'Thanks, darlin',' the soldier replied. 'That means you're the extra, Charlie. Get orf down the train and we'll see yer later, mate.'

'Who are you givin' yer orders?' the other replied but seeing that neither of his friends were about to oblige by giving up the seats they had taken, he scowled and went out.

The soldier with the cheeky grin had chosen to sit next to Beth, his companion sitting in the corner near the door. She felt the pressure of the soldier's warm body as he deliberately pressed his thigh up against hers.

18

She resisted looking at him, returning to her magazine, although it was only a pretence now, because she was conscious of the leering looks the soldier was sending her way.

'All on your own then, darlin'?' he asked. 'Me and me mates are on our way to Torquay. We've got a couple of days leave before we join our units see – going to make the most of our time, if you get my meaning?'

'Really,' Beth said, her heart sinking as she realized that she would have to endure his presence all the way home. 'That will be nice for you.'

'Yeah – find ourselves a few girls, have a bevy or two,' he said. 'Do you come from round there, darlin'?'

'I think that is my business,' Beth said frostily. 'And I would prefer it if you didn't call me darling. I don't know you.'

'Hoity-toity type, are we?' he said and reached across her to open the window on the door. 'Let a bit of fresh air in, shall we?'

Beth ignored him and tried to read her magazine once more. He pressed his leg even harder against hers, then placed a hand on her knee and squeezed it.

'Please don't do that!'

'Only a bit of fun, darlin',' he said leering at her. 'Nothing wrong with that, is there?'

'Remove your hand from the young lady's knee, private,' a clipped order came from the army officer sitting opposite. 'If you can't behave, I suggest you take a walk down the corridor and find yourself suitable company.'

'And who are you when you're at bleedin' home?' The soldier had hardly glanced at the man when he entered the carriage, but as the officer placed his cap on his head he blenched and stood up, saluting. 'Sorry, sir. Didn't realize you were an officer. We'll take ourselves orf. Come on, Fred. Sorry, miss. Didn't realize you were with him.'

As the pair departed, the officer smiled at Beth and leaned across to offer his hand. 'Captain Drew Bryant – short for Andrew. I'm sorry they were troubling you – high spirits, I'm afraid.'

Beth took his hand, liking his firm cool grasp. 'Thank you for your help. I don't suppose he meant any harm, but I prefer not to get involved in things like that...'

'I should think not, nice girl like you,' Drew said. 'I suspect our hero has been celebrating a little too much.'

'Yes, I did wonder when I saw them on the station. I expect it's a mixture of nerves and excitement. I'm Beth Rawlings by the way. I'm going all the way to Torquay so I was afraid I would have his company the whole journey.'

'Couldn't have that,' Drew said and got up to sit next to her, leaving a decent space between them. 'Just in case some of his friends decide to join us. I'm going to Torquay too – to stay at Kendlebury, which is an estate just outside the resort.'

'Oh yes, I know it very well. I visit often.'

'Do you? Then perhaps you may know the

20

family? Harry Kendle and his wife Jessie – and their two sons?'

'Yes. Jessie is a special friend of ours. She and Annabel, my adoptive mother, have known each other for years.' She laughed as she saw the expression in his eyes. 'It is a small world, isn't it?'

Drew looked amazed. 'It isn't surprising that you know the estate, of course, because Kendlebury is pretty well known these days, because of Jessie's efforts to bring in the visitors. But to know the family so well...' He shook his head. 'Jessie is marvellous, isn't she? The way she turned that estate around almost single-handed!'

'Yes, I've always thought so. Harry would be lost without her.'

'I know. Well, that makes it much easier. You see, I'm a friend of their eldest son – Jonathan Kendle. But I'm also a sort of cousin of Harry Kendle's sister's husband. Would you happen to know that side of the family at all?'

'Oh yes, of course,' Beth said and laughed, relaxing as she realized who he must be. 'You're related to Georgie's father, aren't you? Georgie Bridges – she was a Barrington.' Beth was thoughtful for a moment. 'Now you mention it, I think I've heard her mention your family a couple of times. I didn't make the connection at once because I don't think she has ever spoken of you.'

'I doubt if she would. We're very distant cousins,' Drew admitted. 'Several times re-moved as far as I can make out. The families don't know each other well, but I met Jonathan at boarding school and we became friends. He rang and asked me to come down for a few days before I join my unit. He's a year or so younger, but I know he's hoping to join up shortly and wants to talk about the possibilities.'

'Jessie won't be very happy about that,' Beth said and sighed. 'Oh, it's all so horrible, isn't it? Do you believe it will all be over in a few months? I can't see how it can be – look what happened last time.'

'We're more advanced militarily than we were then,' Drew said but he looked serious, his grey eyes the colour of slate. She noticed that a lock of dark hair had fallen forward over his brow and felt a sudden urge to brush it back out of his eyes. Drew did that himself. 'This will have to go when I get back to my proper job. I've been off for a few weeks, seconded to deskwork for some bigwig in London. Now I've got a couple of weeks leave before I move on to further training.'

'Are you a career soldier?' Beth asked. 'You haven't joined up recently, have you?'

'The army has always been my life,' he said. 'It runs in the family all the way back to Wellington's era from what I can make out of the archives. I'm the younger son and that's what we do.'

'I think a lot of the gentry are like that,' Beth said. 'I've been brought up with a rather privileged set but I don't really belong – my mother was an actress.'

'Really?' His eyes lit up. 'Now that's splendid. I wish I had the talent. I always admire anyone with real talent.'

'Yes, so I,' Beth agreed. 'Annabel's sister is an artist. I always wanted to paint but I knew years ago that I'm not good enough – so I'm just a secretary, or I shall be once I can find a job. I was at college until this summer.'

'We can't do without secretaries,' Drew said and smiled at her. 'Is Annabel a friend of yours?'

'She's a sort of adopted mother. Mine died when I was not quite ten and Annabel took me into her family.' Why was she telling him all this? She wasn't sure, except that he was the kind of person she felt she could talk to in a way she seldom did to anyone.

'I'm sorry you lost your mother so young. That's rotten luck. I should be devastated if anything happened to mine. I'm afraid I've been spoiled all my life.'

'It hasn't affected your manners,' Beth said and laughed softly. 'Your mother must have brought you up properly.'

'Oh yes, she did,' he agreed. 'All six of us. There are two sons and four daughters – and all of them married apart from me. I'm the baby of the family, you see.'

'Ah yes, I do see,' Beth said. What a pleasant young man he was, she thought, and was a little disappointed when the woman and her sulky son came back to the carriage.

'Marcus, stop fidgeting,' the woman said and glanced across at Beth, noting the change

23

in seating. 'We had to fight our way back; the corridor is full of rowdy soldiers.'

'Yes, the train is rather crowded,' Beth agreed. 'I think more soldiers got on at the last stop.'

As if to prove her point two young men came in and took the spare seats, both of them armed with newspapers, which they immediately began to read.

Drew Bryant lapsed into silence beside her, and Beth went back to her magazine, managing to read the article she had started, though she wasn't truly interested.

It was about an hour later when the train drew into a station and the other occupants of the carriage got off, Marcus whining and grizzling at being forced to carry some of the parcels.

'I think the crush has finished now,' Drew said glancing out of the window. 'There were only a handful of new passengers to get on this time.'

'Yes, I noticed that,' Beth agreed. 'I suppose it was just the crush in London and everyone has gone their separate ways now.'

'I'm staying with Jonathan's family for five days,' Drew said, hesitating slightly. 'I don't suppose you would consider coming out with me – tomorrow?'

'I...' She was surprised and blushed but then found that she rather liked the idea. He was such an easy companion; she'd been drawn to him at once. 'Yes, I should like that very much. I live at Rowntree House Hotel, which is nearer to Torquay than Kendlebury, but easy enough to find.'

'I think I've heard of it. Some of my mother's friends stayed there and said how pleasant it was – almost like visiting with friends apparently.'

'That's the way Annabel runs things,' Beth told him. 'She really likes people and she enjoys having them to stay. It is more of a private country house than a hotel, and we have the same people staying every year.'

'Sounds wonderful,' he said. 'Better than some of the places I've been unfortunate enough to stay at. I'll pick you up at about twelve then and we'll go for lunch somewhere, then take a spin in the car I hope to borrow.'

'I have my own if you can't manage it,' Beth said. 'Annabel insisted I learn to drive as soon as I was old enough and I was given a small car for my birthday this year. I drive myself most of the time but Georgie's home is a long way and Annabel thought I would be better to go by train.'

'I think Jonathan will lend me something. He told me they have an assortment of vehicles about the place and there's usually something available.'

'How are you going to get there?'

'By taxi I think,' he said. 'Are you being met – or can I give you a lift?'

'We can share the taxi if you like,' Beth said, 'and I'll pay my share. It will be better for both of us that way.'

'Fine, if that's what you want,' he said easily, then changing topic, added, 'I wonder how long it will take them to get the *Wizard of Oz* over here. I've heard they are getting large crowds to see it in New York...'

Beth liked the way he changed the subject. In fact she liked him more the more time she stayed speaking to him and was grateful to the rowdy young soldiers who had brought them together. Had it not been for that incident they might have parted without doing more than nodding in passing.

'Yes, I should like to see that film,' she said. 'I like the cinema – do you?'

'There you are, Beth,' Annabel said as she entered the private sitting room that evening. 'I heard the taxi arrive and thought it must be you, as we haven't any new guests due at the moment. Did you have a lovely time at Georgie's?'

'Yes. I always do,' Beth replied. 'You know I'm fond of her and Arthur – but he isn't at all well. I think she is very worried about him.'

'Yes, I know,' Annabel said and wrinkled her brow. She was an exceptionally attractive woman with sleek, pale blonde hair, which she wore in a shoulder-length bob. Her clothes, shoes, makeup were all immaculate and she looked what she was, a successful woman in her own right, confident and happy. 'She rang me earlier to say you were on your way. She also told me that the doctor wanted Arthur to go into hospital for tests but he refused.'

'He thinks it's a waste of time,' Beth said and looked sad. 'Apparently, the weakness runs in the family and he doesn't believe the doctors can help him. Says he doesn't want to be pulled about for nothing.'

'He might think of Georgie! What is she going to do if he dies?'

'I suppose he believes she will get over it,' Beth said. 'I know she is very upset, but it wasn't exactly a love match, was it – not like you and Paul?'

'No, that's true,' Annabel admitted and wrinkled her brow. 'I believe there was someone else she loved but he was married, and Georgie wasn't the kind to break up a marriage – nor was he.'

In fact the man in question was Annabel's own brother. Georgie had told her about it at the time, but she had never spoken of it to anyone else and didn't intend to reveal any details now.

Beth nodded. 'Well, divorce isn't pleasant, is it? Look at all the fuss they made over the Duke of Windsor and Mrs Simpson. I always felt so sorry for his brother – having all that work thrust on his shoulders because they wouldn't let Edward marry her.'

'The Duke of Windsor made his choice,' Annabel said, an odd look in her eyes. There was a time when she too had had to make her choice. 'It was a question of love or duty and he chose love. I can't blame him, but like you

27

I thought they should have let him marry the woman he wanted and still be the King – but that's only my opinion. The people who mattered didn't agree.'

'Well, that's all over now,' Beth said. 'We've got worse things to worry about, haven't we?'

'You mean the war?' Annabel looked anxious. 'It's coming and soon, I expect. I don't like it, Beth – but there's nothing we can do to stop it. I'm worried about Hetty. I tried to telephone her this morning and couldn't get through. Once the war starts we shall catch it in this country – but think how much worse it will be for her in France.'

'Surely she will try to get home before anything happens?' Beth said and looked at Annabel anxiously. She had made up her mind to tell Annabel this evening that she wanted to look for a job elsewhere. However, seeing how upset she was about the coming war and the very real possibility that her sister was going to be caught up in it, she knew she couldn't add to Annabel's problems. 'Try not to worry just yet. Knowing Hetty, she could turn up on the doorstep at any moment.'

'Yes, that's very true,' Annabel agreed. 'But Hetty is so headstrong. She might decide she is going to stay on in France whatever the Germans do...' A little shiver ran through her. 'I am worried, Beth, I can't deny it – but I'm going to try not to think about it too much.' She smiled at the girl she loved like her own daughter. 'We've been looking forward to having you home. Paula was asking earlier if it was really today that you were coming. I could hardly get her to bed, though she went in the end.'

'I've been looking forward to seeing you all,' Beth said and smothered her sigh. It looked as though she was trapped for the time being at least. 'I've bought her a present – some pretty shoes I saw in London – but if she's asleep she can have them in the morning.'

'Yes, save them until tomorrow,' Annabel advised. 'Otherwise she will want to wear them in bed. You know how she loves new shoes!'

'That's why I couldn't resist these,' Beth said and went to give Annabel an affectionate kiss.

She knew she was lucky to be a part of this family. They were loving and kind and she cared for them all, but she had hoped for a little independence when she left college.

'Did you make any nice friends while you were staying with Georgie?'

'No, not really,' Beth said. 'Georgie didn't entertain much, except for a few old friends of Arthur's. Besides, I was happy just to wander about by myself and relax. However ... I did meet someone rather nice on the train coming home. It was quite a coincidence. His name is Captain Andrew Bryant, and he is a distant cousin of Georgie's father. He is going to stay at Kendlebury for a few days – and he's coming to take me out for lunch tomorrow.'

'How odd that you should meet like that,

but fortunate. It will make a pleasant change for you to go out with a young man, Beth,' Annabel said. 'You mustn't consider yourself tied here every moment. If you want time off I shall understand.'

'Thank you. You are always so generous, but I want to do my share...' While I stay here, she added silently. That wouldn't be forever, but she would wait a while before she broached the subject with Annabel. With any luck they would hear from Hetty soon and then they might all be able to stop worrying.

After all, there was no sense in Hetty staying in France if there was going to be a war, was there?

'But it makes no sense for you to stay here in Paris, *ma chérie*,' Madame Arnoud said and spread her hands in an expression of disbelief. 'You are English, not French. You should go home, get away from this madness before it is too late. Believe me, I am old enough to remember the last time the Germans paid us a visit. It was not pleasant.'

Although well into her middle years the Frenchwoman had a stylish air and was still attractive, her clothes, makeup and dark brown hair immaculate.

'But I feel more French than English these days,' Hetty replied, wrinkling her nose at the older woman's comment. 'I have so many friends here and I love the life I'm leading – why should I give it all up?'

'Because the Germans will make you suffer

if they catch you out,' Madame Arnoud said. 'You will probably be sent to an internment camp, that's if you're not shot as a spy.'

'Perhaps they won't invade...'

'Pouff!' The Frenchwoman snorted her disbelief. 'It is more likely that pigs will sprout wings. They will come, Hetty, believe me – it is merely a question of when.'

They were sitting in Madame Arnoud's private parlour drinking wine, something they often did in the evenings when Hetty called to discuss her latest designs or simply to talk about what she had seen or done. They were good friends and had been for some years, since Hetty had first approached her rather tentatively with a design for an evening gown.

'Yes, perhaps,' Hetty agreed. 'But there's time yet, madame. I shall think about leaving when it becomes inevitable. Not that I've any idea of what I'll do when I get back to England. It will be difficult to settle anywhere else but Paris. Oh, it's such a shame that wars have to happen! Why must the Germans be so awful? Why can't they just leave us alone?'

'If we knew the answer to that the world would be a different place,' Madame Arnoud said and offered a world-weary smile. 'It is men who make wars, *ma chérie*, and we all know about them, do we not?'

Hetty laughed. At twenty-six years of age she had matured into a woman of some style, her hair a rich honey blonde that she wore long and in soft waves rather like Marlene

31

Dietrich, the German film star with the gravelly voice, who had first made her name in the 1930 film, *The Blue Angel*.

When at the age of seventeen Hetty had eloped to France to be with Henri, Hetty had been pretty rather than beautiful, but now she was stunning. Many of the artists she knew begged to paint her portrait, but these days she preferred to use the brush herself and earned a precarious living drawing quick sketches of the tourists; she supplemented her meagre income with the work she did for Madame Arnoud.

'Yes, of that there is no doubt,' Hetty agreed. She had learned how selfish a man could be the hard way, weeping bitter tears the first time she'd discovered Henri had been unfaithful to her with his latest model. He had told her he was sorry afterwards, swearing that the girl meant nothing and that it was her he loved. Hetty had forgiven him but it had happened again, and again, until she woke up one day to discover that he no longer meant anything to her. He was the one who had wept when she walked out on him, begging her to reconsider.

It had been hard at first without Henri, difficult to find work, her income barely enough to keep body and soul together, and lonely too. She had thought about going home to England, but something inside her had refused to give in – just as she had refused all the offers from Henri's friends to take his place in her life. Whether that had been from pride, a lack of interest sexually in the men themselves or her fierce independence she had never been sure, but she had remained alone. And gradually she had found a new life and new friends; she had won respect for her own work, both as an artist on the Left Bank and as a dress designer.

She could have worked fulltime for Madame Arnoud, who had become both a friend and like the mother Hetty felt she'd never had, if she'd wanted to be a model or a venduse, but neither of those things appealed to her. Besides, she now earned enough to pay the rent of her little apartment and to be able to buy food and clothes. She had no interest in more and found the relaxed, pleasant way of living suited her nature.

She might not always have been happy, but her life was busy, interesting, and she made sure it stayed that way. Love was something she'd learned to do without when she was a small child. Her father had been a kindly but remote figure, her mother cold and severe; both Ben and Annabel had been generous and kind but they were twins and closer to each other. In the early years she had wept bitter tears over her mother's lack of affection, but then she had come to realize that it was something lacking in Lady Tarleton: she was a woman incapable of loving anyone other than herself and treated Annabel even worse than Hetty. Becoming independent and resourceful beyond her years, Hetty had found the best times were when she was in the kitchen with cook and the maids who always had a soft word and a smile for her.

Madame Arnoud was still talking to her, scolding her, giving her the advice she knew she ought to take but was stubbornly resisting. Here, in France, she had a life but there was nothing waiting for her in England.

'You are foolish,' Madame Arnoud told her. 'Too stubborn for your own good, *ma chérie*. Paris will not be the same under the heel of the invader. You have no idea how bad it can be. I am thinking of closing my business and going to my sister in the south. If I were not French I would leave the country altogether. You have no real ties here, Hetty. Take my warning – go home while you can.'

'I shall think about it,' Hetty promised, put down her empty wine glass and stood up. 'Now I must go, my friend. I have an appointment for this evening.'

'With a man I hope?'

Hetty shook her head and laughed. She had not taken a lover since leaving Henri and had no intention of doing so for the moment; there was no one who stirred her the way he had at the beginning, and once bitten twice shy.

'With a group of friends. We shall drink wine, listen to music and talk of how the world should be put to rights.'

'Pouff!' Madame Arnoud grimaced. 'Youth is wasted on the young. You have no idea how to live. Find yourself a rich man and marry him, Hetty – preferably an American who will

34

take you somewhere safe and look after you. Americans make good husbands; they are polite and they work hard. The French are too lazy. Be a Frenchman's mistress if you like, never marry one.'

Hetty laughed softly, kissed her friend's cheek and shook her head over that particular piece of advice as she let herself out of the back door into the warmth of a late summer evening. The heat had been oppressive during the day but now it was pleasant, the fragrance of flowers scenting the air. Drifting above the scent of the flowers was a smell that Hetty loved, the smell of the city itself: coffee, fresh pastries and something that was uniquely Paris but indefinable.

How could she leave this – the sunshine and colour, the vibrant city she had adored from her first moment here – and go home to the bleakness of England?

She remembered England as being bleak, though she knew that wasn't entirely fair. It was her home and the woman who had dominated her childhood that had tainted her memories of that country. It wasn't like that at Annabel's home, of course. Her sister's hotel was warm, welcoming and beautiful, furnished with antiques, run efficiently but with all the comforts of home for the guests. And the garden was peaceful. Yes, she had been tempted to stay for a while when she'd visited, but Paris was in her blood and it had called her back. This city was her home, these people her people.

She hated the idea of an invasion. It was hurtful to imagine what it might be like, to think of the people she knew so well being treated as a conquered nation.

Perhaps it wouldn't happen that way. Not everyone held Madame Arnoud's opinion. The newspapers were still talking of France holding firm against any threat, and her friends were full of optimism that the Maginot Line would hold; but the mood of most older people she knew was gloomy. They seemed to think it only a matter of time before resistance crumbled and the Germans marched into Paris as they had in the first World War.

Hetty knew that already many art treasures had been evacuated to the safety of secret hiding places. Many tried to be cheerful but there were glum faces and an atmosphere of apprehension seemed to hang over the city.

The war was inevitable now that the English Government had declared they would fight, of course. Hetty thought about her sister and realized she must write to her, tell her that for the moment she was fine, but if things became difficult she would try to get back.

Two

The few days Drew had planned to spend at Kendlebury flew by. He extended it by another three days, but then told Beth that he couldn't stay any longer.

'I have to go home and see my mother,' he said. 'I doubt we'll get much leave for a while now. I've been expecting a phone call to say this one has been cut short but it hasn't happened, thank goodness.'

Beth was aware of a sinking sensation inside but she smiled and hid her disappointment.

'Yes, of course you must visit your mother. She would be upset if you didn't.' The war had been made official but, although young men were queuing to join up, nothing much seemed to be happening yet. 'When are you leaving?'

'I rang my mother this morning and told her I'd be home tomorrow.'

'So this is our last evening.' Beth swallowed hard. The prospect of parting was more painful than she'd imagined it would be. 'It's been fun. I shall miss you.'

'Will you?' There was an urgent note in his voice suddenly. 'I shall miss you, Beth. I like you an awful lot – more than any girl I know actually.'

Her cheeks were pink as she looked at him, her heart racing like a young colt in spring grass. 'I like you more than any other friend I've had, Drew.' Not that she'd had any real boyfriends before him. She wasn't the type to flirt and had usually gone out in a crowd.

'There isn't anyone else around then?'

'You know there isn't. I wouldn't have gone out with you if there had been.'

'No, I thought not.' He was a little hesitant as he turned to her in the car; stroking her hair gently. 'Would you mind if I kissed you?'

'I think I should like it very much – if you want to?'

'Of course I want to. I've been longing to ever since we met on the train, but I didn't want to seem too forward. You're a nice girl, Beth, and I'd like us to be special. I don't intend to rush things if you're not ready. After all, we don't know each other well.'

He was good looking, intelligent and pleasant to be with, and it seemed that he liked her too. Beth was swept along on a tide of excitement.

'I feel I've known you all my life. Please kiss me, Drew. I want you to, truly.'

Drew reached out for her, drawing her into his arms. His kiss was gentle, hesitant and sweet. Beth trembled inside. She'd never felt this way before and was a little nervous, unsure of how to react. He drew back and looked at her, a tender smile on his lips, aware of her innocence and uncertainty.

'We won't take things too fast, darling. I think I'm falling in love with you and I hope you feel the same way?' She nodded, feeling too shy to say anything for the moment. 'This isn't just a fling. I want to get to know you better, Beth, and one day soon, when we're both sure, I should like us to talk about marriage.'

'Oh Drew...' Beth's face lit up and she looked truly beautiful. 'I didn't dare to hope you might feel the same way about me, though I've felt it for a few days now. I'm not pretty or clever or anything.'

'You're special to me. I think you're lovely, intelligent and warm – all the things I want from my girl. Promise me you will write to me? I can't let my mother down, and it's too soon to throw you into the lions' den, but I'll ring you as often as I can – and perhaps you can meet me in London for a weekend. We'll spend my next leave together.'

'Yes, that would be wonderful,' Beth said, delighted by his plan. 'I've been thinking of joining one of the women's services, doing something useful. Only I have to talk to Annabel first. She's so pleased to have me at the hotel and I feel I shall be letting her down.'

'I like Annabel,' Drew said and ran a finger down her cheek. 'Talk to her, Beth. I'm sure she will understand. Now – what do you want to do on our last night? Go to the pictures or for a meal?'

'We could go to the pictures and cuddle in

the back row,' Beth said and then smiled at him. 'But why don't we go into Torquay, have a walk along the cliffs and then have a drink and a sandwich at the pub? We don't want to waste a moment; time is too precious tonight.'

'That's a wonderful idea,' he agreed. 'We should be able to find a secluded spot for a few kisses, don't you think?'

'Yes, that's exactly what I thought.' She gurgled with laughter, the happiness bubbling inside her as he gave her a broad grin. Drew was so nice. He made her feel warm and secure and cared for. She couldn't believe she'd been lucky enough to meet him and that the feeling between them had been mutual from the start.

Beth had always been a little sceptical about love at first sight, thinking it something that happened only in books or at the pictures, but she'd changed her mind these past few days. It could happen and it did, and it had happened to her.

Arthur was sitting in his favourite chair by the window in the front parlour as Georgie wheeled her bicycle round to the back porch. She was a little late coming back from the meeting at the church hall that evening and her husband would be wondering where she had got to.

The local women had wanted to know what they could do to help the war effort and the Vicar had organized the meeting to set up a committee. There had been all kinds of suggestions as to what they might do; from knitting socks for the troops to hospital visiting when the wounded started to come home. Georgie was sure that once things got under way more useful ideas would present themselves, but for the moment everything seemed to be in limbo.

Nothing much was happening yet. Young men were signing up all the time, of course, and children were being evacuated to the country, but otherwise it all seemed to be taking place abroad and the war still seemed distant. That was a good thing, of course, and she lived in dread of what was to come, but the waiting was bad enough in itself.

She took off her jacket in the hall and went into the sitting room, noticing that the fire she'd lit earlier had almost gone out. Arthur hadn't noticed as usual; he was probably asleep in his chair.

'I thought they would never stop talking,' she said and went over to put a log on the fire. 'Shall I pop the kettle on – or would you rather have a cup of hot milk and brandy?'

Arthur didn't answer. Georgie turned to look at him, feeling a sudden chill at the nape of her neck. He was sitting very still – too still. She knew before she touched him that he had gone. His eyes were closed. He seemed to be asleep. Very peaceful. Perhaps that was all death was, she thought, a final sleep from which one didn't wake.

She felt the sting of tears but blinked them

away, feeling a spurt of anger suddenly. Why did it have to happen while she was at that wretched meeting? She hadn't wanted to leave him alone that evening but he'd insisted.

'You should go,' he'd told her. 'You haven't been out much for ages. It will do you good, old girl. I'll be fine here. I've got the radio and my paper if I want it. I'll just sit quietly by the window and watch for you to come home.'

And that's what he'd done. She'd seen him sitting there as she cycled up the drive but she'd thought he was asleep. His death wasn't unexpected but it was a shock just the same. A part of her was angry with him for leaving so abruptly. There were so many things left unsaid between them. She had waited for the right moment, but she'd waited too long.

'I did love you,' she said fiercely. 'Not in the way you wanted perhaps, but as much as I could. Oh, damn you, Arthur! Why did you ask me to marry you? You knew I could only give you second best. If you hadn't asked I wouldn't have made you unhappy – and I never meant to do that. You must have known I tried my best.'

But that was probably what had hurt him, she thought, the fact that she'd had to try. She had never been spontaneous in bed, always responding out of duty rather than love, lying there afterwards feeling empty because it meant nothing to her – and Arthur had known. Of course he'd known. He wasn't a fool! He was a loving, gentle man and she hadn't deserved him. It had been unfair to marry him knowing she wanted someone else.

It hurt too much to look at him sitting there, quiet and decent and kind, just as he'd been in life; it made her feel guilty.

'You always knew. I was honest with you from the start.'

But she shouldn't have married him. She'd known that on their wedding night.

She left him and went out into the hall to make some phone calls. Later, the tears would come and the grief. For now, there were things she had to do – the last she would ever be able to do for him.

Beth came downstairs with a smile on her face. She was remembering the last kiss Drew had given her, more passionate than any before, his arms lingering around her before he could bring himself to leave.

'I'll phone you from home,' he promised. 'I want you to remember tonight, Beth. We're going to have many more nights like this, I promise you.'

Annabel was just coming from her private sitting room as Beth reached the main reception area, her face wearing an anxious frown.

'I was going to come up and find you,' she said. 'I need to talk to you for a moment – in the office. It's private.'

Beth wondered at her expression and her tone. Had she displeased Annabel in some way? She stood silently just inside the office

43

door, waiting.

'I've just had Georgie on the phone,' Annabel said. 'It's bad news I'm afraid. Arthur died last night and naturally she is devastated. She has asked if I will go up to Yorkshire and stay for a while, and I've said yes – but we're a bit short handed because some of the girls have gone off to do war work. Shirley gave notice this morning and you know Valerie went yesterday. Would you hold the fort for me, Beth? I know you would have liked to go up to Georgie's yourself, but we can't both leave at once. Especially with Paul in America. He has business contacts over there and needs to visit every now and then. It wouldn't be as bad if he was here, but things are difficult at the moment.'

'Yes, of course,' Beth said because she couldn't possibly refuse. She would have liked to see Georgie herself, but she knew that at a time like this she would need Annabel. They had been friends for years and understood each other well. Besides, Beth had only just come back from a visit; it was obviously Annabel who must go. 'Yes, you go and don't give the hotel a thought. I can manage until Paul gets home.'

'I expect him home next weekend,' Annabel said. 'He might be delayed for a day or so if it's difficult to get transport, but he telephoned last night and said he would try to be here by the weekend at the latest.'

'Paul usually does what he says.'

'Yes...' Annabel looked at her thoughtfully.

44

'How did you get on last night, Beth? Did you have a good time?'

'Yes, yes, I did,' Beth replied, a faint colour in her cheeks. She didn't want to share her secret just yet. 'Drew has to spend the last few days of his leave with his family, but we're going to see each other again when he next has leave and he's asked me to write to him.'

'That's nice for you,' Annabel said and nodded her approval. 'I like him very much, Beth. He seems a thoroughly decent young man.'

'Yes, he is,' Beth said, feeling a warm glow inside. Annabel would be delighted if she knew the whole story but Beth wasn't ready to share her feelings just yet. 'When are you leaving?'

'I've arranged for a taxi in half an hour, which gives me plenty of time to catch my train. I shall have to change in London, of course, but I should arrive there this evening. Georgie sounded pretty desperate, though she was trying to hold it back.' Annabel's eyes clouded. 'I don't like pushing all this extra responsibility on you, Beth, but I can't let her down, can I?'

'No, of course you can't. Just tell me anything you think I ought to know and then go.'

'Thank you,' Annabel said gratefully. She hesitated before saying, 'You mustn't think you're tied here, Beth. You're young and I shall understand if you want to stretch your wings a bit – but I'm very thankful for what you're doing now.'

45

'You've done an awful lot more for me,' Beth said, feeling guilty as she recalled the way she had been chafing at the bit recently. 'But now that you've mentioned it – I was thinking I might try to do something for the war effort, in a few weeks or so when things really get going.'

'Yes, I think you should,' Annabel said. 'I'm going to pack. You'll find a list of new guests on my desk, but it's all pretty straightforward, and they are all people who have been before. I'm sure you'll have no trouble.'

'Give my love to Georgie,' Beth said, shaking off her feelings of guilt. There was nothing wrong in wanting a little freedom, and she was suddenly sure that Annabel would understand when she came to tell her that she'd made up her mind to join one of the women's services.

Georgie was at the station to meet Annabel. She felt a surge of relief as soon as she saw her waving and smiling. She'd been feeling wretched since finding Arthur and needed a friendly face, someone she could really talk to, let down her hair as it were.

'Georgie darling,' Annabel said, and dropping her suitcase, hugged her. 'How perfectly awful for you to find him like that.'

'It was horrible,' Georgie admitted with a grimace. Her eyes felt gritty with tiredness. She hadn't slept much at all the previous night and she felt heavy, exhausted, as if she wanted to collapse into a chair but couldn't.

'I didn't want to go to the stupid meeting in the first place but he insisted. I feel cheated, Annabel, as if he slipped out the back door when I wasn't looking. I didn't get a chance to say goodbye.'

'I know it must seem like that,' Annabel sympathized. 'Why do things always have to happen that way? It doesn't seem fair and yet it doesn't really make any difference, Georgie. It isn't as if you weren't expecting it to happen.'

'Soon but not yet. I thought we had a little more time – but we didn't. I can't go back so there's no point in being silly, is there?' She led the way to the car, making a determined effort to pull herself together. Feeling miserable wasn't going to solve anything. 'You said Beth has a boyfriend at last – what is he like?'

'Very nice,' Annabel said as she slid into the passenger seat. 'I liked him. Very suitable for a girl like Beth. And he seemed fond of her. She says he's asked her to write and they're going to see each other next time he's on leave.'

'That sounds promising,' Georgie said. 'She's such a private girl. I've wondered how much she was affected by her mother's murder. It was a terrible thing to have to tell a nine-year-old child.'

'Yes, it was,' Annabel said and her eyes were dark with memories she would rather forget. 'I've never told her that I think Richard was responsible and I don't suppose I ever shall.'

'No point in raking over old hurts,' Georgie

47

said as she started the car, scrunching the gears as she let the brake go. 'It wasn't your fault Richard was a brute. You left him because of it and he got his comeuppance in the end.'

'Yes, he did,' Annabel agreed, giving a little shiver as she thought briefly of her first husband. 'But nothing makes up for what he did, Georgie. I could forgive him for what he did to me – but not for having Alice killed. No, I can never forgive that. I know you are right about Beth. She was always a serious child, but I think the shadow of her mother's murder has hung over her ever since then. And there's something else; she knows her father wouldn't marry her mother and I've thought that might be the reason she didn't seem to want much to do with men. However, she certainly likes Drew and I've every hope that it may develop into a serious relationship. There was a dreamy look in her eyes this morning.'

'And then you had to tell her about Arthur. That would have upset her. I know she was fond of him. He always used to say what a delightful girl she was...' Georgie's voice caught with tears. 'Damn it! I've made up my mind not to be a watering pot. It's ridiculous. We weren't sweethearts, just good companions.'

'You had a wonderful relationship,' Annabel told her. 'I know a lot of married couples who would give anything to be as comfortable and happy together as you two were.'

48

'If only I could believe that!'

'What do you mean?' Annabel glanced at her. 'Arthur told me several times that he couldn't believe how lucky he was to have got you.'

'On the rebound,' Georgie said. 'He said that to me only a few days ago – that he knew he'd got me on the rebound and that I'd never been in love with him.'

'He knew that from the start, but he was content to have what you could give him, Georgie – and from what I could see from the outside that was an awful lot. You got on so well together.'

'But it wasn't enough,' Georgie told her. 'I thought it was until the other day and then I realized that I'd hurt him in some way...'

'You mustn't torture yourself like this,' Annabel told her. 'I'm sure Arthur didn't mean it that way. He was probably just thinking that you'd sacrificed your life for him, because of his ill health. I mean, things have been difficult the last year or so, haven't they?'

'He hasn't been able to do much,' Georgie admitted. 'He couldn't take me dancing or walking – or do any of the things that he liked to do with Geoffrey.'

'There you are then. I expect he was telling you that he was sorry he hadn't been a better husband, and you took it the wrong way.'

'Perhaps...' Georgie looked at her doubtfully. 'I've been feeling terrible about it ever since he said it, but you've made me feel easier. He might have been saying sorry, I suppose.'

'Whatever he meant, you can't change things,' Annabel said. 'Arthur knew when you got married that you weren't in love with him. He took you on those terms and he had no right to feel cheated if that's what he got. Besides, you did love him. Anyone could see that.'

'I loved him, yes,' Georgie said. 'And I miss him like hell – but I wasn't in love. It was never quite what it ought to be in bed, if you know what I mean.'

'There are thousands of marriages like that,' Annabel said, 'and a lot of them start out thinking it's all going to be roses, but it just doesn't work out the way they hoped. You aren't alone, Georgie. At least Arthur didn't hurt you the way Richard did me when we were married.'

'But you and Paul are good together – aren't you?'

'Yes, we are. I'm lucky. But I know a lot of others who aren't, so don't let that bother you. You and Arthur had a good marriage in every other way and most people would settle for that.'

'I had settled for it,' Georgie admitted. 'That's why it upset me so much to realize it wasn't enough for him – but as you said, there's nothing I can do now and I did try to be a good wife.'

'You were a good wife,' Annabel said. 'You are the last person who needs to feel guilty.'

'I'm so glad you're here.' Georgie smiled at her. 'You make me feel very much better.'

'That's what friends are for.'

'I couldn't let Annabel down when she needs me,' Beth said into the phone. 'Please explain to your mother that I would have loved to come down, Drew, but I can't leave the hotel for the moment.'

'She will be disappointed,' he said. 'She told me I should have brought you with me. If you hadn't gone home first you wouldn't have been roped in to help.'

'Yes, I would,' Beth said. 'I should have had to come back if Annabel asked. I owe her everything, Drew. I couldn't be selfish now, not when she is relying on me. She had to go to Georgie and I have to stay here.'

'Yes, I do see that,' he agreed, albeit reluctantly. 'It's just that I'm disappointed. I'm missing you terribly, Beth.'

'I'm missing you too.'

'Do you think you could find work nearer London? I'm likely to be posted not far away for a while. I'm needed for training the raw recruits for the time being they tell me. If you were in London I might get to see you more often. It will be ages before I can get down to Torquay again.'

'I'll try. I was thinking of joining the women's services.'

'If you do that they could send you anywhere. You're a decent driver, aren't you?'

'Not bad,' she replied with a smile. 'Why do

51

you ask?'

'I happen to know someone who needs a reliable driver permanently. He's attached to the War Office – it's all hush-hush and you would have to be vetted, answer a lot of personal questions, but if I can swing it you will be posted in London for the duration. Shall I have a word?'

'Yes, please,' she said, suddenly breathless. 'Do you think I would be suitable?'

'You can type and do shorthand as well, can't you?'

'Yes, I learned all that at college.'

'That might just swing it your way. It won't be a cushy number, Beth – Pearson is the devil to work for – demanding – expects you to be ready at the drop of a hat and put in extra hours if he needs you. He's fair though and you'll get your time off. It would mean that we could be together when I can get a few hours off. I might be able to come up for the odd evening, drive back in the early hours.'

'I would like that, Drew.'

'So would I,' he said. 'I can't promise but if you get an official-looking envelope in the next couple of weeks you'll know what it is.'

'Oh, I do hope it happens,' Beth said on a surge of excitement. 'It sounds interesting and different, just the kind of thing I would enjoy.'

'That settles it then,' Drew said. 'The sooner I can fix it up the better. I can't wait to see you again. I've never felt like this before.'

'I feel the same way about you. It's silly I know, but I want to be with you all the time.'

'Me too – with you. Damn this war! I shall have to report for duty as soon as my leave is up, but if you're in London I can wangle a few hours now and then. I wasn't happy about it when they told me I was being seconded to training raw recruits but now I'm rather glad.'

'Drew, I...' Beth heard the bell ring in reception. 'I shall have to go. One of the guests needs help.'

'I'll ring you this evening at about eight. In fact, I'll ring you as often as I can. I think I'm in love with you, Beth.'

Beth's heart raced. She wanted to tell him she felt the same way but he'd put the phone down immediately. She couldn't get him back because she didn't know the number. Besides, the man in reception had rung twice for attention already.

Going out to the reception area, Beth hardly knew how she managed to answer and deal with a rather disgruntled guest who had arrived without a booking.

'It's always best to telephone first, sir,' she told him. 'I'm afraid we're fully booked at the moment.'

'What a nuisance! You were recommended to me and I've come out of my way to stay here.' His dark eyes glinted with annoyance.

Beth ran her finger down the register. 'We shall have a free room on Saturday, but that's only for one night.'

'No use to me,' he muttered. 'It's just not good enough, that's all I can say.' He was a tall man of spare build and wearing a dark business suit, his hair almost black and slicked down with water to lie flat on his head, his eyes a cool grey.

'We are only a small hotel, sir. I am sure you will find a nice room in Torquay itself.'

'If I'd wanted to stay there I wouldn't have bothered to drive out here.'

Beth remained silent as he left. She couldn't give him a room she didn't have; besides, if that was a sample of his manners she was glad she hadn't been able to oblige.

The telephone rang and she answered eagerly, hoping it might be Drew, but it was another guest confirming a booking. After that two more guests arrived at the desk to ask questions and it was a while before Beth had a moment to herself.

Had Drew really told her he was in love with her? It was almost too much happiness to take in. He had been careful not to rush things on their last night together, but even a few hours apart had made them both realize how strong their feelings were for each other.

Shirley came in after lunch to take over from Beth for a while. She was leaving, having applied to join one of the women's services, but had volunteered to work for a few hours a day until she heard if she'd been accepted.

'I'm going to pick some flowers,' Beth told her. 'I want to freshen the vases in the lounge.

And then I've got a mountain of paperwork to catch up in the office...'

Beth was humming to herself as she went outside. If she didn't get the job Drew had told her about she would be disappointed, but she could find something else. All that mattered was that Drew loved her!

The letter Beth had been hoping for came sixteen days later. It was brief and to the point, almost curt, and asked her to meet Mr Arnold Pearson at his office in Westminster in two days time. It also contained a questionnaire that she was requested to fill in and take with her.

Two days! Beth was stunned. She hadn't really believed it would happen, although Drew had seemed confident when he rang her. He was officially back at the training camp now, finding it frustrating as he struggled to teach raw recruits to become soldiers.

'Some of them are still wet behind the ears,' he'd told Beth. 'It's dangerous to let them loose with a gun, let alone ammunition.'

'I expect they will do better once they get used to it. It's excitement and nerves.'

'Yes, I know. Anyway, I've had a word with Arnold. He's fed up with having temporary drivers and wants someone permanent, as I told you. He's a sort of cousin so he listened when I told him about you. Not that he would do me any favours, but he knows I wouldn't recommend anyone who was likely to let him down.'

'You know I wouldn't do that,' Beth replied instantly.

Only now it looked as if she might have to do just that! Annabel hadn't come back from the visit to Georgie and Shirley had reported for duty at her training base. Beth could hardly walk out and leave them in the lurch. But if she didn't keep this appointment she wouldn't get another chance.

She was frowning over the letter when Paul came into the office.

'Something wrong, Beth?'

'Oh, Paul.' Beth looked guilty. It was on the tip of her tongue to say everything was all right and then she changed her mind. If she didn't do it now, she never would. She handed him her letter. 'I know it's difficult at the moment, but I really do want this job.'

Paul read it through and then looked at her thoughtfully. 'How did you find out about this?'

'Drew recommended me. Mr Pearson is a sort of cousin and he needs a permanent driver and it helps that I can do shorthand as well, apparently.'

'That isn't the only reason you want the job, is it? Drew is based just outside London, I think?' He smiled as she blushed. 'Well, of course you must take this chance, Beth. We can manage here until Annabel gets back. I can hold the fort and I'll ask Shirley's mother to come and give us a hand. I had mentioned it to her and she said she wouldn't mind a few hours. We shall have to find a little army of

56

part-timers to keep us ticking over until things settle down again.'

'Oh, Paul, you are a darling,' Beth said, her face lighting up. 'I was feeling dreadful about leaving you, knowing how things are at the moment.'

'We'll manage,' he said. 'I can do a bit in the office and greet guests if necessary, and I dare say Annabel will be back before too long. She said she was thinking of returning this weekend so it will only be a few days at most.'

'Oh, that's good. How is Georgie? Annabel said she was feeling very low when I asked her on the telephone the other day.'

'I think she is beginning to feel a bit better. It will take time, of course. Annabel has told her she is always welcome to stay here – and I know Jessie and Harry Kendle have told her the same.'

'Staying with friends is nice for a while,' Beth said and looked serious. 'But it isn't the same as being at home. Georgie will need time to get used to Arthur not being there, but I'm sure she would rather be at home. She loves that old house and the garden.'

'Yes, I'm sure you're right,' Paul agreed, thinking what an observant, caring girl she was. 'Well, we shall miss you around here, Beth, but it's good for young people to be independent and see a bit of the world. Keep in touch and come and visit us sometimes, won't you?'

'Yes, of course,' Beth said. 'Thank you for

understanding, Paul. I hate letting you down but...'

'You want to go and it's only right you should – and as for letting us down that is nonsense. Annabel offered you the job here so that you would have security, but she expected you would leave sooner or later.'

Beth blushed faintly, but was saved from replying by a bell in reception. Had Paul and Annabel been aware of her restlessness? Perhaps she should have spoken out ages ago, instead of keeping it to herself.

Beth smoothed the narrow fitting skirt of her best navy blue costume. She had dressed with care for this first interview, her shoes polished until she could see her reflection in the soft leather, her hair done up in a neat twist at the back of her head, instead of allowing it to brush on her collar as normal. She was wearing a small pair of gold clips on her ears that Paul and Annabel had given her one Christmas, and a neat wristwatch. She carried a tan leather briefcase containing her exam results and certificates from college along with her driving licence.

'Will you come this way, Miss Rawlings?'

A young man in a smart navy pinstripe suit came to beckon her from the waiting room. She followed him down a rather narrow, dark corridor to a room right at the bottom marked private.

'Just knock and wait,' the young man said. 'When he's ready he'll come to you.'

'Oh – thank you...' Beth swallowed hard, her knees beginning to shake as she rapped the door once, then hesitated and did it again in case her first wasn't loud enough. Nothing happened. She waited for five minutes, then knocked again, even louder. There was still no answer. Glancing over her shoulder, she looked for help as to what she ought to do next, but finding no one she took a deep breath and opened the door to look inside. A man was sitting at the desk, legs stretched out on the desktop, his head bent and seemingly asleep. Beth was momentarily stunned. What on earth did she do now? Wake him up or go back outside and wait. How long was she supposed to wait?

'Either come in and shut the door or go out,' an irritable voice came from the man at the desk. 'There's a draught and its cold enough in this damned place for a start.'

Beth shut the door. 'I've come for an appointment with Mr Pearson,' she said. 'I knocked several times and I wasn't sure what to do.'

'You were told to wait, I believe?' His eyes snapped open suddenly. Beth felt the shock run through her as she realized that she'd seen him before; he was the guest who had turned up at the hotel without a booking; the one who had been most annoyed because she didn't have a room to offer him. Her heart sank. What chance did she have of getting the job now?

He was sitting up, staring at her, his mouth

pressed into a firm thin line. 'So you're the girl Drew is interested in, are you?' She blushed but didn't answer, convinced that she had no chance of passing this interview. 'Cat got your tongue?'

'Drew and I are friends for the moment,' Beth said recovering her composure. Her head went up, unconsciously proud. 'He told me he would recommend me for the job but perhaps I made a mistake.'

'Not a coward, are you?' Arnold Pearson barked at her. 'You'll be no good to me if you can't take a bit of stick, girl ... what was your name again?' He looked at the papers in front of him, shuffled them and frowned. 'Beth Rawlings. Says here you can drive and do shorthand. And you've been passed by the gods above – no communist tendencies at college or anything like that apparently. So I suppose I'll have to give you a try. Sit down and take a few letters, and then we'll see.'

Beth sat on the chair he indicated. Since he had offered nothing, she took a pad from her briefcase and a sharp pencil, poised ready, waiting for him to begin. He gave a nod of approval and she realized she had passed some sort of test.

For the next twenty minutes he dictated at breathtaking speed. Beth's pencil flew over the paper. She could barely keep up with him, but somehow she managed it, and when he finally finished she saw that he was giving her an odd look.

'Got all that, did you?'

'Yes, I think so, sir.'

'Arnold,' he corrected her. 'Or Mr Pearson officially – can't stand all that sir stuff. That's why I didn't want more army drivers; they bore the hell out of me!'

'Yes, Mr Pearson,' Beth replied. 'Would you like me to type these up?'

'You'd better let me read them when you've finished; I need to see you got it right – then you can drive me to an appointment.' He pointed to a desk in the corner. 'That's yours. Oh, and you'd better sign this...' He pushed a sheaf of papers at her. 'It's the secrecy thing. If you breathe a word of what goes on outside this office they cut your head off...' His grin made Beth sigh with relief. Perhaps he was human after all. 'They'll have my guts for garters if I let you get out without signing it.'

Beth signed after reading the first few lines, and he nodded, taking it back from her and glancing at her signature.

'Readable, that's more than most around here. Get that typing done in double-quick time, Beth. I've got to see the Prime Minister in forty-five minutes.'

'Yes, Mr Pearson.'

'Oh, and Beth...' He gave her a penetrating stare as she looked at him obediently. 'Wear your hair down the way you usually do. It suits you better than that thing at the back of your neck.'

Beth was blushing furiously as she sat down at her desk, head bent over the typewriter. So he had remembered her from the hotel and

61

that was his way of telling her. His manner was a mixture of surly bear and childish glee, and if Beth hadn't wanted this job so badly she would have told him what he could do with his typing!

'Are you sure you'll be all right now?' Annabel asked as she hesitated with her hand on the car door handle. Georgie seemed cheerful enough, but there was no doubting Arthur's death – and the revelations about his feelings of always being second best – had knocked her for six. She felt worried about leaving her alone. 'Why don't you come and stay with us for a while? You know we would love to have you.'

'There's no sense in running away from it,' Georgie replied and smothered her sigh. 'It was good of you to come and you've helped me over the worst of it, Annabel – but I have to face up to things. Arthur has gone and he isn't coming back. I shall probably go down to see Geoffrey in a few days; he wanted to go back to school after the funeral, but he'll be feeling miserable. I shall take him out to tea and talk to him, but he would rather be at school with his friends, and I think he is better off with them for the moment.'

'Yes, of course.' Annabel kissed her cheek. Georgie knew her own mind best, and once it was made up there was no changing it. 'Well, if I'm going I had better make sure I catch my train. Paul is holding the fort for me for the time being but he can't do it forever.'

'So Beth made the break at last then?'

'Yes, it seems like it. Paul says she didn't like letting us down, but that's silly. I didn't expect her to stay if she wanted to do something else. I've never tried to run her life for her!'

'No, of course not,' Georgie said but smiled inside, because Annabel organized everyone without meaning to. However, she'd been grateful for her friend taking over these past couple of weeks and knew that she would have found it impossible to cope with the funeral without her. 'You were just trying to make things easy for her, but she's young and wants to try her wings, I expect.'

'It's because of Drew, of course,' Annabel said. 'I'm so pleased she's found someone at last.' She crossed her fingers, pecked Georgie on the cheek, picked up her suitcase and set off in the direction of the platform. 'See you soon! I'll phone you when I get home.'

Georgie waved to her, then returned to the car and got in. She sat for a moment staring into space before she started the engine. There was no point in moping, because she couldn't change anything.

She headed the car towards her home, and then changed her mind. There was no rush to go home; she didn't have to get back to see to Arthur's dinner. She could go shopping, call in at the library and even have her hair done, if she felt like it.

For the first time in years she was free to do whatever pleased her. She wasn't quite sure how she felt about that just yet. She was still missing her husband and would feel it more than ever when she got home, returning to an empty house. Not that she was frightened of being there alone; she loved the house and all its creaks, and the garden was her pride and joy.

She still had plenty to live for, she supposed. As Arthur had told her, she was young and healthy, and the rest of her life was waiting for her. She just had to make up her mind what she wanted to do with it.

Three

The winter had been cold and bitter in more ways than one, the news becoming increasingly bad as the months passed, both for the Allies and for France. Summer has come to Paris at last, Hetty thought, enjoying the sunshine as she found a table at one of her favourite pavement cafés and ordered coffee and pastries.

Unfortunately, today's news was terrible. She'd bought a newspaper when she saw the headlines – a lot of other people had done the same. There were worried faces everywhere, the mood increasingly sombre since the surrender of the Dutch and Belgians at the end of May. Now, after desperate days of fighting, the British troops had been forced to evacuate from Dunkirk, where they had been trapped on the beaches.

'It is bad news is it not, mademoiselle?'

Hetty's waiter glanced down at her newspaper where it lay on the table; he deposited her coffee and cakes, shaking his head as he stopped to read the first lines of the article.

'We were sure they couldn't break through,' Hetty said, feeling bewildered that it could all change so suddenly. What had happened to all their bright hopes? 'Your eldest boy is with the army, is he not, Marcel?'

'We have heard nothing for weeks,' he replied, shadows of fear in his eyes. 'The British say we should not surrender, but how can we hope to stand against the Germans now? At least if we let them come our children will be saved.'

'Perhaps,' Hetty said. She believed that Marcel was fooling himself. His opinion was very different from that of Madame Arnoud, who had grown more and more gloomy over the winter and was constantly telling her to go home before it was too late.

'You must leave Paris before they come,' she'd told Hetty the previous evening over their customary glass of wine. 'I am closing my business and going south to stay with my sister. To stay open I would have to serve Germans and this I shall not do. Take my advice and leave while you still can.'

'Calais is impossible,' Hetty said. 'I made inquiries and they said there was no chance, but if I can get to Le Havre I might find a ship sailing for England – if I'm lucky. It's getting there; I've heard that the few trains that are still running are overcrowded.'

'You should go by road; the trains may not be reliable and they could be hit from the air. But don't leave it too late.'

'I have my car. It is old and not always reliable but I suppose it might get me as far as I need to go,' Hetty replied thoughtfully. 'I tried to telephone my sister this morning but the lines were busy and it was impossible. I know she will be worried. I suppose I owe it to her to try and get back.'

'You should have gone months ago, *ma chérie*.'

'I didn't want to leave all my friends.' They had all believed, in their brave innocence, that the French line would hold; no one had left the city to start with, not until these past few weeks, but now many of the foreign nationals had gone home. Hetty was one of the few who had hung on right to the end. She was reluctant to leave, even now. 'I shall miss you, madame.'

'I shall miss you, Hetty, but God willing we shall meet again when all this madness is over.'

'When are you leaving?'

'By the end of the week at the latest. I need a few days to settle things here, but there is no need for you to wait. Look around you, *ma chérie*, so many people are leaving and they do so for good reason, believe me. The longer you delay the worse it will be.'

'Yes, I suppose you are right.' Hetty was still resisting the idea even though she knew she didn't have much choice. 'I shall see everyone this evening and make arrangements to leave tomorrow.'

Only her journey had been delayed because the car she had hardly used in years had refused to start. She'd found someone to mend it for her but he'd had to contact his friends to find a new part and it wouldn't be ready for three days. Hetty knew it would be impossible to find another car at the moment, one she could afford to buy anyway. Everyone was thinking the same way and the roads were already becoming increasingly choked with vehicles of all kinds; everything that could move had been snapped up. The Germans were too close for comfort and a lot of people were afraid for their lives. Unless she wanted to walk, Hetty had no choice but to wait.

'Wasn't it wonderful?' Georgie said when she rang Annabel that evening. 'All those little boats going to fetch our men back. It gives me goose pimples all over just to think of it!'

'Yes, I know. I was in tears over some of the stories I read and heard about,' Annabel said. There was a lump in her throat as she spoke. 'They were all so brave. It makes my eyes sting now when I think of all the individual brave acts ordinary men and women performed over there.'

'Have you heard anything from Hetty? I've tried phoning Madame Arnoud a couple of times but there was no answer. I think her phone may have been cut off.'

'Hetty wrote a few weeks ago,' Annabel said. 'She thought Madame Arnoud might close her business if the Germans broke through. She said she was going south to stay with her sister.'

'That was sensible of her. Do you think Hetty might have gone with her?'

'I do hope she has had the sense to leave Paris. Ben was worried about her. He rang me this morning – and you'll never guess why! He has joined the army. I couldn't believe it. He might have got out of it because of the land if he'd wanted but he said he's not needed at the farm and the army might find a use for him if he's lucky. There was some talk of him having flat feet when he went for his medical, but they took him anyway.'

Georgie held her voice steady as she answered, 'I dare say they would take anyone at the moment. Not that I think there's anything wrong with Ben's feet.'

'Well, he's pleased they've taken him. Of course Mother and Helen are both furious with him, but that was only to be expected.'

'He and Helen live almost separate lives these days, don't they?'

'Anyone else would have divorced Helen years ago. She is a perfect bitch to him, Georgie. I don't blame him for spending most of his time in London. Why should he put up with it? I've always regretted that he married her. The money she brought to the estate wasn't that much and her father's money was tied up for his grandchildren in his will; neither Ben nor Helen got a penny. Ben should have sold the estate when he first discovered Father had lost most of the money. I told him so at the time but he wouldn't listen. He admits I was right now. He wishes he'd listened.'

'We all make mistakes, Belle.'

'Yes, I know. I haven't much room to talk, have I?' Annabel gave a rueful laugh. 'I did the same thing, though for different reasons. It's just that I'd like Ben to be happy and I can't see it ever happening – not unless he makes up his mind to divorce Helen.'

'I'm going up to town next week myself,' Georgie said, changing the subject because it made her unhappy to hear about Ben's problems. She'd thought herself long over all that, but it seemed she was still affected. 'There's a conference for the volunteer services and I've been elected as our local representative. We're doing various things to help out, knitting, collecting scrap metals, holding bring-and-buy sales, all the usual stuff. But I thought I would like to do a bit more so I'm going to see what's on offer.'

'I feel terribly lazy. I haven't joined anything at all. Paul is on firewatch twice a week and he made enquiries about the Home Guard and various other things, but I've been busy at the hotel. The new regulations take up all my time, with the blackout restrictions, rationing and checking papers. There's such a lot to sort out these days. I thought we might have to close for the duration but everyone wants to come just the same. They don't seem to mind the rules and restrictions, and we do have hens of our own so that provides a few eggs. I suppose it's all a matter of doing what we can. Jessie sends me some game over now and then, when she has spare, and Paul is good at wangling a bit extra here and there so we're managing well.'

'Yes, I think we do better in the country than they do in town, but that doesn't make it any easier to bear. I just wish it was all over,' Georgie said and sighed. Sometimes at night with the curtains closed and only the radio to keep her company she found the silence unbearable. At least when Arthur was alive she'd had someone to talk to, someone to fuss over, even if life had been more worry than pleasure these past few years.

'Are you all right there on your own? You could come to us, you know.' Annabel was picking up vibes despite Georgie's attempt to hide her feelings.

'I would like to come for a visit in July or August and bring Geoffrey, if I may? He loves Torquay and likes to see your two when he can.'

'You know we would love to have you both. The children get on so well together, though they won't be able to run free on the beach as they've done before this year. We've got restricted areas and barbed wire in places, but you can still get on safely if you know where.'

'Then I shall definitely come,' Georgie said. 'Oh, there's the door. I had better go. I hope you have news of Hetty soon – good news.'

'Yes. I've got my fingers crossed. Bye for now.'

Georgie put the phone down and went to answer the door.

'You've got a glimmer of light showing through your front window, Mrs Bridges,' the

ARP warden said. 'If my superior saw it you'd get a heavy fine. I should paint the edges of your window black if I were you – or stick some tape on it. You don't want Jerry to drop a bomb on your lovely house, do you? Be a real shame that would, after it's stood here all those years.'

'No, I don't want that to happen,' Georgie agreed and smiled at him. The war had given Tom Bradbury a new lease of life. He was seventy-three and took his new duties seriously. 'Thank you very much for telling me, Tom.'

'Pleasure, Mrs Bridges. If it were some I'd have reported them straight away, but I knew you would take notice if I told you.' In his opinion she was a nice little widow and a bit of a looker, and he didn't want to get her into trouble if he could help it.

'Yes, I'll put it right immediately,' Georgie promised and shut the door. The heavy curtain in the front parlour had snagged on a vase of flowers she'd placed in the window earlier so she removed them. There was no point in tempting fate after all.

The old house was sturdily built of grey stone with ivy trailed walls and she had always loved it, though its situation just beyond the edge of the village did make it a bit isolated and she'd felt lonely during the past winter. Still, she would hate something that had been in Arthur's family for years to be destroyed by her carelessness. It would go to Geoffrey one day and he loved it as much as she did.

Georgie was over the first tearing grief of her bereavement. She often felt restless in the evenings and she still missed Arthur, but she was learning to fill her life with other things. The winter nights had been the worst, but now she could work in the garden until quite late in the evening, and she went to committee meetings at least two or three times a week.

It still wasn't enough, of course. She knew something was missing but for the moment she wasn't sure what she could do to fill the gap Arthur's death had left in her life. She supposed she needed a job of some kind. Something worthwhile that would make her feel she was really living rather than just passing time.

'It was good of you to meet me at such short notice,' Georgie said as she kissed Beth's cheek outside the small, discreet restaurant they had chosen for their lunch later that week. 'I rang on the off chance, thinking that you would probably be too busy, so this is a bonus for me.'

'My boss – Mr Pearson – has important meetings right through the day today and so he won't need me until this evening. Then he will have masses of notes for me to take down in shorthand and then type up so we may be in the office until past midnight, but that's how it works out. If he doesn't need me I have several hours off but I have to be prepared to stay when he does.'

'That's a little awkward at times, isn't it? Supposing you wanted to go out with friends?'

'I don't bother much unless Drew can get a pass, and he usually lets me know the day before. So far it has fitted in well. He was here the day before yesterday actually. We went for a walk by the river, had a pub lunch, and then he had to get back and I got on with the typing I knew Arnold wanted by the morning. I didn't mind working at night because I'd had my free time earlier.'

'Do you call your boss Arnold?' Georgie asked as a waiter showed them to their table by the window. 'I thought it was all official and call me *sir* at the War Office?'

'Well, I suppose it would be with most people,' Beth said and gave an odd laugh. 'Arnold Pearson isn't like anyone else I know. One minute he's a slave driver, biting my head off and the next he does something really nice. He bought me a huge box of chocolates the other day. They came from America. He was given them by an American diplomat and he passed them on to me, said he didn't like them, but I left them open on the desk and I noticed he ate two as he was dictating. It slowed him down for a few minutes, gave me time to catch up.'

'He sounds rather an oddball,' Georgie said. 'Now what shall we try? The chicken salad with new potatoes – or the meat pie?'

'The chicken sounds best. At least you can

see what you're getting,' Beth said with a wry grimace. 'You never know what is in the pie. It could be anything.'

'Yes, I think you're right,' Georgie agreed. 'Someone told me they had a whale meat casserole the other day at a Lyons Corner House. Apparently, it wasn't bad, but I don't think I should fancy it. I suppose I'm spoiled living in the country. I've got my own hens and ducks, and I can often buy a rabbit or a pigeon. I was given a lovely plump pheasant the other day. They take a while to pluck and prepare, but I always think it's worth it in the end.'

Beth nodded her head. 'Fresh eggs are becoming scarcer in London. As soon as the shops get supplies of anything a queue forms, everyone joins it even if they don't know what they're queuing for and they've often run out before you get to the end.'

'The merchant navy has taken a terrible battering from the U-boats and since the Germans started attacking neutrals as well it has made the problem worse. Our navy has been making gains against theirs, or so one reads in the papers, but those damned U-boats are a menace on the Atlantic run.'

'Yes, I know.' Beth coloured and took a sip of water. She probably knew a lot more about that particular problem than Georgie possibly could, but Arnold Pearson would have her guts for garters if she let a word slip. She turned to something safer. 'Don't you think everyone was simply marvellous the way they

75

turned out to bring our men back from Dunkirk?'

'Yes, just superb. Did you know one of Paul's friends took his river cruiser over? I think that was terrible brave. Rather foolish in a way, because those boats aren't intended for ocean going, but someone up there must have been watching over him. He made it there and back and rescued three men from the sea.'

'There are so many stories like that,' Beth said, then a shadow passed over her face. 'It's awful news from France. They say the Germans will be in Paris within days or perhaps hours. Annabel is very worried. She hasn't heard a thing from Hetty.'

'That foolish girl makes me so angry! She might have come home weeks ago. She must know everyone is concerned but she has always been the same. What she wants is all that matters. I think she is totally selfish.'

'That's a bit harsh,' Beth said. 'I've never thought Hetty was selfish, not really. She can be thoughtless and impulsive and she does live her life the way she pleases – but is that so very wrong?'

'No, I suppose not, when you think about it. I may have been a bit harsh, but I think it is careless of her not to at least let Annabel know what is happening to her.'

'Perhaps she can't,' Beth said. 'It must be absolute chaos out there. Just imagine what it would be like if the Germans were about to march into London.'

'God forbid!' Georgie shuddered. 'I pray that never happens.'

'Let's hope it doesn't,' Beth said. Arnold had told her it could and might happen and she knew of some of the contingency plans for the Government and important personages if it did. Naturally, she couldn't breathe a word of that to Georgie. 'Well, I just hope that wherever Hetty is at the moment, she is safe and on her way home.'

'I'll second that,' Georgie said and took a sip of water. 'Here comes our meal. It doesn't look too bad. Let's hope it tastes all right...'

Hetty broke a piece of croissant and popped it into her mouth. She was hungry but didn't want to stop just yet because at last she was on her way, a reasonably empty road ahead of her. She'd left Paris early in the morning, taking two suitcases of clothes, a few of her favourite pictures and all the food she'd had in the house. Everything else had had to be left behind. A friend had offered to store some of her things, but she'd given most of it away.

'After the war I'll start fresh,' she told her friends as she said her farewells. 'I'll be back as soon as I can, believe me.'

Her heart remained in Paris. She felt angry and hurt that she'd been forced to leave but everyone told her to go.

'You're British. They will arrest you.'

'It would be foolish to stay.'

'You should have gone long ago.'

How true that was, Hetty thought ruefully. It had taken ages to come fifty miles. The roads leading away from Paris were so congested that she was often obliged to let the car engine idle or stop altogether to save petrol. There was no guarantee she would be able to fill up the tank when she needed to and she couldn't afford to waste it. Her radiator was playing up and she'd had to fill it with water after it had got too hot. If she'd left a few days earlier it would have made all the difference, but there was no point in worrying about that. What did worry Hetty was the plight of some of the other people fleeing from the city.

There were so many: on foot, on bicycles, pushing handcarts, driving a horse and cart or even a donkey. She had particularly noticed one old man struggling with a heavy handcart, his wife limping painfully beside him. She could see that they were of Jewish origin and understood their panic after the reports of atrocities against Jews elsewhere. Her heart wrenched with pity for the elderly couple; they were too old to be forced onto the road like this, but there were many others in the same situation. Madame Arnoud had warned her against picking up strangers.

'Think of yourself for once, Hetty. I know you have a kind heart, *ma chérie*, but if you try to help one they will all try to get into the car. They will demand food and money, some may be desperate enough to rob you. Stay inside the car and keep your door locked; it isn't safe for a young woman alone in these times.'

It was good advice, but Hetty felt guilty as she passed a tired women carrying children. Her back seat was piled with things she wanted to keep but the front passenger seat was empty. She could take a woman and perhaps a small child. Her conscience pressed more as the day wore on, and then she saw *her*. A woman of perhaps thirty-something with a small girl. She was sitting by the side of the road, her feet bare, obviously bloody and painful, and the child was crying and pulling at her skirt. The woman looked so despairing that Hetty stopped the car and called out to her.

'How far are you going? Can I give you a lift?'

For a moment the woman stared at her dully. Hetty had spoken in French and yet she seemed not to understand. Perhaps she was just too weary and dispirited to listen.

Hetty tried again, 'Do your feet hurt? I have water. You can bathe them when we stop later.'

At the mention of water the woman's head came up. She got to her feet and limped towards the car, her feet obviously causing her terrible pain.

'Forgive me. I do not hear you at first. We have been two days on the road. I have no food or water for the child.'

'Get in,' Hetty said and leaned over to open the door. 'She can sit on your lap. We'll get a

79

bit further while we can and then stop for a meal. In the meantime have this...' She handed the woman a bag of pastries and a half-empty bottle of water.

'But this is your food ... you will need it yourself.'

'I have enough to share,' Hetty said and felt pity as she saw the woman's eyes fill with tears. God, this bloody war! It made her want to hit somebody but there was nobody around who deserved it. This poor woman had suffered so much. 'It isn't possible to help everyone, but you looked as if you needed it more than most.'

'My name is Marie Rybach,' the woman said. 'I am French but my husband is part Jew. He went to fight for the French but there has been no word in months. I am trying to take Kristina to my family in Rouen.'

'That is a long way to walk, Marie,' Hetty said. 'My name is Hetty and I am English. I am trying to get to Le Havre. I don't know how far this old car will take us, but you are welcome to ride with me for as long as we keep going.'

'God bless you, Hetty. I have a little money. I will gladly pay.'

'Keep it for food until you get home. The food I have will last for a couple of days, but after that we shall need to buy more, that's if we can find someone to sell to us.'

'I tried to buy from a farm back on the road but he threatened us with a shotgun. Even for money he would not give me as much as a cup of milk for the child.'

'I have no milk,' Hetty said regretfully. 'There is some condensed milk in the boot. She can have that mixed with a little water – or do as I do and eat it with a spoon. I've always liked it, though most people say it is too sweet.'

'Kristina likes it too,' Marie said and kissed the top of the child's head. Kristina was eating one of the pastries with every sign of enjoyment. 'Say thank you to Hetty for your pastries, darling.'

'Thank you, mademoiselle. I was very hungry.'

'You are welcome,' Hetty said, her eyes moist. For the past few kilometres she'd been travelling at a reasonable speed, but ahead of her she could see that the traffic had come to a standstill again. A lorry had shed its load, blocking the narrow road. There was noise and confusion, horns blowing as frustration boiled over in the heat of the afternoon sun.

'Well, we're obviously not going anywhere for the moment,' Hetty said and stopped the engine. 'We might as well have something more filling to eat than cakes. I could do with a cup of coffee. I've got a little picnic stove in...' Hetty's nape prickled as she heard the noise of a low-flying plane overhead but she tried to ignore it. It surely couldn't be a German plane! 'You could bathe your feet, Marie. I've got some soft muslin...'

The rest of Hetty's words were lost as they suddenly heard the roar of the guns firing at

81

the parked vehicles. They saw the plane swoop low over the road and then there was another burst of fire from yet another direction. Kristina screamed and pulled at her mother in terror.

'It happened yesterday,' Marie said, her face white. 'They came out of the sky suddenly at us. She saw terrible things.'

'We should get out of the car,' Hetty urged, thinking of the extra cans of petrol she was carrying in the boot. The first plane had turned ready for another low swoop over the people who were panicking, running for their lives. They could hear screaming and witnessed the confusion as bullets caught out those who stood dithering, uncertain of which way to go. Some had run for the fields on either side of the road, looking for protection from the deadly onslaught. There was more screaming, even more terrible as the bullets ripped into soft flesh. 'Come on, Marie. Give me Kristina. I can run faster than you.'

'Yes, take her into the ditch,' Marie said. 'I'll follow.'

Kristina was screaming and crying as Hetty snatched her up and sprinted for the ditch. The German plane was shooting at people as they ran, almost as if playing some malicious game, deliberately going for the most vulnerable it seemed. Hetty saw old men, women and children fall in front of her and felt the whistle of bullets so close that she didn't know how they had missed her. The gorge

82

rose in her throat, but she kept running instinctively, throwing Kristina into the ditch and covering her with her own body for the next few minutes.

For a while it was like a vivid nightmare with the screams of the wounded and dying all around them, and then, all of a sudden, the roar of the engines faded and the bullets stopped; the planes had gone. It seemed strangely silent for a moment, and then Hetty became aware of the child whimpering and asking for her mother.

'Yes, darling, we'll find her,' Hetty said and climbed out of the ditch, taking Kristina into her arms and holding her tightly. 'It's all over now. We're safe.' She looked around her as those that had survived started to come out of the ditches and take stock of what had happened. There were bodies lying on the ground, some of them twitching, some moaning, but most still, their clothes and bodies ripped apart by the deadly hail of bullets. 'Let's look for mummy. Marie ... Marie, where are you?'

Kristina was sobbing, clearly distraught. Hetty kept her face pressed against her, protecting her from the worst of the horror as she made her way back towards where she'd left the car. Thankfully it was still there. She thought it might have gone up in flames, because she'd heard an explosion, but the car burning was some distance behind her in the queue.

The German pilots had certainly chosen

their moment well, Hetty thought bitterly, when the traffic was trapped with no way to go.

'Marie...' She turned her head to the right and saw the body lying there face down. Marie hadn't even had time to get away from the car. With her feet cut to ribbons she hadn't stood much chance. A sob caught in Hetty's throat. 'Oh, Marie...'

What did she do now? She couldn't bury Marie herself; she didn't have the tools and she didn't imagine she had the strength either. Yet she felt awful about just leaving the poor woman lying there.

She ought to make sure she was dead. But what about Kristina? How was she going to protect her from seeing her mother's body, riddled with so many bullets that there wasn't much chance she was alive? She had just decided to put Kristina in the car and then investigate when she saw the man open the back door of her car and begin to pull things from the back seat.

'What the hell do you think you are doing?' she demanded. She put Kristina down and went to try and protect her property. 'Those things belong to me. Just keep your filthy thieving fingers off them!'

'There's nothing of any value here,' the man said as he turned to her. She saw that he had blood smeared over his face and hands. 'My friend has been injured. If I don't get him to a doctor he'll die – what are a few amateur paintings compared to that?'

He stared at her from angry blue eyes, his mouth set in a thin line of disgust, which made Hetty lose her temper further.

'They happen to represent years of my life,' she told him, piqued that he'd described her work as amateur. 'That's some of my best work.'

'Well, if you painted them you can do it again,' he said and ran impatient fingers through dark blond hair. 'For God's sake, woman! Jean is going to die if we don't help him. And you should attend to your child if you don't want her to look at dead people.'

'Oh my God!' Hetty cried, whirling round to see Kristina bending over Marie's body. 'She isn't my child and that is her mother. I think she's dead but I'm not sure.'

'Take it from me she is,' he grunted. 'Grab the girl before she gets too near ... too late.' Kristina had started to scream and wail. Glaring at Hetty as if it was her fault, he went over to the child and snatched her up. Coming back, he thrust her into Hetty's arms. 'Get in the passenger seat with her. I'll put Jean in the back and I'll drive.'

'This happens to be my car. I'll drive.'

'Across there?' He nodded towards the fields. 'Or are you going to wait in line for the road to clear – let the German bastards come back and finish off what they started, why don't you?'

'Oh damn you!' Hetty said and got into the car. She was furious with him for taking over her car and discarding her possessions, but the pictures were less important than a man's life and she couldn't deny that. Besides, Kristina was sobbing wildly and calling for her mother, and it was all she could do to hold her as she struggled to get back to her maman.

'It's all right,' Hetty crooned as she held the girl to her, feeling the deep sobs as they shook the child's body. 'It's all right, Kristina, Hetty will look after you now.'

'Maman ... maman...' the child wailed. 'Want my maman...'

'Yes, I know,' Hetty murmured and stroked her hair, kissing the top of her head as she buried it into her breast. Kristina's tears were soaking through the thin material. 'Maman will be looked after by the nice people who will come soon.' She prayed that she was right. Surely when it was safe someone would come to bury the dead? 'Try to sleep now, dear ... shush...'

The child felt thin and vulnerable as she held her and Hetty's heart was wracked with pity. It was useless trying to soothe her. Her tears had soaked into Hetty's silk blouse, her nose running, face sticky with spittle as she wept and screamed in despair.

'Hurry up,' Hetty said to the blue-eyed man as he returned to the car carrying his friend, who was bleeding badly and moaning but clearly still alive. 'I want to get away from here.'

'That's more like it,' he said as he settled his friend on the back seat. 'Hold on, Jean. I'll have you safe soon. Don't give up, my friend. It's going to be all right.' He glanced at Hetty briefly before starting the car. 'I am Pierre de Faubourg, and my friend is Jean Renoir – no relation to the artist. My apologies if I was harsh just now, but I wasn't even sure the owner of the car had survived.'

'So that gave you the right to commandeer it, I suppose?' Hetty glared at him. Why did men always imagine they had the right to whatever they wanted? 'Supposing I'd wanted the space for a wounded friend?'

'Then we should have had to get them both in somehow. I am sorry about your friend...' He nodded at the child. 'How old is she?'

'I have no idea. I picked her and Marie up a few kilometres back on the road. I'd never seen them before.'

'And now it looks as if you're stuck with the child, at least for the moment. You've no idea where the father is, I imagine?'

'He went to fight some months ago. Marie said she had family in Rouen. I could try to find out something perhaps.'

'Do you know her second name?'

'Rybach, I believe.'

'Ah, I see,' Pierre nodded his understanding. 'Those dark eyes and that curly hair are a giveaway. No wonder they were desperate to leave Paris.'

'Yes, Marie mentioned it. She was French but her husband is half Jewish.'

'Or was,' he murmured. 'I don't think Marie's family will be too anxious to claim

87

the child at the moment. You'd better give her to the nuns.'

'That's hardly appropriate, is it?' Hetty gave him a scornful look. 'I'll take her to England with me. I can find a place for her in my home and after the war I'll see if I can trace her people.'

Kristina was still sobbing but much more quietly. Hetty continued to stroke her hair and felt that she might sleep soon; her excess of grief had exhausted her; the combination of the fear and horror of what she had witnessed on the road.

Hetty hadn't taken much notice where they were going at first. Now she saw that the car had traversed the larger part of the open fields and was headed towards a wood.

'Where are you going?' she asked alarmed. 'You can't get through there. It's impossible.'

He shot her a challenging look. 'You think not, mademoiselle?'

'You will get stuck in the wood if you're not careful and then we shan't get anywhere.'

'Trust me,' he said. 'You didn't give me your name, mademoiselle?'

Hetty was tempted to reply rudely but decided against it. Like all men this one had taken without asking, but in the circumstances she couldn't really blame him. Besides, she could hear gunfire back on the road and realized that it made sense to take cover in the trees if only for a while.

'It's Hetty Tarleton,' she said feeling sick at the thought of what might have happened if she hadn't let him take over. The Germans were going back to finish what they'd started. 'I didn't believe they would come back for more. Haven't they done enough harm for one day? We're not soldiers. What good has it done them to kill ordinary men and women?'

'It's sport to some of them,' Pierre said grimly. 'They probably invited some of their friends to join the party.'

'God, I hate them! Until now I didn't feel much about the war, one way or another. Some of the younger people I knew in Paris thought we ought to let them in from the start; they saw no reason for France to fight against their close neighbours. They thought we had much in common with them.'

'Communists,' Pierre said and his mouth hardened. 'There isn't much to choose between them if you ask me.'

'That's not fair,' Hetty objected and glared at him. 'My friends wouldn't fire on innocent men, women and children.'

'Maybe not, but wait until you see what crawls out of the woodwork once the Germans are in power. There will be plenty that agree with them and suck up to them then, do their dirty work.'

'Not after word gets out of what they're doing.' Hetty glared at him angrily. 'Most of us will fight if we get the chance.'

'But you're not French. You're leaving for England – and that's the best place for you. The Germans will shoot you as a spy if they catch you.'

'You are as bad as my friend Madame Arnoud,' Hetty said, her eyes flashing blue-green fire. 'I've lived in France for ten years now – why shouldn't I want to fight for it?'

'Because it is not your country. You should go home, Miss Tarleton. It's where you belong.'

'Go to hell!' Hetty muttered. She glanced down at the child as she caught the sound of regular breathing. 'I think she is asleep. She was worn out with all the walking and now she is exhausted.'

'Perhaps it is just as well,' he said. 'The worst time will be when she wakes up and realizes her mother isn't coming back.'

'Poor little thing,' Hetty said and blinked as she felt the sting of tears. They had entered the wood, which wasn't as thick as she'd imagined from a distance. She acknowledged that it *was* possible to drive through the trees, though it involved some sharp twists and turns, which drew a few cries of pain from the man lying on the back seat. Hetty turned to look at him. In her concern for Kristina she hadn't thought about him much. 'He's holding on – but I think he is in a lot of pain.'

'Of course he's in pain! God damn it! He has three bullets in him, woman! You would be in pain if you had been hit.'

'There's no need to bite my head off,' Hetty said. 'You took over my car but you could at least be polite.'

'Forgive me, I don't suffer fools lightly.'

'I'm not a fool – just concerned about

90

someone in pain.'

'There's nothing either of us can do about it until I get him home. He's just going to have to bear it.'

'Home – does he live close by?'

'Jean doesn't but I do,' Pierre said. 'You'll see in a little while. We haven't much further to go – providing the bastards haven't bombed it by now.'

Hetty saw the hard jut of his jaw and lapsed into silence. He was rude, overbearing and bad-tempered, but perhaps she'd feel the same way in his shoes. After all, it was his country that was being invaded, his friend who had been badly wounded. She was upset enough over Marie, and she didn't even know her.

'Perhaps we should start again,' she said with a grimace. 'I was angry when I saw you pull my pictures from the car, but you were right – a man's life is more important. I may be able to go back and paint the pictures again one day.'

'I'm sorry if they meant a lot to you,' he said and sent a rueful smile her way. 'But all I could think of was that there was a car, no people and a way of getting Jean to safety quickly.'

'We'll call a truce,' Hetty suggested. 'Once you've got your friend home I can go back and pick up my things if...' She broke off as she caught a glimpse of a large house through the trees. Surely that wasn't where they were headed? 'Is that a château I just glimpsed?'

'That is Château de Faubourg,' Pierre said, a faint smile on his lips. 'It belongs to my grandmother, the Comtesse. It was passed on to her through her husband's family not through my father. He took her name because she was the last of her line and she wanted the name to continue.'

'Oh...' Hetty saw that the track they were following now had widened out and had been used frequently by vehicles in the past, possibly for collecting fallen trees. 'It's beautiful...'

'It is also falling down in parts,' Pierre said. 'Not that you would notice it from the outside, but one wing is too damp to use, and some of the ceilings could fall on your head if you were foolish enough to venture there – so don't try it.'

'No, I shan't,' Hetty murmured. Considering she did not intend to stay more than a few minutes, it hardly applied. 'Why don't you have it repaired?'

'We have a very big house but very little money,' Pierre told her with a wry grimace. 'My father was unfortunately not a good businessman. I had hoped to improve the family fortunes when I took over after his death – but unfortunately Hitler intervened.'

'That must have been inconvenient for you?' Hetty smiled as he lifted one eyebrow. She was beginning to like his sense of humour, which had been sadly lacking at the first moment of their meeting.

The drive leading up to the château was

long and grand, and it was easy to see that the house had been magnificent once. There were some signs of neglect outside, but nothing that would suggest the serious decay Pierre had mentioned inside.

'We are art dealers,' Pierre said. 'Not just pictures but objects of beauty of many kinds: bronze, glass, china, even some furniture. War is not a good time for our trade. Most of our stock has been hidden away in dry cellars where we hope it will be safe for the duration. That is why the château looks more forlorn than usual.'

He drove round to the back of the house and honked loudly until drawing to a halt outside what was clearly the kitchen quarters. A door flew open and two men ran out, closely followed by three women.

'Monsieur!' one of the men cried. 'We heard that there was an attack on the road and saw smoke rising. Your car was hit?'

Pierre smiled at the elderly man, who was his grandmother's most faithful servant and had been in her household all his life.

'It went up in flames. It was all that petrol you had saved for me, Bernard,' Pierre told him. 'We would have gone with it if we hadn't made a run for it – but Jean was hit. We need a doctor and fast.'

'Of course, monsieur.' Bernard gave orders as willing hands reached for the wounded man, then turned to Pierre. 'You will please come in – are you wounded yourself? And the others?'

93

'Take Mademoiselle Tarleton to my grand-mother,' he said. 'She was good enough to lend us her car. Madame de Faubourg will want to thank her – and I dare say she is hungry. Perhaps someone could see to the child? She is sleeping but she has seen her mother killed; she will be in shock when she wakes.'

'*Mon Dieu!*' The old man looked horrified and beckoned to one of the women, telling her to put the child to bed and stay with her.

'Tell me if she wakes,' Hetty instructed. 'She will be frightened and at least she knows me. I shall come if she needs me.'

'She sleeps deeply, mademoiselle,' Bernard said. 'It is the good God's mercy on her. She has seen something that no child should ever have to see.'

'Yes, she has,' Hetty agreed. 'But I am tired, shocked and hungry. I should like to rest for a while before I leave.'

'You will not think of leaving today,' a new voice said. Hetty turned to see a tall, white-haired woman. From her manner and bearing it was obvious that she was Madame la Comtesse de Faubourg. 'It would be too cruel to make the child go on when she is so tired – and you should rest, mademoiselle. My grandson has told us that you have helped him, and we are glad to offer you our hospitality for a few days – or as long as you wish.'

Her eyes were not as blue as her grandson's but they might have been once, Hetty thought. The remnants of her beauty were still there, and her pride was unbent despite the years. Although autocratic and undoubtedly demanding, there was something about her that appealed to Hetty and she found herself smiling and thanking her for her hospitality instead of refusing.

Four

'Georgie! Georgie, wait a moment.' Hearing the man's voice call to her as she left her hotel, Georgie turned and saw him walking towards her, her heart suddenly leaping and beating much faster than normal. The noise of the traffic seemed to fade away and all she could hear was the drumming of her heart. He was smiling as he reached her, the smile she had remembered all these years. 'Annabel told me you were in town and I thought it was you. I was going to call at reception and ask if you were in. It seems I just caught you. Were you going somewhere important or have you time for a coffee or something?'

'My meetings are all finished,' Georgie told him when she could control her breathing enough to speak. 'How are you, Ben? Annabel told me you have joined the army?'

'Yes.' He grinned at her just the way he had when she'd taken him for a spin in her car all those years ago. The years spun away, and she was a girl again on the verge of life, entranced by a young man's easy charm. He'd captured her heart then and in a way it had ruined her life. 'I've been told to report in two days. I expect I'm just going to be pushing a pen at some office somewhere or in charge of moving stores. I doubt they will think I'm much good for anything else, but I don't mind. I just feel I want to do something to help.'

'Yes, I know exactly what you mean,' Georgie told him. 'I've been working with our local women's group, doing all the usual things, but I wanted something more. That's why I came up this week to attend meetings. I hoped they might give me a job of some kind.'

'And did they?'

'Not yet,' she said and laughed at her own innocence. 'It's not that easy it seems, but I was told about several avenues I might try. Apparently, there are lots of committees, a bit like you've been saying, Ben. They say I might have a chance of driving an ambulance, or volunteer driving anyway. It seems at the moment that it's the ordinary hospitals that are most in need; their staff have been pretty well poached by the military. I thought that might suit me well, taking people with no transport of their own back and forth.'

'That sounds excellent,' Ben said looking at her. Georgie's stomach lurched. 'I'm free all day. You wouldn't spend it with me I suppose – for old time's sake?'

'We didn't really have any old times, did we?' Georgie looked rueful. 'We were both young and full of ideals.'

'I was a bloody fool! I should have asked you to wait until I could get a divorce. It hurt when you married Arthur, Georgie. I didn't know it was going to feel that way, believe me. I've regretted letting you go all these years.'

'Oh, Ben...' Georgie's heart felt as if it were being squeezed. 'I should never have married him. It wasn't fair to either of us. He wasn't happy. I thought it was working out until just before he died and then I realized that he felt cheated. I felt cheated too, Ben.'

Ben looked concerned for her. 'I'm so sorry. I thought you were happy with him.'

'I learned to be content in time,' Georgie said. 'But don't let's talk about the past, Ben. You've become successful and famous these past years. Tell me about your work. I went to see both your plays when they were on, you know.'

'What did you think of them? I suppose they did all right – better than I ever expected anyway. The short stories have sold well and the magazine work keeps me going. It hasn't made me rich, but I'm making a reasonable living. I've bought back some of the land my father sold and the farm is more prosperous because of it, so Mother and Helen have no complaints in that direction.'

'I'm glad you've done something for yourself,' Georgie said. Taking his arm, she smiled up at him. Her heart was behaving more normally now but a warm feeling was spreading through her and she felt happy, as if she had somehow shed her cares. 'What shall we do? I was thinking of visiting a museum to pass the time. But I just like walking really, taking in the sights like any country bumpkin up for a visit, and shopping – though there isn't the choice there used to be. I did think I might treat myself to a new dress, if I can find one I like.'

'We'll do all those things, why not?' Ben said. 'I feel like a schoolboy playing truant. If you like, we'll visit one of the museums, providing it's still open – or there's a rather nice art gallery I know of that has a show on at the moment. The artist sent me tickets. Perhaps you would like to come and meet him? I know him quite well actually. His name is Henri Claremont.'

'Isn't that Hetty's...?'

'The lover she left home for? Yes, as a matter of fact it is. We've met several times over the years. I quite like him, though I know he didn't treat Hetty as he should, too selfish – but he says he has news of her for me so I think it might be a good idea to put in an appearance.'

'I thought she left him ages ago?'

'Yes, she did, but amazingly they are still on friendly speaking terms. She just didn't want to live with him any more, and I can't say I blame her after the way he behaved. He expected her to wait on him hand and foot, pose for him, be his mistress and put up with his straying, and in the end she got fed up. I asked her to come home when I was last out there, but she adores Paris. I know she want-ed to stay until the last moment. I'm hoping that Henri can give me some news of her.'

'Then I think we should go to his show,' Georgie said. 'It would be wonderful to have news of her, because Annabel has been very worried.'

The art gallery had several visitors and some of them appeared to be buying despite the uncertain times. Henri Claremont was a popular artist, particularly with the younger generation. Georgie found his style a bit too modern and harsh for her taste, but despite her prejudice against him she found him extremely handsome, and began to see why the youthful Hetty had run off to France to be with him.

He had included two pictures of Hetty in his show; one of them when she was about sixteen, the other more recent. Georgie looked at it with interest.

'This is very attractive,' she said to Ben. 'I haven't seen Hetty for a while – does she really look like this?'

'Yes, she does actually. She has changed quite a bit since she left Henri, grown up I think – matured. I saw her a few months before the war started, which was when this was done I should imagine. She was wearing that same dress.'

'You should buy the picture, Ben.'

'Henri won't sell it. He says Hetty was the love of his life and she broke his heart when she left him.'

'You don't believe that?'

'I'm not sure. I think he probably did love her in his way. He just couldn't be faithful to her. Some men are like that – but he's seen us. He's coming over.'

'Ben, *mon ami*,' Henri said and kissed him on both cheeks in what Georgie thought was a rather theatrical way. 'I am so glad you came. The show is a success, *non*?'

'It certainly seems to be,' Ben agreed. 'Georgie was just admiring the pictures of Hetty. Georgie knows Annabel well, of course, but she hasn't seen Hetty for a while.'

'Ah, my darling Hetty, she is so beautiful, *non*? Everyone admires her, they all want to buy her picture, but me, I cannot part from it. It means too much to me.'

'I told Ben he should buy it,' Georgie said. 'It is an exceptional painting, monsieur.'

'You are too kind, madame. It was done from the heart, you see, and I can never sell it – but you will want to hear news of Hetty. I saw her a few days before she left Paris. She came to say goodbye and told me to take care of myself. I also was leaving but I was given a flight in a private plane. I would have taken Hetty but it was not in my power, you understand? I had to come to London for my show; it was important.'

'More important than saving Hetty's life?' Georgie asked sharply. 'If you'd given her your seat she might have been here now.'

'Hetty would not have accepted it,' he told her. 'You do not understand. She is the free spirit ... she does always as she wants. Besides, she understood the show was important to me. She told me I should go, that it

101

would be better for me to leave Paris before the Germans came.'

I'll just bet she did! No doubt Hetty hadn't been given the choice. This man thought only of himself. Georgie didn't voice her angry thoughts aloud though she might have if Ben hadn't given her a warning glance.

'So you don't know when she left Paris for sure?' Ben asked. 'If you had left before her?'

'One of my friends managed to telephone me yesterday,' Henri told him. 'He knows that Hetty had to wait for her car to be repaired but her apartment is empty and she asked someone to store some of her things for her. I know she intended to make for Le Havre. They say it is still possible to get a ship for England from there.'

'Then we shall hope to see her before too long,' Ben said. 'Thank you for the information and for letting us see your show, Henri. We have a lot to do today so we must get on. Good luck with everything.'

'Do you intend to return to France?' Georgie asked.

'No, not while it is under the heel of the jackboot,' Henri said sorrowfully. 'They are philistines and my art would suffer. I have been invited to give a show in New York soon and I think I may settle there for the time being.'

'Very wise,' Ben said and took Georgie's arm before she could say more.

'Trust him to choose a safe haven,' she said as Ben drew her outside. 'If you hadn't jumped in I might have told him just what I thought of his behaviour, Ben.'

'I thought so,' he replied and laughed. 'He can be a pain in the backside at times, I know – but he is charming in his own way.'

'Totally selfish!'

'Oh yes, no doubt of that,' Ben said. 'Shall we have lunch now? We could go to a concert this afternoon – or we could...'

'What?' She looked up at him, her heart beating very fast. 'Finish what you were going to say, Ben.'

'We could always listen to the music on the wireless at my apartment.'

'Yes, we could do that,' Georgie said and smiled at him. 'I think that sounds absolutely lovely.'

'I happen to have a rather special bottle of wine I've been saving for the right occasion. So we'll have lunch first – at the Savoy I think. They are kind to me there and look after me so we'll be sure of a decent meal, and after that...'

'After that,' Georgie said, 'we'll let *after that* take care of itself I think, don't you?'

Georgie gave a little scream of pleasure as she came to a glorious, shuddering climax, clinging to Ben as he collapsed against her when their fierce and urgent loving was done. She felt the tears begin to trickle down her cheeks as she realized that for the first time in her life she had experienced the true pleasure and meaning of physical love.

'Oh, Ben...' she whispered chokily as he raised his head to look at her, an anxious, tender expression in his eyes. 'I didn't know ... I'd heard but I never knew it could be this way.'

'It doesn't often happen like that for me either,' he admitted and smiled. 'I think it was special for both of us, Georgie. We had been waiting a long time.' He rolled over on to his back and reached for a pack of cigarettes beside the bed, lighting one, which he offered to her. She took a short puff and handed it back. She didn't often smoke, but this seemed the appropriate time for it.

'Yes, too long,' she said and sighed. 'I feel as if we've wasted the last ten years, though that's a wicked thing to say, and it isn't really true. We both have children, and parts of my marriage were good.'

'Like the curate's egg?' Ben suggested and gave her a naughty grin that made her laugh, banishing her faint feeling of guilt.

'Yes, just like that,' Georgie agreed. 'I suppose there was too big a gap in our ages. Annabel thought so at the time and so did my mother – but I wouldn't listen. All I wanted was to get away from the anguish of knowing the man I loved was married to someone else. I thought that if I married Arthur I wouldn't be miserable.'

'And were you?'

'Yes, dreadfully so. Especially at first. I couldn't get you out of my mind I suppose and every time he touched me I wanted it to be you.'

And there had been other things; Arthur's annoying little habits that she had tried to ignore over the years but which had driven her nearly mad. He always left the top off the tin of toothpowder so that it got wet and became unusable, but then saved little bits of soap in a dish in case some use could be made of them, and there had been other habits that she found irritating. Of course she wouldn't tell Ben that, because it would be a betrayal, and perhaps she'd had habits that had annoyed Arthur – like when she made shelves full of preserves and then gave them away to her friends because they couldn't possibly eat them all themselves.

'Poor Arthur,' Ben said and kissed the end of her nose. 'That couldn't have been easy for him, knowing you were thinking of another man.'

'No, it wasn't,' she admitted. 'Things got better though. I can't say I ever looked forward to his loving but I tried to respond as much as I could. And I did try to make up for it in other ways – though I don't think I succeeded. He felt cheated.'

'It was all my fault,' Ben told her. 'I was weak and indecisive when I should have been strong. I knew before I married Helen that I wasn't in love with her. I think I started to fall in love with you when you took me for a spin in your car, Georgie. I should have broken off my engagement then, but I was an idealistic prig and felt that would be dishonourable. So

105

instead I made you miserable and gave myself years of hell – until I'd finally had enough. I told Helen I was moving out of our room and that I would be living in London for most of the year.'

'Did she object?'

'She told me that she would never give me a divorce because she wasn't prepared to let her children bear the stigma of such a shameful act, but that in every other respect she was glad that our marriage was over.' Ben laughed ruefully. 'A pretty pair we make, don't we, Georgie?'

'I might not have loved you so much if you'd been other than you were, Ben,' she said. 'You weren't prepared to break your marriage vows then, and you ought not to now. This afternoon is special, something to keep in our memories, to cheer us up when we're low, but it can't drift into a proper affair. Helen is right about the scandal reflecting on the children. If she isn't prepared to divorce you it would just become messy and uncomfortable and we might end up hating each other.'

'You know that's not true, darling,' Ben said and kissed her neck, his hand moving idly over her thigh. 'I could never hate you and I don't think you would hate me, but you're right about a hole in the corner affair. I don't want that for us.'

'What else could it ever be?'

'I'm not sure at the moment,' he admitted. 'Let's just forget about it for the time being, shall we? As you said, this afternoon is special; it's our time and I want to savour it and you, Georgie. Once isn't enough – could never be enough after all those years of wanting and longing.'

'Oh, Ben...' Her guilt fled as she turned in his arms, giving herself up to the pleasure of his loving. He was a strong man, his body muscled and hard beneath her stroking hands, and his flesh felt firm and satiny close to hers. She felt the rising tide of passion inside her as she arched into him, a moan of pleasure escaping as his tongue circled her nipples, bringing her to an aching awareness of her need. 'Oh, Ben, yes please ... that feels so good ... so very good.'

Her packing finished, Georgie tested the weight of her suitcases and found that she'd bought more than she'd imagined on her shopping spree. These were heavy and she hoped there would be a porter at the station, otherwise she was going to have difficulty in getting them home.

It was no problem from the hotel to the taxi or at Liverpool Street Station, but at home it might not be so easy. If there was no one available she would simply have to leave one at the station office and make two journeys to the car.

'You always buy too much, Georgie, old girl.'

'Don't scold me, Arthur.'

She spoke aloud before she realized

Arthur's voice was only a memory. Of course, she was feeling guilty this morning. She had known she would even as she lay in Ben's arms, glorying in his lovemaking. The largest part of her guilt was not that she had been to bed with Ben, but that she had given herself to him in a way that she had never been able to give herself to Arthur. She was aware that her own failure to respond had been the root cause of much of the problem and it hadn't been fair to blame Arthur for her lack of pleasure.

'Oh damn,' she muttered. This wasn't getting her anywhere.

She lifted the telephone and rang down for the porter. This visit to London had been enjoyable in many ways, but she needed to be at home so that she could think things through.

Nothing had changed in all these years really. Ben was still tied to Helen and his duty, and she couldn't see that changing. What had changed was his willingness to have an affair. She knew that he wanted their relationship to carry on, even though he had agreed that they should both stand back and take their time. She'd meant it when she'd said it should end here, but Ben had just been trying to make the decision easier for her. He was looking to find some happiness with her. His marriage had been far worse to endure than hers, which had really been quite good in many ways.

'Oh damn, damn, damn!' she muttered

again. Why did she have to have this wretched conscience that wouldn't let her be? Arthur was dead. She couldn't hurt him now, whatever she did. A part of her wanted to telephone Ben and ask him to get in touch whenever he could, but she held back.

She would wait, give herself time and think it over.

'Why not stay here with us for a while?' Madame de Faubourg said to Hetty. They were watching Kristina playing happily in the nursery with toys left behind by generations of the de Faubourg family. 'The child seems easier now, I grant you, but to take her to England where she will not understand what anyone says ... that seems unkind. I have told you that there is a home for you here with me. The house is so big that we need never meet if you wish it that way.'

'I could never wish that. You have been kindness itself, madame,' Hetty said and realized that a part of her was responding to that and wanted to stay. 'But I was intending to return to England to see my family. They will be anxious for me.'

She had already delayed three days, because Kristina had been too distressed and screamed whenever they went near the car. It had been the Comtesse's idea to bring her here to the nursery and it seemed to be helping the child. In playing with the toys she could forget the terrible sights she had witnessed.

'I am sure there is a way of letting your

family know you are safe,' the Comtesse said. 'I dare say letters can still get through. Our telephone has been cut as you know, but there are always some who can contact London.'

'What my grandmother is trying to say is that she wants you to stay,' Pierre said as he came to join them. 'Jean seems better this morning. If he continues to improve we shall be on our way in a week or so.'

'I am glad Jean is better,' the Comtesse said. 'But I do not see your hurry to leave, Pierre. We have been forced to sign the surrender in the most humiliating way, but what can you expect after the Government ran away? It is shameful! They should have defended Paris to the last man.'

She was talking about the armistice, which the French had been forced to sign at Compiegne, where the German surrender had taken place in 1918. The German troops were now parading along the Champs Elysees, the French Government having left for Bordeaux days earlier. They had heard that heavy restrictions were already in place, cinemas, restaurants and some shops reserved for German use.

'It would have been a waste of lives,' Pierre told her but smiled fondly. 'You are too fierce, *ma chérie*. If we had an army of men like you we should never have let the Germans put one foot on French soil.'

'Pah!' She made a grimace of disgust. 'As always it is bad planning, no backbone to speak of at the top. They were too willing to lie down and let the Germans walk all over them. And now what will you do? You hurry to return to your unit but for what? To surrender like the rest of them?'

'No, I shall never do that, Grandmère,' Pierre told her, mouth set in a harsh line. 'There is still some fighting going on, and when that is crushed, as it will be, I shall join the secret resistance. I would rather my blood was spilled on the ground than surrender to the enemy.'

'Now you speak like a man,' she said approvingly. 'That is what you must do – what all of us must do. We must resist with all our strength, be it great or small. They should be made to understand that we are not all willing to be their slaves.'

'I am sure there are many who think as we do,' Pierre said. 'We could not hold out against them because they were too strong for us, but that doesn't mean we have all given up the fight.'

'I shall never give up,' the Comtesse declared, her eyes flashing. In that moment Hetty saw echoes of the splendid woman she must have been when she was younger. 'Let them do what they will to me, I shall fight them until I am dead.'

'Bravo, *ma chérie*,' Pierre said, his eyes warm with affection. 'Perhaps Hetty will stay and help you?'

'You told me I was British and should go home!' Hetty gave him a challenging look.

'That was before I knew you,' he said, his smile teasing and warm. 'My grandmother likes you and she means what she says. You told me you love France, that you had lived here for ten years – stay and join in the fight with her.'

'No, Pierre, you speak too fast,' the Comtesse said, shaking her head at him. 'Hetty must stay for a little; to bide her time and think about what she wants to do. Then, if she wants to continue her journey, we shall help her.'

'I think I must stay for a while,' Hetty admitted. The Comtesse was someone she admired. Already she felt drawn to her and there was no way she could leave until Kristina was less nervous. 'If a letter could be sent to England I should be grateful, or a message of some kind. My family will be worrying, because they must know that the Germans are in Paris, and they cannot know that I escaped before that happened. Kristina isn't ready to leave yet, and I can't abandon her. Who knows what might happen if the Germans found her? So I shall avail myself of your hospitality and stay for a while, thank you.'

'Good, that is settled,' the Comtesse said with a satisfied smile. 'Now you will leave me alone with the child and you two will go for a walk. Pierre should show you certain things that you may need to know if the Germans come here.'

'Yes, Grandmère is right,' he agreed.

112

'Come, take a stroll with me, Hetty. I should like to show you a little more of my home.'

There was no doubt that he could be charming when he chose, Hetty thought. He reminded her a little of Henri when they had first met. They were not really alike in looks, for Pierre was a much sterner man, more aristocratic, more cultured and knowledgeable. Henri had lived only for his art. She ought not to think of them as being alike for in truth they were not – except for just now and then when she was aware of something in Pierre that made her think he might not be all that he seemed. Yet perhaps she was too sceptical because of Henri's betrayal.

'Perhaps you should tell me what to avoid in the old wing,' Hetty suggested. 'I remember you saying that parts of the ceiling are unsound.'

'I warned you not to go there and that still applies,' he said, 'but there is something about the old wing that you should know in an emergency...'

'You intrigue me,' Hetty said looking at him curiously. 'Tell me what you mean?'

'I think I would rather show you,' Pierre said, his smile positively Machiavellian. 'In this instance, actions speak louder than words...'

'Your French is excellent, Tarleton,' the officer said looking at him speculatively. 'Spent much time there?'

'Several holidays when I was younger,' Ben

113

said. 'And I've been a few times in the last few years, to see my sister. She has been living out there for some years. Her French was so good that it made me take more pains with my own, though I couldn't rival Hetty. She sounds like a native.'

'Your sister is still living there?'

'I wish I knew,' Ben said and frowned. 'We haven't heard from her since the Germans broke through the French lines. Someone told us he believed that she left Paris before they got there, but we don't know for sure. We've had no word as yet.'

'There may be a way of finding something out – is she married?'

'No, she's still Hester Tarleton, Hetty for short. She had a lot of friends in Paris, but if she has left there I'm not sure where she would go. I imagine she might try to get a ship, but there's no guarantee she would make it that far. Her car wasn't much use. I offered to buy her a better one once but she refused, said she never needed a car in Paris.'

'Well, I can't promise anything, though we do have contacts.'

'Yes, sir. I understand this interview is something to do with liaison work? Because I speak French reasonably well.'

'I'm not at liberty to tell you any more at the moment. Though, you will have to undergo some basic training first – but if we wanted you to go in, would you be prepared to do so?'

'Go in under cover?' Ben stared at the

officer in surprise and with a flicker of excitement. He'd been warned that because of a defect with his feet he wouldn't be much use for ordinary duties as a soldier. He had been prepared for some basic army training and then being transferred to some dead-end job as a pen-pusher for the duration, but this was beyond anything he'd imagined. 'I'm not sure my French is good enough for that – but I'm prepared to give it a go, sir.'

'Just like that? Most of my operatives want time to consider. I won't beat about the bush – a lot of them don't make it back. They slip up and that's curtains. We provide you with a suicide pill in case of torture...'

'Yes, I imagine that might come in handy, sir.'

The officer smiled. 'Well done, Tarleton. That floors some straightaway. We hope you won't have to use it, but the first thing you learn if you join us is that you owe loyalty to your comrades. The one thing you never do is talk – so there's an easy way out if you can't take it.'

'Understood, sir.'

'Still want to go ahead with the training?'

'Yes, sir.'

'We'll give you ten days to consider, visit family, friends, anybody you care about – but you can't breath a word of this to anyone. Understood?'

'Can't say I know much yet, sir,' Ben said and smiled oddly. 'I'm not likely to tell anyone what you've told me.'

'You'll have to sign the Official Secrets Act, of course.' The officer offered his hand. 'Ted Barker. I shall be your mentor in all this, Tarleton. We shall meet again next in Scotland. I'm here to recruit a small team of operatives, but the training is north of the border. You'll arrive by train and be met in Edinburgh; from there you'll be taken by car to the secret location. Rather pleasant surroundings. We treat our operatives well during training, though it isn't easy to get through the course. Even if we take you on it doesn't mean you'll pass.'

'The condemned man ate heartily, sir?' Ben raised his brows. 'That rather puts us on our mettle, doesn't it? I'll look forward to seeing you in a few days, sir.'

'That's the spirit, old chap. Off you go now and enjoy your leave. It might be a while before you get another one.'

'Thank you – and thank you for giving me this chance, sir. I didn't expect it.'

'Thought we'd put you behind a desk moving records around, did you? You might wish we had before you're finished, Tarleton.'

'No, I don't think so,' Ben said. 'Always did enjoy exploring the French countryside, sir.'

'By moonlight?'

'I should imagine the last thing I need to wish for is the moon.'

'Perfectly right,' Ted Barker said. 'Glad you spotted that – it shows you think with your brain and not through various other parts of your anatomy.'

Ben smiled. Having already been put through several weeks of marching and various other delights by an army drill sergeant, whose face looked as if he drank vinegar for pleasure, he had no doubt what part of his anatomy was in question.

'I try not to, sir.'

'Get off then – you're wasting my time and your own.'

Ben saluted and left the office. He was feeling a bit stunned as he went out into the warmth of a perfect summer day. He had ten days. He ought to go home and see the children, but he wouldn't stop for more than a day. It was just possible that he wouldn't get another chance and he knew exactly what he wanted to do with the remainder of his leave.

'You've had a letter from Hetty?' Georgie was pleased; she could hear the relief in Annabel's voice. 'That's wonderful. When did it arrive?'

'Only this morning. Someone came into reception and asked for me, then gave me the letter. It hadn't been through the normal post and it looked a bit grubby, as though it had passed through a few hands, but the main thing is that she says she's fine. She isn't in Paris but she can't tell me where she is for security reasons. She says she's with friends and that she may stay for a while...'

'Why on earth doesn't she come home? If she can get a letter out there must be a way of getting back. I know some people managed it after the Germans first invaded, though it must be more difficult as their patrols spread out through the country. I expect their grip is tightening all the time.'

'You know Hetty. She is always so independent and if she has found somewhere safe for the moment that's all that matters. She says she was caught up in an unpleasant incident and that she is caring for a child whose mother was killed in an attack from the air.'

'Yes, I read about something like that in the paper,' Georgie said. 'They flew over the people leaving Paris and shot at them – one report said several were killed.'

'Yes, I know. It gave me nightmares for days, but now I can relax for a while, thank goodness.'

'You're sure the letter came from Hetty?'

'Yes, of course. She mentioned something only she and I know – about Mother actually. She says she's met a lady who would put Mother in her place in five seconds flat, but that she's brave and wonderful and she likes her very much.'

'She doesn't tell you who this lady is?'

'No – she doesn't give any names. I'm not sure what she's up to, Georgie. I've been told that the French are forming a secret resistance to fight against the Germans.'

'Who told you that?'

'A friend of Paul actually. I don't suppose it's all that secret really. That French general de Gaulle was on the wireless telling his people to carry on fighting and how he is forming an official resistance.'

'Yes, that's rather different though, isn't it? He's over here and Hetty is there. I hope she has the sense not to get involved in anything like that, Annabel. It would be terribly dangerous.'

'Hetty has always been brave, you know. It took a lot of courage to run away as she did with Henri. I don't think I would have done it in her place.'

'I call that reckless and headstrong.'

'Yes, but brave too. I think it would be just like her to help with the resistance if she could – and the letter that came, well, it didn't get here through the usual channels.'

'No, that sounds pretty much as if...' Georgie heard the doorbell ringing and frowned. 'This always happens to me when you telephone, Annabel. I shall have to go. I'll ring you back later if I can.'

'Well, I've told you my news. I've been trying to get Ben, but I haven't managed it yet. Bye for now.'

The bell was ringing again. Whoever was there was very persistent, Georgie thought as she went to answer it. Opening the door, her heart caught and she stared in surprise as she saw him.

'Ben ... what are you doing here?'

'I thought you might be pleased to see me? I have nine days leave, Georgie. I thought we might spend some of it together.'

'Ben...' She felt breathless, the excitement rising inside her in an overwhelming tide. 'Come in and we'll talk about it. I was on the

119

telephone to Annabel when you arrived, that's why I was slow to answer – she's heard from Hetty at last. She's out of Paris and staying with friends.'

'That's a relief,' Ben said and gave her one of his special smiles. 'I'll ring her later so that she can tell me the good news herself – but I thought we might go for a little holiday together, Georgie. Just throw a few things in a case, get in the car and drive. I'm not sure where we'll end up, probably the sea somewhere as the weather is so nice at the moment.'

'Yes...' Georgie had been longing to see him again. She might feel guilty afterwards, though there was no real reason why she should. 'Yes, I should love to come away with you, Ben. I've been hoping you might telephone.'

'I thought about it,' he admitted, 'but there didn't seem much point until I could get away for a few days. The training has been pretty tough and that was only the beginning; they're sending me somewhere else at the end of my leave for more training. I can't tell you much about it, but it's not quite what I thought.'

'Don't even try to tell me,' Georgie said and held out her hands to him. 'I'll put the kettle on and while it's boiling I'll go and pack my case. Geoffrey went to stay with his school chum two days ago so that's one problem out of the way. I see no reason why we shouldn't enjoy ourselves as we please for the rest of your leave.'

'That's what I thought,' Ben said. 'We're both adults and I think we would be mad to let our consciences dictate to us, Georgie. We made a mistake years ago. If I'd gone to bed with you then I should never have let you go again. I've been thinking of you constantly day and night. I was afraid that if I rang you might tell me I shouldn't so I decided to come and carry you off by force if need be.'

'No, I shan't tell you to go away,' she said and reached up to brush her lips softly over his. 'I've been missing you. I love you, Ben. It was always you I loved and I shouldn't have married. If I'd waited you might have divorced Helen in time.'

'That's another thing I want to talk about,' Ben told her. 'It can't happen while there's a war on, Georgie, but I've made up my mind that I'll sort things out when it's all over. I refuse to waste the rest of my life in a relationship that is meaningless and empty. I love you and I want you to be my wife. It won't be easy, but somehow I'll do it. I promise you that, my darling. Do you believe me?'

'Yes,' she said. She trusted him but it wouldn't be easy and she wasn't sure he would be able to carry it out, but she knew he meant it and that was what counted. 'Yes, I believe you, my darling – and I love you.'

Georgie knew she would always remember those eight precious days spent with Ben.

They had decided not to stay at one place all the time, and drove as far as they wanted each morning, stopping at country pubs for bed and breakfast and in a caravan at Flamborough for two days. Set high on a chalk headland, it was a village rich in folklore about the sea and the people who had served it for generations. For more than two thousand years the headland had seen duty as a fortress, guarding against the invader, and Danes Dyke stood testimony to the vigilance of the villagers throughout the centuries.

The weather was perfect for much of the time and they walked a lot, on the beach where they could or in quiet woods, seeking out beauty spots away from the crowds who flocked to the more popular resorts just up the coast on the bank holiday weekend.

'It would have to be this weekend,' Ben groaned after they were turned away from one small hotel.

'We'll choose out of the way places in future,' Georgie said and they had.

It was just as good between them in bed every time.

'I thought it couldn't always be like this,' she admitted when they'd been together for three days, 'but it just seems to get better.'

'That's because we're in love,' Ben said and touched her hair with the tips of his fingers. 'We were always right for each other. We both knew it at the start, but we made a foolish mistake. At least I did, because you wouldn't have if I'd asked you to marry me.'

'We've come to our senses just in time.' Georgie raised her head to kiss him. 'So many years wasted but that's all over, Ben. We'll be together as often as we can in the future and one day it will all work out right for us.'

'This war is a damned nuisance,' Ben said. 'But in a way it brought us together so I shouldn't complain. I'm not sure when we'll be able to be together again, darling.'

'But you're going to be doing some sort of office work, aren't you?' She felt him go still and a prickle of fear started at her nape. 'Or has that changed?'

'I can't tell you,' he said. 'I'm sorry but it's a part of the job. All I can say is that I'll telephone you as much as I can, Georgie.'

'Are you going to be in some sort of danger?'

'It's best you don't ask. For the moment I'm simply going for more training.'

Which meant that the job was dangerous, Georgie realized, the fear seeping into her bones. She'd believed that Ben would be safe doing a nice little job at the War Office or something, rather like Beth's boss, but obviously his role wasn't going to be like that at all.

A surge of rebellion went through her. Ben must have been singled out for this special work, whatever it was. She wanted to protest, to tell him he mustn't let them use him. It wasn't fair! It just wasn't fair that she might lose him before they'd had any time together.

All those wasted years and now ... but she

was being foolish and selfish. She couldn't wrap Ben up in cotton wool and keep him safe, any more than thousands of other women could keep their men safe. No matter how unfair this all was, the war was happening and she couldn't do anything to stop it.

'Oh, Ben,' she said and pressed herself against him as if she wanted to imprint the feel of his flesh so deep that she would never lose it. 'I do love you so very much.'

'I love you, darling. I promise I'll keep in touch and if I get more leave before … then we'll meet in London next time. Go to a show or something?'

'Yes, that would be nice.' She clung to him, knowing that she had to play the game, pretend that everything was fine. She wasn't the only woman who felt this way. There must be thousand of others all over the country in the same situation. 'I'm hungry, are you?'

'Yes.' Ben laughed and kissed her. 'Get out of this bed, woman. You promised to cook me a meal if we took the caravan, and I'm not in the mood for going out this evening. It wastes too much time – time we could spend more pleasurably.'

'I'll do steak and chips with mushy peas, onion rings and mushrooms, shall I?' she teased. 'Or will you settle for bacon and eggs – and I do have some mushrooms I picked in the wood.'

'Are you sure they're edible?' He grimaced. 'They look a bit odd to me.'

'Trust me,' she said. 'I've used them all before. I know my fungi, Ben. I shan't poison you.'

'I'll trust you,' he said. 'After all, you sweet-talked that farmer into selling you the eggs.'

'Duck eggs too. I'm going to make a delicious omelette. Just stay where you are and I'll call you when I'm ready.'

Georgie left him in bed, walking naked into the kitchen area of the caravan. She'd drawn the curtains earlier, but there was no one else around. The farmer who owned the van lived some distance away. He'd told them that the field had been full of tents and caravans earlier in the week, but everyone had gone back to work now.

Their holiday was over, and Ben's would be soon. Then it might be ages before she saw him again – if she ever did. It was possible that he might be killed doing ... whatever it was he couldn't tell her. And how was she going to feel then?

Georgie blinked back her stupid tears. She'd made the excuse that she was hungry because she'd been frightened she might give herself away, but she wasn't going to cry. She knew from experience that it never helped.

'Oh, Drew,' Beth said as she ran to greet him outside her lodgings that afternoon. It had just started to spit with rain and was cooler than it had been of late. 'I thought Arnold was never going to let me leave. I told him you had just forty-eight hours and he agreed

125

to my having the time off, but then he just kept finding things for me to do.'

'Well, you're here now,' Drew said and pulled her into his arms. He kissed her hungrily. 'And we've still got forty-seven hours and twenty minutes – and I don't want to waste a second.'

'Drew?' Beth felt a little shiver of apprehension as she looked at him. His expression was so serious that it frightened her. 'Is something wrong?'

'I'm being transferred to active service. A chap who has seen action and been injured is taking over my job and I'm being moved on. That's why I got the two-day pass. I want us to get married, Beth. I know we were going to wait until Christmas, but we've got all the necessary paperwork in hand and I don't see why we should wait any longer. I'm sure of my feelings – aren't you?'

'Yes, of course I am,' Beth said. 'You know I am, Drew. We were only waiting because Annabel and Paul wanted to give us a nice wedding at the hotel.'

He frowned slightly. His mother had wanted to give them a big wedding too, and it was awkward.

'You can telephone them, tell them to save it for when I get leave. We can invite all our friends to a reception then if you like?'

'Yes, of course we can,' Beth said and smiled at him. 'What do we have to do? Don't we need a special licence or something?'

'I've had that for a while,' Drew told her.

'And I rang to make sure it was possible – the registrar can fit us in tomorrow morning at ten thirty.'

'Oh, that's lovely,' Beth said swallowing her disappointment. She'd been looking forward to buying the material for her wedding dress, saving the coupons until she had enough for her needs, but now she wouldn't have to.

'I know it isn't what you'd hoped for,' Drew said, sensing how she felt even though she was doing her best to hide it. 'But I want us to be together, Beth. We've waited even though we've both wanted to make love, but we've held back – and I don't want to wait any longer. I love you and I want you very much.'

'Yes, I know. I want you too, darling.'

Beth knew he'd been marvellously restrained and patient. A lot of the girls she saw at the office talked about sleeping with their boyfriends quite openly. They didn't seem to see anything wrong with it.

'Got to give him something to remember – something to make him keep his head down and come back in one piece,' were frequently used phrases in the tearoom.

Drew hadn't wanted that. He loved her and respected her, and wanted to wait despite their growing frustration. Kissing and heavy petting wasn't enough for either of them any more.

'You aren't too disappointed about not having a big wedding, Beth darling?'

'Not, of course not,' she said and smiled at
127

him. 'Annabel will be disappointed I know, but all I want is to be your wife.'

Especially if he was being sent abroad. Beth felt a sudden chill of fear as she realized what that meant. They had always known it could happen but she hadn't expected it so soon.

'Why don't we spend tonight at a hotel?' she said. 'It's only a few more hours to our wedding and we haven't got that long, have we?'

'If you're sure?'

She could see that it was what he wanted and she smiled lovingly, lifting her face for his kiss.

'Yes, of course it is, Drew. I suppose we've been old-fashioned and silly to wait all this time. All the other girls I know sleep with their boyfriends.'

'I don't want to marry them,' Drew told her, his eyes warm with love. 'You are sweet and precious, Beth, and I want you just the way you are.'

After that, Beth would have been stupid to regret the glamour of a big wedding. She knew how lucky she was to have found Drew, because she'd never felt in the least like this about anyone else.

They were lucky to have this little time together and they had to make the most of it. She wouldn't think of anything else but being with him, loving him. It would be time to think of the future when he'd gone.

'Let's go and find that hotel,' Drew said and held out his hand. 'I've got a present for you, Beth. I was going to give it to you tomorrow, but I want you to have it today, my darling.'

'But you've given me lots of presents,' she said her eyes bright. 'What is it this time?'

'Ah...' He laughed as she pouted. 'It's something rather special – but you are just going to have to wait and see...'

Five

'Why did you show me the secret caves, Pierre?' Hetty asked as they were walking back towards the house. She had been in the woods picking berries and he had met her, taking her basket from her. 'Don't you realize I could sell your family to the Germans and get rich?'

He quirked an eyebrow at her, seeming amused at the suggestion. 'Somehow I don't see that happening, Hetty. Why did I show you? I suppose because Grandmère needs you to stay with her. She pretends to be strong and independent, and she means it when she says she would rather die than give into them, but I don't like the idea of her being alone here. I know her people are devoted to her, but she needs someone she can talk to sometimes. Besides, there is a possibility that I might die fairly soon, and someone will need to do something about the caves after the war. Grandmère won't be around forever.'

'Supposing you were both dead?' Hetty asked. 'What would you want me to do with all those treasures? You told me you didn't have much money, Pierre – but that stuff must be worth a fortune.'

'Yes, I suppose it is,' he said and pulled a face. 'A lot of it is family heirlooms and Grandmère would never part with it simply to repair the roof, but I had planned on making changes. Hopefully, I shall, when it's all over.'

'And when do you suppose that will be?'

'A long time, I dare say, unless the British fold under the pressure and let the Germans win – and somehow I doubt that. But it could happen, of course. Now that France has fallen Hitler is bound to turn his attention on them.' Pierre sighed. 'But I didn't answer you about what you should do with the stuff. I have lawyers in England. I shall give you their names before I leave and hope that you will get in touch with them if both Grandmère and I are no longer here. They will know what to do, but they don't know where to look for the stock – I didn't dare share the secret with too many people. But someone ought to know in case of my death.'

'Please – don't talk that way,' Hetty pleaded. 'You're going to fight them, Pierre. You shouldn't be fatalistic. In all probability you will find that your unit has surrendered and then you can come back to us and join your grandmother's fight against them here.'

'The secret resistance?' Pierre smiled wryly. 'It sounds brave and wonderful, doesn't it? But what do you think a few men and women can do to halt them? They are ruthless, Hetty. Grandmère talks of defying the enemy, but she doesn't see what kind of retribution will fall on those who get caught.'

'But they have to catch us first,' Hetty said, a naughty smile curving her mouth. 'And you might be surprised what a few women can come up with if they put their heads together, Pierre.'

'Nothing you did would surprise me,' he said and turned suddenly towards her, pulling her hard against him, a hungry light in his eyes as he gazed down at her. 'You've only known me a short while, but there's something between us – don't you feel it, Hetty? You're a special woman and I want to make love to you.'

'Do you, Pierre?' She looked into his eyes. 'Tell me, honestly, is it really me or would any woman do to fill the emptiness inside you? Isn't it just physical?' Something inside her was warning her not to get involved, and yet he was going away and might be killed. It wouldn't hurt to relax her guard for once.

'I could go to any brothel for that,' Pierre replied. 'I've been wanting to kiss you since we first met and you accused me of stealing your things.'

'Well, you were,' she said but her eyes were bright with laughter. She had come to like Pierre these past weeks and he was right, the physical attraction was there between them, had been from the beginning. She wasn't sure about love. Her experience with Henri had taught her to be wary of giving her heart too easily; she had been hurt and she didn't want that to happen again, but she knew that she wanted to go to bed with this man. It was a long time since she'd been close to anyone and she needed the comfort of physical contact.

'I sent some of the servants to look on the road for your pictures,' Pierre told her ruefully. 'I'm afraid there was nothing left of them but a few shreds of torn canvas. Everyone had trampled right over them.'

'Possibly the best thing that could happen,' Hetty said. 'At least I still have my paints. I can do some work here – a few pictures of your château perhaps.'

'That would please Grandmère.' His eyes darkened with passion as he bent his head towards her. 'You haven't said yes...'

'But then again, I haven't said no,' Hetty said and reached up on tiptoe to kiss him. 'Perhaps you ought to see if you can persuade me?'

Hetty lay looking up at the silken canopy of the four-poster bed while Pierre slept beside her. A little smile curved her mouth, for their lovemaking had been both pleasurable and satisfying. Pierre was a good lover, skilled and passionate – a better lover than Henri had ever been, because he had tried to please her before seeking his own release. Henri had only ever thought of himself.

Hetty hadn't known it was possible to feel quite such exquisite pleasure and she was glad that she had not refused him. She didn't

133

believe that she was in love with him. From what she recalled of her first feelings for Henri they had been very different. Love made you afraid, excited, nervous; she'd gone on loving Henri for a long time despite his faults and the hurt he'd caused – but she wasn't experiencing any of those emotions at the moment. Pierre had made her happy, as she had made him happy; it was a fleeting thing but something to be enjoyed and forgotten.

She gave a sigh of pleasure. She had quickly grown fond of the Comtesse, and she enjoyed Pierre's company. She had promised she would stay on for as long as possible, and she knew Kristina had found a safe haven, for Madame de Faubourg loved her. They were together much of the time; child and old woman, hand in hand in the gardens, enjoying the sunlit, peaceful days. The château had a timeless feel, as if life went on in the same way endlessly, passed by as the world rushed to chaos; as if by her strength of will alone the Comtesse could hold back change.

If only it could stay this way forever, Hetty thought, knowing that it could not last indefinitely. The Germans would come and when they did ... Madame talked of killing them, but Hetty was more wary. They could fight in secret ways, were already making plans to make sabotage attacks on German trains, but they could not hope to repel the Germans if they came to the château in force.

They were as Pierre said, only a few women, old men and boys.

'What are you thinking?' Pierre asked and kissed her neck.

She had thought him asleep, but obviously she was wrong.

'I was just thinking I should like to lie here with you forever.'

'You are a siren, Hetty,' he told her with a throaty chuckle. 'In olden days you would have lured Grecian sailors to your island and kept them prisoner there.'

'And what does that mean?' she bristled.

'It means that I agree with you. I wish I could stay here forever, just like this.'

'But you can't – because I'm going to do this!'

Hetty laughed huskily and rolled him over on to his back, beginning to kiss his body, trailing her lips and tongue down from the hollow at his throat, past the narrow arrow of hair to the growing evidence of his need. She took him into her mouth, her teeth grazing the delicate flesh and making him cry out as his back arched in response to her teasing. Her tongue aroused him further, bringing cries of pleasure from his lips. And then she was sitting astride him, arching her body over his, lowering herself slowly, oh, so slowly, on to his hard, throbbing shaft. She fit him like a moist, silken sheath, surrounding him in warmth, making him writhe with the pleasure of her tantalizing movements. One moment she was bent over him, her firm taut breasts

135

making tempting fodder for his eager mouth and tongue, then in the next moment she sat back, arching away from him as his hands moved down her slender body, then lifted her and brought her down on him hard.

'*Mon Dieu*, Hetty!' he gasped as his body shook with the force of his release. 'I've never known anyone like you ... never!'

'You are a wonderful lover, Pierre,' she repaid the compliment. 'You have made me happy.'

'I am glad,' he said and pulled her close, burying his head in her breasts. She had her own perfume, a delicious fresh scent that mixed with the musk of her sex and was irresistible. 'One day I should like you to be my wife.'

Hetty gave a little chuckle. 'I'm not an innocent virgin to be placated with offers of marriage, Pierre. You owe me nothing – this was an exchange of pleasure between a man and a woman, that's all.'

'You are a free spirit,' Pierre said and seemed amused. 'I do not offer out of guilt or conscience, *ma chérie* – but because I should like to keep you all for myself.'

'We shall see,' Hetty said and rolled away as he tried to grab her. 'Enough for now, my impatient lover. I'm hungry. I want something to eat. Come, dress yourself. Grandmère will be wanting her supper and she will wonder where we are.'

'If I know anything, Grandmère is well aware of where we are, Hetty. She has already told me that I would be a fool to waste my chances. I don't know what it is about you, but she has taken to you as if you were her own. She has already told me that I should marry and produce an heir for the family – and I think she has you in mind.'

'As I said, we shall see,' Hetty said. 'I am going to wash and dress – and I advise you to do the same...'

Hetty was thoughtful as she left the bed. Pierre would return to the French army now. She would remain here with the Comtesse, but she would not be idle.

Georgie was on her knees weeding in the rose beds when she heard the telephone shrilling through the open French windows. She put her trowel down hastily and hurried inside, her heart racing. Would it be Ben? It was only a couple of weeks since they'd parted, but she was missing him terribly. He'd managed to ring three times, just for short periods, but he couldn't tell her much, just that he loved her and missed her – but that was enough. She was hungry for the sound of his voice.

'Georgie?' Annabel's voice came over the line. 'I've managed to get you at last. This must be the tenth time I've rung you – have you been away?'

'Yes, I did go to stay with a friend for a few days after Geoffrey went back to school,' Georgie said. 'He enjoyed his few days with you and your family, Annabel. I only had a short break away myself. But I've been out a lot since I got back. I've been driving an ambulance, just a small emergency one, more like a converted van, really. Still it does the job for wheelchairs and less urgent cases. I need to take a further driving test before I can graduate to a proper ambulance, but I think I shall go on with it. I didn't realize how desperate they are for volunteers.'

'Yes, that's what Paul says. He was turned down by the army – a bit too old, they said. That rankled, I can tell you! But he found himself a job doing part-time driving for the Fire Service. So at the moment he does two nights on firewatch and three mornings a week driving for emergency services. And that's besides a bit of training with the Home Guard.'

'Good gracious! How does he fit all that in with his own work?'

'Oh, he manages,' Annabel said and laughed. 'He was determined to do something after they told him he was too old for active service. He's only about ten years older than Ben, as you know.'

'I think Ben only got in by the skin of his teeth,' Georgie said, deliberately casual. 'Have you heard from him recently?'

'Not for some weeks,' Annabel replied. 'But Ben is like that. You don't hear a word for ages and then get three phone calls in a week!'

Georgie smiled to herself. She hadn't done too badly then, though it wasn't nearly enough. She changed the subject, not wanting to show undue interest in Ben.

'I went to the pictures with a friend the other day. We saw *Gone with the Wind* again.'

'Yes, I saw that with Beth the first time and cried buckets. Oh, I drove over to see Jessie yesterday.'

'How is she?'

'You know Jessie, active, fit as a fiddle. I don't think she's aged a day in the last ten years. Unfortunately, I can't say the same for Harry. He isn't much older than Jessie but he looks drawn and tired. Jessie says he's worried about the boys. He didn't want either of them to go through a war; he had enough himself in the last one. As you know, Jonathan joined the airforce last month, the second they would take him, and now Walter is talking of doing the same thing. He has another two years to wait but the way things are going I can't see this being over by then.'

'Oh, please don't say that. It's too awful.'

'Let's hope I'm wrong.'

'Have you heard anything more from Beth?' Georgie said, feeling she needed to change the subject once more.

'No, not since she rang to tell me that Drew had gone,' Annabel said and sighed. 'She didn't sound too happy. I'm worried about her alone in London, Georgie. We keep hearing rumours about London being in for it one of these days, and I've asked her to think about coming home now that she can't see Drew, but she says her work is important and she can't let Arnold down.'

139

'You know how stubborn she can be,' Georgie said. 'Besides, they said London would catch it at the beginning and it hasn't happened yet. They seem to be concentrating more on the airfields and the ports than the city centres.'

'Bad as that is, I would rather it stayed that way for Beth's sake. Oh dear, that sounds awful, doesn't it? Of course I don't want anyone to be bombed! I hate this war.'

'Don't we all? I suppose you haven't heard anything more from Hetty?'

'No and I don't really expect to, Georgie. Hetty let us know she is out of Paris, and she won't bother trying to get another message out. She will either stay where she is until it's over or come home – that's if she can, which I doubt.'

'I dare say it's a bit late now,' Georgie agreed, 'though I suppose there are ways.'

'Yes, perhaps, but Hetty isn't likely to get that sort of priority.'

'No, that's reserved for a special breed of people – and we shouldn't talk about that on the phone, or anywhere else come to that. You know what they say, keep your mouth shut for Britain.'

'We aren't likely to know any secrets, are we?' Annabel laughed. 'Oh, well, I just wanted to make sure you were all right. You can always visit again soon if you're feeling a bit fed up.'

'Yes, I know, thanks. I'm fine at the moment. Too busy to be lonely.'

It wasn't quite true. She was lonely for Ben, but she couldn't tell his sister that; it was their secret for the moment and it had to stay that way for everyone's sake.

'Well, that's what I wanted to hear. I'm glad you're feeling better, Georgie. I hope Beth will come and stay at Christmas if she can get leave. You might think about bringing Geoffrey and making it a family party?'

'Yes, perhaps,' Georgie said. 'We'll talk about it nearer the time, Annabel.'

'Well, I shall have to go. Paul just came in and he will be wanting something to eat and a chat before he goes out again. He's on firewatch this evening.'

'Bye then.'

Georgie sighed as she put down the phone. Annabel was a good friend and she didn't like keeping secrets from her, but she could hardly tell her she was Ben's lover, could she? She used the word lover in her own mind because she didn't like the alternative.

If only Ben had been given the desk job he'd expected to have when he'd joined up! He would have been able to telephone and to visit more often. Georgie pulled a wry face. She ought to know that life wasn't like that. It had a habit of smacking you in the face just when you thought everything was fine.

Surely she couldn't be pregnant! Beth came out of the bathroom, wiping her mouth, the horrid taste still on her tongue. That was the worst thing about living in lodgings, she thought, as she saw her landlady's husband glance at her curiously when they passed on the landing – there was no privacy!

It wasn't fair that she'd fallen pregnant so quickly, Beth thought. She felt a little resentful. They'd only made love a few times – and the first had been so awful. It had hurt so much! She hadn't been able to stop herself shrinking away and giving a cry of pain, and then of course Drew had been wretched. He'd apologized over and over again, and that only made her feel worse.

'I'm so sorry, darling,' Drew kept saying. 'I was impatient and you weren't ready.'

'It isn't your fault, Drew. I was nervous, that's all. It will be better next time.'

She'd been a silly little virgin, of course, but she did love Drew so very much, and it *had* been easier the next time. Except that Drew had waited so long because he wanted to be sure she was ready that it had been over too soon. So he'd ended up apologizing again. They'd got it more or less right after that, but just as they were beginning to relax with each other and enjoy themselves, Drew had had to leave.

'I wish we could have longer together, darling. I hate leaving you.'

'I wish you didn't have to go, but we both know you do.'

'What are you going to do now? Shall you stay in London or move back to the country? I would feel happier if I knew you were safe.'

'I'm as safe here as anywhere.'

142

'Mother would love to see you. I'm sure you could stay there until I come back if you wanted.'

'I shall write and thank your parents for sending me those pearls, of course.' Beth avoided his eyes. She wasn't sure why but she was nervous of meeting his parents, though they had been perfectly sweet to her over the hasty wedding.

Drew's surprise present had been a wonderful pearl necklace. Beth had never seen any as fine and she'd known before he told her that they were family heirlooms.

'Mother said I should have them when I told her we were getting married,' Drew confided, looking proud and pleased. He'd gone to the bank to fetch them before meeting Beth that afternoon. 'I know she will love you, Beth. You must promise to visit when you have time.'

'Yes, of course I will,' Beth agreed, though it was something she was reluctant to do. It wouldn't have been so bad if Drew had taken her himself, but to go on her own would seem an intrusion. 'But I can't take more time off yet. Arnold relies on me.'

'I almost wish I hadn't got you that job.' Drew looked at her with a hint of jealousy. 'Don't get too close to him while I'm away.'

Beth stared in astonishment. Surely he couldn't mean that?

'You can't imagine I would think of Arnold in that way? No, Drew, that's too silly!' She went into a peal of laughter. 'He's at least twelve years older than me for a start. Besides, he's not my type. You can't think either of us would be interested? Arnold is a confirmed bachelor.'

'No, he isn't actually,' Drew said wrinkling his brow. 'He was married for a brief time when he was about your age. His wife died of a lung infection a few months later.'

'Oh, Drew!' Beth was shocked, her eyes opening in dismay. 'That's terrible. I had no idea. He never mentions her – but then, he never speaks of his private life at all. I thought he was only interested in his work.'

'I expect that's why. He went very quiet after her death, as you might imagine. Mother said it changed him completely. Before that he was a rather happy-go-lucky type apparently.'

'Losing someone you love would change anyone.'

'Yes, you're right. I should hate to lose you, Beth.'

Beth had simply put her arms around Drew and kissed him. They'd made love again and it had been the best of all. She thought now that it might have been then when her child was conceived. Always supposing that she was pregnant, of course. The sickness might be caused by something she'd eaten. She would have to see a doctor as soon as she could manage to make an appointment.

Suddenly the wail of an air raid siren sent a chill down Beth's spine. Surely they weren't going to be bombed at this hour of the morning?

For the past few nights the sirens and bombing had become a part of all their lives. London was really catching it now. She hoped Drew didn't know it was happening because he would worry about her.

'You'd better come down to the shelter, Mrs Bryant,' her landlady called up to her. 'It might be a false alarm but you never know.'

'Yes, thank you. I'll come now.'

Beth grabbed her coat and bag from the bed and went out. If it really was a raid she was going to be late for work, but with any luck the all clear would go before too long.

'I'm sorry I'm late,' Beth apologized as she went into the office after the all clear. Arnold was bent over his desk, one lock of dark hair falling over his forehead as he read through some papers. 'I got caught in a false alarm before I left my lodgings.'

'Just as well it was a false alarm. Did it upset you? You look a bit peaky, Beth. Not ill, are you?'

'I don't know. I was sick this morning. I'm not sure what caused it.'

'Something you ate?' He raised his brows. 'Or are you pregnant?'

The direct question made her blush. 'I suppose I might be. It's a bit soon though, isn't it?'

'It happens,' Arnold said wryly. 'It happened to someone I knew.'

Beth had the oddest feeling that he was talking about his wife. Drew hadn't told her

145

that Mrs Pearson was pregnant when she died. That must have made it even worse for Arnold. She felt her heart wrench with sympathy for him but didn't say anything. If he wanted to talk he would when he was ready.

'What will you do if you are?' Arnold asked. 'Will you want to leave immediately?'

'Not unless you want me to?'

'I'd prefer you to stay on as long as you can manage. You've been useful, Beth. I shall be sorry to lose you.'

'That's very kind of you. I shan't leave until the work becomes too difficult.'

'I can get another driver when I need to, but you could carry on with the other work for some months, couldn't you?'

'Almost to the end I should think – that's if you can put up with me.'

'Let's see how it goes. It might just be a tummy upset.'

Beth had a feeling that he hoped it would be exactly that, but she wasn't sure how she felt herself. If Drew had been home she would have been pleased. Somehow it didn't seem right to have to go through nine months of carrying his child without him being there to comfort her.

'Can you take dictation now?' Arnold asked. 'I have an important meeting later with Churchill and I want to show him this report. My writing is atrocious. I can't read half of what I've written myself. I shall have to dictate and improvise what I can't make out.'

'I'm fine now,' Beth said. It was the first time he'd asked her if she was ready to take dictation. He usually just took her for granted. She was rather touched by his concern. 'Thank you. If you have a meeting, would it be all right if I took an hour or so off to see a doctor?'

'Of course. You have to take care of yourself, Beth. I don't want you to make yourself ill.'

'Oh, I shan't do that,' she said. 'I'm quite ready – if you are?'

His smile warmed her and suddenly she didn't feel quite as alone as she had earlier that morning.

Hetty was relieved that her monthly flow had come as usual. The complication of a child at this time was the last thing she needed. She had hoped there might be a baby when she was living with Henri but it hadn't happened. She thought that perhaps it wasn't possible for her and was a little sad. Yet she knew that she would not have wanted to have Pierre's child at this particular moment in time. It would be too awkward and constricting, especially at times like these.

'Are you listening, Hetty?' The man's impatient voice brought her thoughts to earth with a bump. 'The device is set. All you have to do is get down to the line and place it where we arranged without being seen.'

'You make it sound so simple, Bernard,' she said. 'Supposing I set if off by accident?'

147

'If you'd been listening you would know that isn't possible. You unravel the wire as you come back up the bank. I shall attach it to the remote detonator and...'

'Boom!' Hetty said and grinned at him. 'As I said, it sounds so simple.'

'As it will be if you are careful. I would go myself but you are more nimble. If anyone saw me I would be too slow to hide. Besides, Louis and I will be on the watch up here with the guns. I do not think you would be able to shoot anyone if it became necessary.'

'I should miss if I tried,' Hetty retorted. 'I need a lot more lessons before I can get the aim right. No, we agreed that I should be the one to place the device. You've told me what to do six times, Bernard. I shan't forget.'

'If you're challenged you must run away at once. Don't let yourself be caught, Hetty. Get rid of the explosives somehow and run as fast as you can.'

'I know. You've told me. Stop worrying. I know exactly what to do.' Sometimes Bernard was an old woman!

'It's time to start down now. You have fifteen minutes to get down there, wedge it on to the line, bring the wire back to me so that we're ready when the train comes through.'

'You're sure you'll know it's the right one?'

'I'll know.' He looked grim.

Hetty started off down the incline. It was almost dark, the moon obscured by helpful clouds. She was praying it would stay that way. She could see just enough to find her

148

path down the steep embankment. They had practised this several times. Hetty had carried a basket, pretending to be picking wild herbs. She'd tried the descent with her eyes shut and knew she could do it, her feet sure and safe as she went down. Finding the right spot on the line was more difficult. Bernard had told her it must be against the inner rail so that the train caught the full blast. It was only capable of causing a small explosion in itself, but the German train was carrying ammunition and should go up like a firework display according to their information.

She found the right spot and placed her package. Her fingers shook a little and her heart raced as she began to unravel the wire. This was the danger time if she was spotted from the station just up the line. She held her breath as she began to climb back up the steep bank, expecting to hear shouting or gunfire, but there was nothing and she reached the top without incident, flopping down on the grass beside Bernard.

'Good,' he said, a note of satisfaction in his voice. He was making the connection and the plunger was ready, fully extended. They all heard the train coming and looked at each other expectantly. 'Go now, both of you.'

Hetty hesitated, but Louis grabbed her arm, pulling her to her feet.

'Come, it is dangerous to be seen together. There will be fire.'

'But your grandfather?'

'He will follow.'

Hetty allowed the youth to urge her towards the shelter of the trees. She heard the first explosion seconds later, and then after a short delay, a series of huge ones, sounding like a fantastic firework display. The sky was suddenly red and orange as a fireball shot into the air behind them. It was awesome and frightening; Hetty was shocked that they had managed to do something like this. Until this moment it had been almost like playing a game, but now, suddenly, it had become reality.

'We must hurry. If we are seen we shall be suspected.'

'Bernard...'

'Knows these woods better than you, Hetty. Save your breath and run.'

Hetty did as she was told, blocking thoughts of what was happening behind her. The train was manned by Germans because they didn't trust the French. Bernard had told her so and she had to believe him. It didn't matter how many Germans were killed, because they were the enemy. They were killing anyone they pleased, ruthlessly and in cold blood. She hated them. They had killed Kristina's mother and probably her father too.

Louis stopped her when they reached the edge of the woods close to the château. He took his gun and hid it in a hollow tree. In the faint glimmer of moonlight his eyes held the glitter of excitement.

'Now do not forget, we have been visiting

150

my great grandmother who is sick, Hetty.' He handed her the basket she had left earlier by the tree. 'You have been tending her. She lives five miles in the opposite direction from where we blew up the train.'

'Yes, I know,' she said. 'I don't know what all the fuss is about. No one would betray us, Louis. They all hate the Germans.'

'We must be careful. They will come, Hetty, after this they will assuredly come. We must give them no reason to be suspicious or they will shoot us all.'

'At least we have done something tonight – struck a blow for France.' She felt strangely elated as if she would have liked to shout her triumph aloud.

'Oui, mademoiselle.' His manner had become that of the respectful servant once more.

Hetty walked a little behind him, her head bent in thought. It took only a few minutes to reach the servants' entrance. Once they were inside she breathed a sigh of relief.

It was short-lived. Louis was talking to one of the women and she could see their anxious faces.

'What's wrong?'

'A German general is here,' Louis told her. 'He came in a staff car with two junior officers. More men will join them in the morning.'

Hetty felt the chill at the nape of her neck. 'How long have they been here?'

'A few minutes only,' Louis said. 'The story is changed, mademoiselle. You have been lying down in your room. You had a headache but Madame la Comtesse has sent to ask if you will come down.'

'I shall use the back stairs. I must change my dress and I shall leave my shoes here. Where is the general and his staff?'

'In the green salon.'

'At the front of the house?' Hetty breathed more easily. 'They would not have seen as we returned. It is fortunate that they came on ahead of the others – I wonder why they did that? It is more usual for them to sweep in and take control with no warning.'

'General von Steinbeck has stayed here before as a guest of the family. He wanted to warn the Comtesse without alarming her that her house was to be inspected. They are looking for somewhere suitable to set up their headquarters in this area.'

'Tell me the rest later. I must hurry.'

Hetty ran up the stairs, making her way swiftly to her own room. She tore off her dress, which might show signs of where she'd lain on the grass waiting for the train. Selecting a heavy linen dress with a demure white collar and short sleeves, she found a pair of black satin shoes and then dragged a brush through her hair. She decided against makeup. If she looked pale so much the better. She was supposed to have the head-ache.

Her heart was thumping as she walked down the main staircase and turned towards the green salon. She had always known the

152

Germans would come one day, but that it should be this night! Her guilt lay on her heavily, but she fought it down. What was done was done and for France. The door of the salon was slightly open and she was surprised to hear the sound of laughter. She paused outside to catch her breath and then went in. The Comtesse had brought out a bottle of the best champagne.

'Marguerite,' she said, turning as Hetty came in with a smile of welcome. 'Please come and meet my good friend General von Steinbeck. He was a particular friend of Pierre's father, you know.' She smiled encouragingly at Hetty. 'General – my great-niece, Marguerite Lebrun. How is your headache now, my dear?'

'A little better,' Hetty said. She felt as if she were in a nightmare. She had just been the cause of death and destruction to this man's comrades and here he was being treated as a favoured guest at the château. Yet what else could the Comtesse do? She had no choice but to follow her lead. 'Forgive me for keeping you waiting, General von Steinbeck. I was asleep.'

'And we have woken you! Forgive us, mademoiselle. Your great-aunt insisted that you would want to come down, though I told her it could wait until tomorrow.'

'It is all right, Marguerite. I have shown General von Steinbeck your papers. Everything is in order. He understands why you have come to stay with me, my dear.'

'I was afraid you might be lonely.' Hetty smiled and went to kiss her cheek. She glanced at the two younger men. They seemed more interested in the General than her and she realized that they were homosexual, and possibly the General's lovers.

Someone knocked at the door and Bernard entered.

'Your rooms are ready, gentlemen,' he said smiling easily.

Hetty wondered how he had managed to get back in the time and still manage to look so relaxed. 'General, you will not remember me, perhaps?'

'Certainly, I remember. You looked after me very well when I last stayed here. I apologize for being the bearer of bad news, but I shall make the inspection as easy as possible for you. And now – if you will excuse us, madame, mademoiselle – we shall avail ourselves of your excellent hospitality.'

He picked up the champagne and started towards the door, where Bernard awaited him. 'I have myself been preparing for you, General, or I should have been here sooner. The meal we have for you is but simple food but the best we have available at such short notice. Tomorrow we shall do better.'

'Ah yes, I have made arrangements. Supplies will arrive. You know my tastes, Bernard. I am sure you will look after me.'

'Everything you eat or drink will be supervised by me, monsieur. You have no need to fear while you are a guest here.'

154

'As Madame de Faubourg assured me on my arrival. We can be civil to one another even though our countries are at war. We Germans and French must work together for a better future – do you not agree.'

Madame de Faubourg lifted her glass in salute. 'I shall drink a toast to that, General von Steinbeck.'

'Thank you, madame.' He bowed and went out, followed by the two young men.

Hetty glanced at the Comtesse but she shook her head.

'Are you sure your head is better, dearest? You look very pale.'

'It is still quite painful but I thought you would expect me to come down, Tante Adele.'

She went to the door and peeped out. The German general could be heard talking to Bernard from the first landing; he was laughing and teasing his friends, completely at ease, thinking himself amongst friends no doubt.

'It is all right, madame. They have gone with Bernard.'

'I was praying you would return in time. I was afraid to tell them you had gone to visit Louis's sick grandmother in case you were blamed ... All went well?'

'Very well.'

'So now we must wait and see.'

'Yes,' Hetty agreed. 'Now we must wait and see what happens next.'

★　★　★

Fate had been kind in sending them General von Steinbeck. A man devoted to his own comfort, he took a tour of the old wing and shook his head in distress at the neglect. It was plain to see that he was shocked at the depleted state of the château's former glory. So many of the château's treasures had been removed that it seemed an empty shell compared with his memories.

'I am sorry to see you like this, mademoiselle,' he told Hetty. 'I had remembered something vastly different.'

'I believe Monsieur le Comte was not a good businessman, General. His son-in-law was no better. Things have been sadly neglected for too long and with the unfortunate happenings of the last few months...'

'We shall say no more, mademoiselle,' he told her. 'This is not the place I remembered and will not serve my purpose. I have another château to inspect. My men and I will move on this afternoon.'

'It is sad to see such neglect is it not?' Hetty said. 'I know my great-aunt will be disappointed you cannot stay. She had thought we might be safe if you were quartered here, General.'

'I think you will be safe enough. Once my report is entered I dare say you will be left in peace.'

'You are so kind.'

'It is my pleasure. I was looking forward to staying here...' Hetty caught her breath. Had she pushed her luck too far? But no, she

156

could see that he was thinking of his own comfort. 'However, it is not to be. We shall leave in two hours.'

Hetty contained her delight beneath a grave face. If they were to get away with this visit so lightly it would be nothing short of a miracle.

Two hours later the German patrol was lined up in the courtyard, ready to leave. The General's car was stacked with three cases of their best champagne and a small Renoir he had taken a fancy to and been given as a present. He came out on to the steps to take his leave of them, kissing both the Comtesse's and Hetty's hands.

It was all going so well! Hetty was on thorns, afraid that suddenly they would change their minds and start tearing the place apart, but it seemed the Germans were ready to leave

Then it all changed. Suddenly, Kristina ran out of the house; she clawed at the Comtesse's skirt as she saw the German cars and lorries and started to scream and sob.

'What is wrong with her?' General von Steinbeck's eyes narrowed as he looked at her, taking in the dark eyes and curly hair. 'She looks...'

'Her mother was killed in an attack from the air,' Hetty told him quickly. Her nails were turned into her hand but she didn't feel the pain. He must not harm the child! 'It was as I was on my way to join my aunt – I snatched her up and ran to safety with her, but her mother died.'

'She is the daughter of a *Jew*,' he said, his smile disappearing. 'We shall take her with us. Such children pollute this country and you cannot want her here.'

He moved to grab hold of the child but she screamed and ran off across the courtyard just as one of the patrol vehicles started to move forward. It hit her small body with a sickening thud, sending her flying. Hetty gave a scream and would have gone to her at once, but the Comtesse put out a hand to detain her.

'Bernard – see to the infant,' she commanded, not the flicker of a muscle to betray her feelings for the child. She turned her imperious gaze on the General. 'It was an accident. You can have no use for her now. You will leave her to us.'

'Yes, of course.' Hetty noticed that he looked sick as Bernard lifted the child's limp body in his arms and ran with her to the back of the house. 'It was an accident as you say. Please accept my apologies. I had no intention of hurting her. She would merely have been sent to a camp with her own people.'

'Yes, I understand, General. We have enjoyed your visit and we are sorry it has been so brief.'

He bowed his head, but Hetty noticed that he did not look them in the eyes as he ran down the steps to his car. She waited until he had been driven away before going into the house. Bernard had taken the child to the servants' hall, where she lay on a horsehair sofa, her face as pale as snow.

'How is she?' Hetty started forward. 'Is she badly injured? Have you sent for the doctor?'

'It would be useless, mademoiselle,' Bernard said. 'I am very sorry.'

'You can't mean ... not dead?' Hetty moved towards where the child lay, looking down at her. She could see a dark mark on her forehead where the heavy vehicle had hit her and a sob rose in her throat. 'Poor little Kristina. First her mother and now her ... I hope they rot in hell!'

'Be careful, Hetty.' The Comtesse spoke from behind her. 'You hate them for what they have done, but don't let hate rule you. You can do more damage if you use your cunning rather than brute force. We were lucky this time, but Kristina paid the price.'

'It was my fault, madame,' one of the women said. 'I should have been looking after her but she slipped away and I did not know where she was. She came looking for you...'

'As she always did, my poor little one.' The Comtesse was grey with grief but she did not weep and her head was up, body stiff with pride. 'They will pay for this, Hetty, believe me – they will pay.'

'I was sorry for them when the train exploded,' Hetty said, her voice thick with controlled anger. 'They were the enemy and I knew that it was necessary, but still I was sorry for them – in future, I shall not be.'

Inside her head she was vowing to kill every German she could.

'Do not let it make you bitter,' the Comtesse said and sighed wearily. 'I know you loved Kristina, as I loved her – but we shall recover. It is always so. And now I must rest. I am tired.'

Hetty knew that the old woman's heart was breaking. She, more than anyone, had loved the child, taking her everywhere with her, teaching her things, entertaining her so that others could get on with their work.

Hetty looked at Bernard after she had gone. 'Will you teach me how to use a gun properly?'

'If it is what you want?'

'It is exactly what I want. A life for a life, Bernard. Every French life they take wantonly shall be repaid in German blood.'

Bernard nodded. 'In this Louis and I will help you all we can – but we must find others to make our group stronger.'

'Who can we trust?'

'I know of one or two. Others are bound to come once they learn what is happening. I promise you, mademoiselle – we shall see that Kristina is revenged.'

Hetty nodded, a cold smile on her lips as she walked into the main part of the house and up the stairs. A deep searing hatred was growing inside her, hatred that would last until they had rid France of the invader.

Six

Georgie straightened up with a sigh, putting a hand to her back. She had been working in the garden clearing leaves and other debris for most of the afternoon and what she wanted most now was a nice hot bath. She replaced her tools in the shed and went into the house just as Mrs Townsend was finishing for the day.

'I've baked you a nice fatless sponge and left it on the kitchen table to cool,' she told Georgie. 'I thought you would decide on the filling yourself.'

'Thank you. I was wondering what to have for tea. I was given a little pot of clotted cream this morning so I might just have some of that. It's such a treat that I've been wondering how to make the most of it.'

'When you think of all the cream Major Bridges used to like on his scones. Doesn't bear thinking about!'

'No, it doesn't,' Georgie said and sighed. 'But from what I've read in the paper things are going to get worse before they get better.'

'I expect you're right. I'm off then, Mrs Bridges. I might be a bit late in the morning, but I'll make up for it later.'

'Oh, yes, your grandson has to go to the dentist.' Georgie nodded as she recalled her housekeeper telling her. They always had a good chat first thing in the morning and Georgie caught up on all the local news. 'Don't worry about it, Mrs Townsend. The house is clean and I can get myself a light meal.'

The other woman shook her head and looked sorrowful. 'That's your trouble. You don't eat properly unless I look after you. Whatever the Major would say I don't know.'

Very few remembered that Arthur had once been a major in the army, but Mrs Townsend was one of them. Over the years Georgie had almost forgotten it herself. When they'd met he'd seemed quite dashing in his way and the age gap hadn't seemed to make that much difference. His illness had changed him too much – but it was good that someone remembered how he'd been once.

'Arthur would have scolded me, Mrs Townsend. He was always a good trencherman, until the last year or so anyway.'

'There you are then. You mustn't neglect yourself.'

Georgie smiled but made no reply as her housekeeper left. It was true that she didn't always bother with big meals these days, but she was busy and it was easier to snatch a snack on the run some days. This evening, however, she had nothing much to do but relax with the wireless. She thought she might do tomatoes on toast and follow it with a piece of Mrs Townsend's cake.

She was just turning on the taps for her bath when the phone rang. She hesitated, tempted to ignore it, but then she turned the tap off and went down to the hall.

'Hello, Georgie Bridges here.'

'It's Ben.' Her heart did a flip as she heard his voice. Thank goodness she hadn't ignored the phone! 'How are you, darling? Sorry I haven't been able to ring for some days.'

'I was a bit worried about you,' she said. 'How are you, Ben? You haven't been ill, have you?'

'No, just up to my neck in this wretched training business,' he said. 'Look, they've given us a couple of days' leave. Could you meet me in London, day after tomorrow?'

'Oh, Ben!' Georgie felt a surge of delight. 'That's wonderful. Yes of course I'll be there. Where shall we stay?'

'At my apartment? We can have more time to ourselves there. You've got a key if you're there before me.'

'I'll go up tomorrow afternoon,' Georgie said. 'Tidy things up a bit for us and get some food in – I can take some stuff from here.'

'I might be able to scrounge a bit my end,' Ben said. 'And we'll go to the Savoy for a meal one evening. I love you, Georgie.'

'I love you too.'

'What are you doing? I like to picture you at your home, it makes us seem closer at times.'

'I've been in the garden this afternoon, making a pile of leaves ready for the bonfire.

And now I'm going to have a bath, then eat my supper by the fire in the sitting room and listen to the wireless.'

'What a perfect way to spend the evening,' Ben said. 'I wish I was there with you, darling.'

'So do I – but at least we'll be seeing each other soon.'

'Yes, that will be marvellous. I had better go because another chap wants to use this thing now. See you soon.'

'Yes, of course,' Georgie said. 'I can't wait.'

She was smiling as she replaced the receiver. She would do some shopping in the morning, see what she could find going under the counter to make Ben's leave as special as possible. But most of all she just wanted to see him and hold him, to rediscover the happiness she'd known in his arms.

It wasn't until she was soaking in the bath, having indulged herself with slightly above the recommended level of water, that she wondered why he had sounded a bit odd. Almost regretful ... or was she just imagining that tone in his voice?

A chilling certainty that Ben had been given leave before being sent on a mission of some kind had lodged in her mind and wouldn't be shaken. It was what usually happened to men when they were being sent off for active service. Ben wasn't in the regular forces, but she had a good idea of where he was going and what kind of work he'd been trained for.

He hadn't ever said anything to her about

164

his training when he rang, but it was obvious that if it needed to be so hush-hush it was both secret and dangerous work. Ben had visited France quite often in the past; he knew the people and he spoke the language better than most British people she knew. No, it didn't take a degree in mathematics to work that one out.

Ben couldn't tell her, and she wouldn't ask, but she was sure in her own mind of what was about to happen.

She mustn't let him know that she'd guessed or that she felt wretched about it, Georgie decided. She must just make the most of the time they had together and hope for a brighter future for them all.

The shops were dressed for Christmas, Georgie noticed as she finished her shopping and then caught a bus to the corner of the street where Ben's apartment building was situated, feeling relieved to see it was still standing. It seemed sad not to see all the pretty lights of previous years in the shops, but at least some had made an effort to ignore the war in their window displays. They might not have the stock to offer they'd once boasted, but they weren't going to give up without a struggle.

It was the famous British fighting spirit, Georgie reflected. What were a few bombs and a blitzkrieg to Londoners? Their mood was belligerent, their general answer two fingers up accompanied by a rude word!

165

However, it seemed that for the moment the worst of the bombing was over for London since the German bombers had been turning their attention of late to other cities and Coventry had recently received one of the worst attacks of the war so far.

Georgie had telephoned Beth and asked her to meet for tea that afternoon; she was pleased to see the girl waiting for her when she arrived at the small hotel they'd arranged. Beth's pregnancy was showing, but not too much. She went to give her a hug and handed her a big parcel of baby clothes she had knitted.

'Oh, that's so lovely of you,' Beth said. 'I've bought a few things but nothing much yet.'

'I've used lemon wool,' Georgie said. 'I bought it to make a cardigan before the war and then never got round to it so I've been able to make quite a few things. I thought I would do first and second sizes, and I've got enough to do a third a bit later.'

'I'm getting thoroughly spoiled,' Beth told her. 'Annabel has managed to find me several things that are waiting for me at home. She says there's no sense in bringing them up until I know where I'm going to be living afterwards.'

'Surely you will go home to your family?'

Georgie looked at her. She knew Annabel was expecting it and that she would be disappointed if it didn't happen.

'Drew's mother has asked me to go there,' Beth said and looked less than happy at the idea. 'I've said I shall go down for a few days at Christmas. Arnold has been invited too and he's going to drive me down and bring me back, save me bothering with the train, he says.'

'I thought he didn't drive? Isn't that why he needs a driver?'

'Well, he doesn't drive often. Actually, he hates it, but he can when he wants to apparently. He's offered to take me because he knew I was reluctant to go. Whether I shall end up doing most of the driving remains to be seen. Not that I shall mind particularly if he does leave it to me. I'm still able to fit behind the wheel, so far.'

'Why don't you want to visit your mother-in-law?'

'It was just being on my own with them that I didn't fancy. It's a big house and...' Beth sighed and Georgie guessed she wasn't quite sure herself. 'I think it will be all right for a holiday, and I know it is what Drew wants – but I'm not sure I want to live there. It wouldn't be too bad if he was here, but...' She pulled a face. 'How did you get on with your in-laws, Georgie?'

'I didn't have any,' Georgie said. 'That was one problem I never had to face, and neither did Annabel. I often wished Arthur had had more of a family, but of course I had my own – still have, of course. Mother has invited me there for Christmas. I've said I shall go. It's the first time for years. Arthur liked to be in his own house. He always made a big thing of it. So we stayed at home and had friends over on Boxing Day or at New Year.'

'It will be your second Christmas without him.' Beth looked at her oddly. 'You stayed with Jessie and Harry Kendle last year, didn't you?'

'Yes, just for a few days. It was good of them to ask me. I didn't want to be alone, but I didn't want to face my family. This year it's better.'

'It's my first with Drew gone,' Beth said and Georgie understood her earlier expression. 'I miss him so much, Georgie – but I had a letter from him yesterday so that cheered me up a bit.'

'At least you've got the baby to think about,' Georgie said and smiled at her. 'That must keep your mind occupied.'

Beth's mouth screwed up in a wry grimace. 'If I'm honest I wish I wasn't having a baby just yet. I know that sounds awful, but I'd rather it hadn't happened so soon.'

'I suppose it is a bit of a nuisance with things the way they are.' Georgie noticed the dark shadows under her eyes. Perhaps Beth was suffering more than she let on. 'You look tired, my dear. Has it been terrible with all the bombs? Annabel wishes you would go home. She worries about you being up here the way things are.'

'I know. She says the same thing everytime I telephone – but I don't want to go, Georgie. I'm not ready yet. I like my job and I like being a part of things. I should feel bored with nothing to do all day.'

'I think Annabel could find you enough to do,' Georgie said. 'She has a terrible problem finding sufficient staff these days.'

'Yes, I suppose so,' Beth said. 'But that's not very exciting after...' She shrugged. It was impossible to explain to Georgie why she didn't want to go back, perhaps because she didn't really understand it herself. 'Well, we'll see when it comes to it. Arnold is relying on me at the moment and I'm certainly not leaving until I have to.'

'Oh, well, you know what you want,' Georgie said and the subject was dropped. Annabel wouldn't have it, of course, but the girl had been spoiled. She seemed a little bit selfish to Georgie, but perhaps that was unfair. After all, she had her own life and perhaps it was wrong to expect her to drop everything and go home. Yet it surely couldn't be that wonderful living in lodgings and having to run out to the bomb shelter most nights of the week?

Georgie wondered what on earth made the girl want to stay in London at a time like this. It wasn't as if she could see Drew. He wasn't likely to get home leave for months.

Georgie spent the evening getting the apartment ready for Ben's leave. She heard the wail of an air raid siren in the distance but didn't bother to look for a shelter. To her way of thinking, if the Germans hadn't managed to knock the place down in the two months

169

since September they weren't likely to just because she was staying there for one night.

The awful sound of a bomb dropping a few streets away made her shiver. She turned off the lights and went to look out. The sky had turned red and she knew that someone's house was on fire. Somehow reading about it in the paper hadn't brought it home as much as that sinister glow in the sky and she felt her eyes sting with tears.

Pulling on a coat and scarf, Georgie went out into the streets. The all clear had sounded now but she could hear the wail of a fire engine and as she turned the corner she saw that a whole row of shops and flats had been demolished. Men were already there with water hoses and policemen were organizing a search and rescue team of ordinary members of the public. Georgie went up to one of them and asked if there was anything she could do.

'We think most places were empty, miss,' he told her. 'But they're looking for volunteers down at the shelter to make tea and cut sandwiches. It's down the road, left at the corner. The Sally Army building. Anyone will tell you.'

'Yes, thanks. I'll go and see what I can do.'

The scene of devastation had shocked her. Her throat felt scorched by the heat and the acrid smoke and she hurried in the direction she'd been sent. When she got there, she saw that the large numbers of people needing help, some of them still in their nightclothes, had overwhelmed the workers.

'What can I do?' she asked a harassed-looking woman.

'The kitchen is through there,' the woman replied. 'You'll be given a job if you ask.'

Georgie went through the door pointed out to her, and saw that three women were trying to cope with mounds of bread and margarine and huge teapots.

'Can I help to make sandwiches?'

'Sure – there's Spam and a few tomatoes, and some fish paste,' one of the women told her. 'Use the Spam sparingly. We were given a case by an American officer but when it's gone it's back to jam or Bovril if they're lucky.'

'Yes, of course,' Georgie said, and taking off her coat she joined one of the other women at the table. 'Shall I fill? If you cut the Spam you'll know how much for each sandwich. Do I put anything else in?'

'We don't use mustard,' the woman told her with a friendly smile. 'There's some out there in pots while it lasts, but some don't like it.'

'I think it makes it a bit more bearable if you put home-made pickles in it,' Georgie said, 'but we don't have any of that here, do we?'

'Up from the country are you, luv?'

'Yes, just for a couple of days.'

'Staying with friends?'

'No. I've come to meet my friend.'

'Going to have a little fling with your feller?' The other woman grinned at her. 'It's all right, luv. We're all in the same boat. My feller

171

was home last month. I shan't see him no more for a year worse luck – still as long as he gets back in one piece that's all that matters, ain't it?'

'Yes, of course it is,' Georgie said and smiled. 'We've had it easy where I come from compared to you. We've seen a few dogfights and a German plane crashed into the field near my house. It went up in flames. I don't think anyone got out alive. They searched in case but they seemed to think they had all died in the flames.'

'Poor buggers,' the woman said. 'My name is Dot, luv. I know I didn't ought ter feel sorry for the bloody Jerrys but I 'ate ter think of any man dyin' like that.'

'I'm Georgie. Yes, I agree it's horrid to think of anyone dying like that – except that it makes you hate them more when you see what happened tonight just round the corner.'

'We don't none of us know what's comin' next,' the other woman agreed. 'My parents lost their 'ouse last week, but they got out all right so that's all that matters. They've moved in with friends. I told them to leave and go live in a cottage in the country and they told me they bloody well wasn't going to let that Hitler win, so what can you do?'

'Not very much,' Georgie said. 'Other than what you already are, keeping going despite it all.'

'That's right,' Dot said. 'Well, that's the last of the Spam then. We shall have to start on the paste next and then it's jam. Still, that's better than we got when we were kids. A bit of bread and scrape if we wus lucky. I tell yer, the kids these days don't know they're born!'

'Well, I think you were brave and foolish to go out after a raid like that,' Ben said, his arms protectively around her as they lay side by side in bed. 'It can be very dangerous, Georgie. Bombs don't always go off immediately, you know. And there are gas leaks and explosions to say nothing of danger from fires and collapsing buildings.'

'Well, I was fine so there's no need to worry,' Georgie told him. 'I was telling you about Dot. She's a really funny lady. She had me laughing all the time. It didn't seem as if anything out of the ordinary had happened. She took it all in her stride.'

'Salt of the earth some of these Londoners,' Ben said, holding her closer. 'I'm just glad you're all right. I couldn't have stood it if anything had happened.'

'Silly,' Georgie said and pressed herself against him, lifting her face for his kiss. They had already made love twice since he'd got here. It seemed that they just couldn't get enough of each other, and it just kept getting better and better. 'I love you so much, Ben. I know I shouldn't say it, but I hate being on my own now. I miss you so very much when you're not there. It's daft considering that until a few weeks ago I hadn't seen you in years, but that's the way it is. I hate this war

173

for taking you away from me!'

'It will be over one day, darling. I promise you,' Ben said. His hands were firm and gentle as they stroked her back. 'I'm sorry I wasted all those years when we might have been together. If I could go back to the beginning I would do it all differently, believe me.'

'It wasn't your fault, Ben. Things were stacked against us. One day we'll be together and then we'll look back on this time and think how romantic it was.'

'Well, at least Jerry seems to be giving it a rest tonight,' Ben said and began to kiss her neck. She could feel him harden against her thigh and knew he wanted her again; she was ready too, and put out her hand to caress him and show him that he wasn't the only one who felt that way. 'I'm like a man dying of thirst in the desert,' Ben said with a laugh. 'But I promise I'll take you somewhere tomorrow. I want to buy you a present. Something nice for Christmas.'

'I've got you a present,' Georgie said. 'And I managed to get a nice duck. We'll make it our Christmas tomorrow, shall we? A Christmas dinner in the evening with all the trimmings we can find, and presents.'

'Yes, that's just what we'll do,' Ben said before he covered her with his body. For a while they both forgot that when Christmas actually came they would be apart.

Georgie went back to the flat after she'd seen

Ben off at his station. He wasn't returning to Scotland, but somewhere down south. He hadn't told her exactly where and she hadn't asked.

'I'll be thinking of you all the time, darling,' he said as he held her for one last embrace. 'Take care of yourself, Georgie.'

'I shall think of you always,' she said. 'Come back to me soon, Ben.'

'Of course. As soon as I can.'

He hadn't looked at her as he said it and she felt an awful chill in her bones. Ben didn't need to tell her he was about to do something dangerous; she knew. He was nervous but also excited; she had picked up the vibes despite his efforts to control them.

He hadn't wanted her to wait until the train left so she'd walked away as soon as he boarded. Her eyes were bright with tears, but she hadn't cried. She didn't cry until she got back to the flat and found one of his socks lying under the bed. She picked it up, and on impulse shoved it into her coat pocket. Stupid of course, but it was all she had left of him. The presents he'd given her were beautiful, and included a soft cashmere coat that they had been elated to find and a gold bracelet.

'But that's far too much,' she'd protested when he'd given her both presents. 'The coat alone is very generous, Ben.'

'I want to make up for lost time,' he told her. 'For all the years I wanted to give you a present and knew I couldn't. When I come home you're going to be one spoiled lady, my

175

darling.'

'Just love me, keep loving me as much as you do now – that's all I ask.'

'I shall love you until I die, and if it's possible afterwards.'

'Do you think it's possible, Ben?'

'I don't know – but if it is I shall, scout's honour.'

They had laughed and made love again, so many times that Georgie had lost count. It had been the most wonderful two days of her life and she would treasure the memory. Pray God it wouldn't have to last her for the rest of her life, Georgie thought as she locked Ben's apartment and went out – but she mustn't let herself think like that or she would break down in tears. And she wasn't going to cry any more!

'You are my A student,' Ted Barker said to Ben as they smoked a last cigarette and drank a glass of wine together. 'I despair of some of them ever getting it right. The main thing is to keep your wits about you and remember what we've taught you. For God's sake don't do what that ass Forsythe did last week. He started to speak English to me when I offered him an English cigarette. Even if you think they're all right, stick to French and be certain. They know we're sending teams of French-speaking operatives over there and they'll catch you out if they can.'

'*Merci, monsieur,*' Ben said and grinned at him. He liked the man and felt flattered that he had been picked for this urgent mission. 'I know where my brains are, thank you, sir, and I'm not likely to make that mistake.'

'Anyone can have an unguarded moment,' Ted said and frowned. 'The last man completely messed up, that's why we're having to send you in so soon. I wanted you to have more training on the explosives, but there's no alternative. Foxcub needs you and you're the only one who can remember the new codes. We're reluctant to transmit them because we think they may have his frequency. Foxcub is going to change it when you get there and we shall wait until we hear the signal before we reply.'

'What about the other supplies he asked for? You were waiting for clearance on those, weren't you?'

'We'll be sending them a day or so after we get the new codes in place. Otherwise they could be waiting to pick them up – and they may be waiting for you, Ben. Just be aware that instead of Foxcub's men you could find a very different welcoming party.'

'Yes, I am aware of that, sir.'

'If the pilot suspects danger he will divert and you'll be dropped at another location. If that happens it means you will have to make your way to the original dropping zone yourself or if that fails keep the rendezvous at the second location. You have the references in your mind – you know what to do if it all goes pear shaped?'

'Yes, sir.' Ben tapped the side of his head

and looked confident. 'I know the area Foxcub is using. It isn't far from Paris and I used to drive out there with Hetty for picnics. That's why I was able to assimilate the details so easily.'

'Good man. It's your experience on the ground as well as your grasp of the language that makes you so useful to us – but I wish you'd had more time on the explosives. You'd better tell Foxcub that you didn't finish the course, ask him to fill you in on anything you're not sure of. He's an excellent man, the best of our contacts over there. Some of the groups are disjointed, amateur affairs; there's one in particular that has caused us a few headaches in the past. Foxcub isn't sure where they're working from or he would have told them to fall into line and co-ordinate their attacks. They mean well and they've had some success, but they work on their own and they messed up an attack Foxcub had planned last month. They didn't know, of course, but they blew up a patrol the night before a special person was due to pass through and compromised weeks of planning. He was furious about it, but until he can make contact there's not much he can do to stop them. He's heard a woman is running the show, but it may just be rumour.'

'Sounds a bit unlikely, sir,' Ben said. 'Still, if things haven't been going just right it may be that a woman is behind it – though Georgie would have my guts for garters if she heard me say that.'

'Friend of yours?' Ted Barker raised his brows.

'Yes...' Ben slipped a hand into his cheap, French-made suit and took out an envelope. 'This is for Georgie if anything happens. I was thinking of leaving it in my room, but you'll see she gets it if necessary?'

'Yes, of course. Not carrying anything else that might give you away, are you? You've got rid of all your English stuff as instructed?'

'Yes, sir. It was just this.'

'Well, it's probably time you were on your way, Ben.'

'Yes, sir. It looks like being a dull night.'

'All the better for you.'

They shook hands and Ben went out into the raw cold of a bitter night. The aircraft was waiting and he ran across to be greeted by the pilot and a junior officer who helped him to board.

'Put these on, sir,' the young officer said and handed him a fur-lined helmet and gloves. 'You'll find it a bit cold up there tonight.'

'Thank you.' Ben took them gratefully. It was bloody stupid to feel an attack of nerves now. He'd gone over this a hundred times in his mind. He was already trembling inside with nerves and he hoped it didn't show. 'I mustn't take them with me, though.'

'No, sir. Good luck, sir.'

The pilot turned round to grin at him and the gunner in the tail fin put his hand up in a salute as Ben scrambled on board and sat down. His stomach was tying itself in knots. It was one thing to talk this thing through with his commander but very different on a cold December night to be actually doing it. The navigator was helping him to fasten his parachute.

'This is for an emergency. In case we can't put you down. You have practised this, I hope?'

'Yes, of course. We covered all emergencies.'

Ben hoped it wouldn't be necessary. The plan was to land on a strip prepared by Foxcub and his men, but there was a chance he would have to drop in.

'We'll soon have you there, old chap,' the pilot said. 'First time up in one of these birds, is it?'

'I've been up in a few, but not one of these,' Ben said. 'Looks like it's a rough night?'

'Just right for what we want,' he said. 'Hold on tight. We're getting the signal for take-off.'

Ben sat back and held his breath, closing his eyes until he felt lift-off. He willed himself to think of something other than what was happening. He mustn't lose his bottle; they were all relying on him, he mustn't let them down. As a child his mother had often made him feel he was letting her down; he'd tried hard to make up for it after his father's death but he knew he could never measure up to her expectations. Helen had been much the same, always dwelling on his failures rather than his few triumphs. Not that there had been many of them, apart from his writing.

Maybe that was why he'd welcomed this chance to do something with his life, to show himself that he was capable of being both brave and decisive.

He thought about Georgie, about her lying in his arms, kissing him. He remembered the taste and feel of her, her own special scent, and wondered what she was doing that night. Would she be making toast in front of the fire? Would she be thinking of him?

He imagined the two of them toasting bread together. Where would they choose to live after the war? If he was as successful with his writing as he had been before the war, he could buy them a small place of their own. Helen and his children would have Tarleton Towers, of course. He wasn't sure what Georgie would want to do about her own home...

They were up and on their way. The nerves that had attacked Ben on take-off were under control now. He felt a return of the excitement he'd felt about making the trip and settled down. He had everything clear in his mind. It was all going to be fine.

By the time they reached France the mist had settled thickly over the land. The pilot circled lower and lower, looking for the flares that would tell him he had found the right dropping zone, but there was no sign of anything.

'It's right according to my references,' the navigator told the pilot. 'Something must have gone wrong.'

'Shall we abort the mission and try again

another night?'

'No, that is out of the question,' Ben said. 'Double check your references and, if you're sure this is it, I'll go in.'

'You'll never find your way in that, sir. Wouldn't be able to see your hand in front of your face in mist as thick as that.'

'I'm going in,' Ben said stubbornly. He wasn't going to fail again! 'This can't be aborted. It has to be tonight.' If he went back it would mess all their plans up and he refused to give up at the first hurdle.

'You're the boss,' the pilot told him. 'I'll take us up to the proper height, sir. This is as close as we're going to get to where you should be dropped, but I don't like the idea of you taking pot luck without the signal.'

'I know how to find my contact,' Ben said. 'We arranged a secondary meeting in case this was aborted. Just drop me and get out of here before something happens.'

'I think that's an open field down there,' the pilot said as for a moment the mist seemed to clear. 'You know what to do? Is your parachute secure?'

'Yes, it's all done,' Ben said. 'I'm ready now.'

'Tally-ho then, sir. Good luck!'

He prayed silently as he jumped from the plane, a sick feeling in his stomach. This was another thing he hadn't had enough practice at unfortunately. They had been certain it wouldn't be necessary, but they hadn't bargained on the fog being this thick or Foxcub letting them down. Thankfully his chute opened properly and he floated down slowly, feeling like he was in some kind of nightmare.

He landed with a sickening crunch on his right ankle; the pain told him immediately that he had damaged it, though when he tried getting up he discovered that he could just about put it to the ground so it probably was not broken, but a nasty jolt that would hurt like hell if he had to walk far. He told himself to keep calm and take things slowly. He could still walk so it might have been worse. All he had to do was find somewhere to rest for the night. By the morning his ankle might be better and he could find his contact easier once the mist had lifted.

But first of all he had to get rid of the parachute, helmet and gloves. He'd meant to leave the helmet and gloves behind, but the chute was a giveaway in itself. He had to find a thick bush to hide the stuff. The mist seemed a little thinner from the ground than it had from above, and he saw a ditch just ahead of him. He would dump the things there and tell Foxcub where to find them. Someone else could come back and make a better job of covering them. He wasn't about to try digging with his bare hands in ground as hard as this. It was freezing!

He hobbled as far as the ditch and dumped all the stuff in it and then turned away. His ankle hurt more than he'd imagined and he realized it might be a minor fracture after all. He swore as he got out his compass and found the glass had cracked when he landed.

He could just about see the needle and hoped it was still working properly. If the pilot had got his references right, he needed to head due north from here.

Ben started to walk in what he hoped was the right direction. His best bet was to keep moving and watch out for German patrols. He shivered in his thin clothes. They were cheap and they felt it! Cursing beneath his breath, he wondered why he was stuck in alien country on a night like this instead of in a nice warm bed back home. His teeth gritted against the bitter cold, he regretted his own thick overcoat, which was hanging in the wardrobe in his apartment, and then told himself not to be a misery guts.

He reflected wryly that he must be all kinds of a fool to have got himself into a mess like this. Yet he knew he'd had no alternative but to go on with his mission. Aborting it wasn't an option; they'd lost too many operatives of late for it to be coincidence. Somehow the Germans had got hold of their codes and they had to be changed. But it was one hell of a night to be out on his own with no clear idea of what he was going to do if he couldn't find the second rendezvous.

No good worrying about things like that. He could put up with a little bit of cold. The main thing was that a hail of bullets hadn't met him when he reached the ground. He checked his compass again, wishing for a moon so that he could see more than a few inches in front of his nose, then he laughed as he checked himself. A moon was the last thing he needed. If he could see so could the Germans.

He paused to get his breath and look about him. He was coming to the edge of what looked like a thick wood. He'd been walking for ten minutes or so, maybe a bit more, and the pain in his ankle was becoming chronic. He wasn't sure he could manage to go much further without a rest. And he thought that the mist might have started to clear a little, which meant he had to be more careful.

Why the hell hadn't Foxcub been here to meet him? Was it possible that this whole thing was a set-up? Was that the flash of a torch or a car's headlights? He stiffened, suspecting a patrol. Now what did he do? Go on or change direction? He hesitated, uncertain what he'd seen through the trees. He had been heading for the wood hoping to find a hut where he could shelter for a while, but now he was unsure what to do.

Damn, his ankle hurt! That bloody parachute. It was one of the things he hadn't been good at – like the explosives. He'd never been an action man, no good at sports at school but top of his class when it came to anything that needed a good memory. The other boys had thought him a bit of an ass really, and he suspected his father might have too. But he'd made it this far and he was going to make it the rest of the way to the second rendezvous if it killed him – which it might if this pain in his ankle got any worse!

He swore silently and stopped for a breather, leaning against a tree for support, and then instantly went still, his heart thumping as he heard a voice near by. Crackling sounds told him that there was more than one person. A German patrol! No, they were French voices – but that could be a trick. Yet he would swear that one of them was a woman's voice.

He strained to hear what she was saying, then picked up the gist of it and smiled to himself. She was telling the others that she was sure she'd seen a parachute come down somewhere nearby. And she was very close to him now. He could see the little group of three men vaguely through the mist and a woman nearer, ahead of the others, just feet away from where he was hidden.

'I know I saw something when the mist lifted for a moment,' she said. 'If it was a parachute it will be an English airman. He must have been in trouble to have bailed out like that in this weather. We're going to search for as long as we can, Bernard. We can't just leave him out here. You know there's a patrol stationed in the village at the moment. If he walks into that he'll be finished.'

'But you could look all night, Mademoiselle 'Etty...'

'If we have to we will.'

'Mademoiselle 'Etty, you can't be sure you saw it,' said another voice, younger this time.

'Go home if you want, Louis. I'm going on.'

Ben was stunned with disbelief. Had he

heard right? Surely he was dreaming? Yet he was sure the men had called her Mademoiselle 'Etty and that rang bells. He'd heard that name before, when visiting his sister in Paris. 'Etty could mean Hetty! Ben felt the thrill of elation shoot through him. He had thought the woman's voice strangely familiar and now he was almost certain. The woman was his sister. Yes, he was sure of it.

He was going to have to take a chance. He stepped out from behind the tree, lifting his hands in the air in submission.

'I surrender,' he said in French. 'Can you help me?'

'Who are you?' a suspicious male voice demanded.

'Ask your female friend if she knows of Tarleton Towers ... and if she still remembers Benedict...'

'Ben – is that you?' Hetty stepped towards him. At least the woman vaguely resembled his sister, but not as he'd ever seen her. She was dressed as a man, her hair hidden under a black beret, her face smeared with dirt. 'My God, it is you! What the hell are you doing here? Don't you know there's a war on? You could have run into a German patrol just down the road!'

'Hang on a minute, Hetty,' Ben said and grinned at her. It seemed that the gods were looking after him after all. 'I could ask what you're doing wandering around dressed like that in the dead of night, but I won't. I shall take it for granted that we both know what we're doing. If you could give me a bit of a hand, please? I've dumped my chute in a ditch back there and I seem to have landed badly. My ankle hurts like hell.'

'It serves you right for playing games and putting the wind up us,' Hetty said but grinned at him. Her disbelief was fast turning to pleasure though she couldn't understand why he was here. 'My friends will see to your debris. Can you manage to hobble if you put your arm around me – or do you need to be carried?'

'It depends how far it is,' Ben said truthfully.

'We've got a truck in the woods. I'll get you home and my men will follow us later, when they've checked to see if your arrival was noticed.'

'Your men, Hetty?' Ben asked, giving her a quizzical look as he put his arm about her shoulders. It was still painful to walk but he wasn't going to show it faced by his little sister toting a gun over her shoulder. My God, it was almost unreal! And he had to admit the greatest stroke of luck for him. He'd been wandering about like a fool rather than using his brains. Instead of Hetty and her friends, he could have bumped into the patrol she was talking about. 'Do you know how to work that thing you're wearing?'

'Of course – do you?'

'Just about – but I haven't actually used one in action.'

'Still wet behind the ears, are you?' Hetty

188

smiled oddly. 'Well, I suppose you are here for a reason. You can tell me when we get home but keep quiet from now on just in case. We may not be the only ones to have spotted your chute.'

Ben smiled but didn't answer. He had begun to wonder whether Hetty's little group might be the mavericks who had caused HQ all the headaches of the past few weeks. Knowing her temper from old, he didn't fancy the job of telling her but it would have to be done.

'What the hell are you talking about?' Hetty said angrily. Her cheeks were flushed, eyes snapping with temper. 'I don't know who sent you, Ben, but they've got their facts mixed. We've done a lot of good work these past months and we don't need anyone else telling us how to do our job, thanks all the same.'

'Don't fly off the handle,' Ben said. 'No one is blaming you, but the plain truth is that you messed up an important raid last month. You and your men took out a small supply patrol the night before an important attack had been planned. It meant weeks of planning were aborted and the target HQ was after was diverted.'

'And who the hell are HQ?'

'If you were working with the proper contacts you would know,' Ben said. 'We know you're trying to help, Hetty, but you could do more good if you worked in conjunction with another group who are based in this area.'

'I told you, we prefer to be independent.' Her eyes flashed angrily at him.

Ben groaned inwardly. He was sitting in front of a warm fire with his ankle expertly bound by the man she called Bernard, and drinking cognac. He was grateful for her help, but it seemed she was as stubborn as ever.

'Perhaps you should listen to him, mademoiselle,' Bernard said. 'We are too few to tackle anything more than small patrols and they guard the line too heavily now for us to blow up another train.'

Hetty's mouth set in a thin line. She didn't answer back immediately so Ben knew she was thinking it over.

'I've got to make contact with someone tomorrow morning,' he said. 'It's important, Hetty. This ankle should be easier in the morning. If you could get me a part of the way there...'

'I'll go,' she said. 'I'll make contact with this person who says I've been interfering with his work and bring him back to the château. You can tell him what you have to say then.'

He looked at her dubiously. 'I'm not sure he will trust you.'

'I am not sure I should trust him,' she retorted. She hated it that he was making light of her achievements, bringing her down to the level of a younger sister again. It was time he learned she was a woman and a confident, independent one at that, well able to think for herself and the group she ran. 'If you weren't my brother I wouldn't trust or believe you.'

'Hetty...' Ben sighed and then smiled at her. No point in antagonizing her! He didn't think his ankle was going to recover in time to make that second meeting point. 'You haven't changed much.'

'You have,' she told him. 'The old Ben would never have got involved in something like this. When I first realized it was you I thought you must have come looking for me.'

'You were the last person I expected to see. I've been hoping for news of you, but I'd given up expectation of anything – at least until you were ready to let us know. Annabel worries about you, Hetty.'

'It's difficult to get letters out,' she said evasively. 'I told her I was safe. I don't see why you worry so much over little things.'

'Safe?' Ben's brows rose. 'I'm not sure that what you're doing is exactly safe, Hetty. You spoke of a patrol earlier this evening – supposing they had been where I was?'

'We would have shot them.' She smiled as she saw the disbelief in his eyes. 'We were just an advance party, Ben. There are more of us, believe me.'

'I can't believe you would shoot a man.'

'Can't you?' Her mouth twisted in a strange smile. 'You haven't seen what they do, Ben. We blew a train up some months ago. In retaliation they took six men and two women from a village ten miles from here and shot

191

them. They were all innocent of any crime. None of them even knew why they were being punished. We had several new members from that and we attacked a patrol a week later and killed all of them – ten or twelve men, I'm not sure. We take a life for a life where we can.'

Ben wrinkled his brow as he looked at her, trying to see beyond the mask she was determined to wear. 'Where does it end? They probably shot some more innocent victims in revenge for that little episode.'

Hetty shrugged. 'They kill when they choose anyway. We do what we can for France.'

'Then make the most of what you do by co-ordinating with another group. Make sure that every German you kill is killed for a purpose. The mission you aborted would have taken out an important person and perhaps have shortened the war.'

'You're just saying that to make me feel stupid!'

'You know me better than that, Hetty. Don't worry, we'll get him or his replacement another time – but think about what I'm asking. Please?'

'I'll think about it,' she said and moved to the door as the younger man, he heard her call him Louis, came to give her a message. They whispered together for a moment and then she nodded and returned to the fireplace. 'Louis says the Germans were searching for you. They've found your chute. You didn't make much attempt to hide it.'

'I couldn't with my ankle the way it was.' Ben frowned. 'Will this make trouble for your people?'

'They may search the villages nearby and eventually they may come here. We have somewhere we can hide you if it comes to it. You'd better get some sleep now. It isn't very pleasant where you're going to be hiding so make the most of this while you can.'

'I'm really sorry to have brought this on you,' Ben said, feeling guilty. 'I didn't think they would find the chute that easily.'

'If we hadn't been looking for you they would have found you too,' Hetty said. 'We may be a group of bumbling amateurs as far as you and HQ are concerned, but we probably saved your life tonight.'

'Yes, I think you probably did,' Ben said. 'Don't be angry with me, Hetty. I can't tell you how glad I am to see you again.'

She stared at him for a moment longer and then the anger faded. 'It's good to see you too, Ben. And it's not your fault that this other French operative claims we've messed up his plans. If he knew who we were, why the hell didn't he make contact?'

'I dare say he had his reasons,' Ben said. 'Anyway, you can ask him when you see him.'

'So you agree to my going to the rendezvous in your place?'

'Yes, I don't see why not,' Ben told her. 'I can't give you any messages to pass on, I'm afraid. Other than that I need to see him urgently and I'm not very mobile at the moment.'

'I'll bring him here,' she said. 'He may not trust me but if he wants to see you he hasn't much choice.'

Seven

Hetty walked into the café carrying a basket over her arm. She was wearing a dark coloured coat in a cheap material and short white socks with flat black shoes that had worn down at the heel. She had borrowed them from one of the maids at the château and the Comtesse had protested at her wearing them.

'It doesn't look like you, *chérie*,' she told her. 'I don't like the idea of you doing this. It could be dangerous for all of us.'

'It will not be dangerous,' Hetty promised. 'I know where to go and what to say, and I shan't get caught.'

Bernard had driven her to the village. It was a place she and Ben had often visited when he had come to visit her in Paris. It was some ten miles or so distant from the beautiful little town of Louviers, where they had loved to stroll and admire the charming half-timbered houses; it had been on their route because they chose quiet country roads. Many people would not even have known it was there. In fact, she and Ben had discovered it by accident. They had sometimes stopped at an inn here for lunch, because the food was of the peasant variety and always good, as was the wine

'If there is any sign of a patrol come straight back,' Bernard warned her when she got out of their car. Like the Comtesse he had not wanted her to come.

'There will be no Germans,' she said confidently.

The first thing Hetty had noticed was that the inn was closed and shuttered. Perhaps they had no trade now – or perhaps there was a more sinister reason behind the closure. A family had run it by themselves. The parents were elderly and their sons and daughters-in-law had taken over most of the work. She believed there were grandsons but had no idea how many or whether they had followed their parents into the business.

She'd told Bernard there would be no Germans. In fact she had passed two young soldiers near the closed inn, but they had been with French girls, clearly escaping from the routine of army life to be with the girls. One of them had given Hetty the eye only to have his arm pulled by his companion, who was clearly jealous. Hetty wondered how the girls could go with them. Didn't they know what brutes they were? But it wasn't for her to judge. Perhaps they had their reasons.

As she had her reasons for being here. It was important to act naturally and not show fear. She walked into the café just as the church clock was striking the hour of eleven. Ben had been most particular about that and she'd waited outside the village until exactly the right moment.

Two men were inside, sitting at different tables. Both were drinking coffee. One was older than the other, but she avoided looking at them as Ben had instructed.

Walking up to the counter, she asked for black coffee, and then, when the small cup was put on to the counter, she hunted in her basket for her purse and gave a cry of dismay.

'I have lost my purse,' she said. 'I am sorry. I cannot pay you.'

According to Ben, her contact would offer to pay. She waited for a moment, but apart from a glare from the assistant behind the bar, who whisked the cup away and put it under the counter, nothing happened.

Hetty wondered what to do now. She hesitated, but neither of the men sitting at the tables had either looked her way or moved. It was obviously a mistake. Ben must have given her the wrong password, or it was a different café or something. Even as she hesitated, Hetty heard laughter and saw the two German soldiers and their companions enter the café. She shrugged her shoulders and went out.

It was clearly useless to wait here and hope something happened. Ben must have given her the wrong password she thought again … but no, she recalled now. *She* had made the mistake. She was supposed to say money and she'd said purse instead, but a man wouldn't have a purse. Ben would have said money.

How could she have been so stupid as to forget?

She looked round, wondering if she should go back, but the Germans were in there and the bartender would say something if she tried it again. As she hesitated a man came out of the café. It was the younger one. She waited instinctively as he came up to her.

'I am sorry you lost your purse, mademoiselle,' he told her. 'Perhaps I could buy you a coffee?'

'I should have said I had lost my money. He told me but I forgot and said purse. I'm sorry.'

The man's forehead creased as he looked at her. She sensed hostility in him.

'Who are you? I've seen you before. I'm certain of it.'

'I used to visit here before the war,' Hetty told him.

'No, not here – somewhere else. Who told you to come here and give that password? I was expecting a man.' He looked furious, as if it was her fault there had been a change of plan, and she felt the resentment stir inside her.

He took hold of her arm as two more soldiers walked towards them, smiling at her and steering her down the street towards the river. There were wooden seats on the grassy bank but no one was sitting there.

'Sit down and tell me everything,' he instructed. 'Make it look as if you're flirting with me.'

'I'm not sure I want to do that,' Hetty said and gave him a teasing smile, her tone belying her look. He was much too sure of himself, much too arrogant for her liking. 'You hurt my arm, you pig. You didn't have to manhandle me like that!'

'You look so beautiful when you are angry,' he said and Hetty was surprised until she saw an old man was walking past them. His eyes stabbed at her, angry and demanding. 'I asked who gave you the password?'

'If you want the truth it was my brother.' She reached towards him, planting a kiss on his cheek and smiling in a way that seemed beguiling to passers-by. 'He dropped in out of the mist last night and we found him when we were in the woods.'

'What were you doing in the woods?' He took her statement without a blink, which surprised Hetty. She had thought he would disbelieve her whatever she said, which is why she'd told him the plain truth.

'Looking for Germans to kill,' she hissed in his ear. 'Just as you would if you're the person I'm looking for.'

'I knew I'd seen you!' he said and reached out to trail a finger down her cheek. 'You're one of the ones who have been messing up my plans these past few weeks. I caught sight of you last month running away from the scene of your stupidity.'

'And you're a self-satisfied pig,' she replied and jerked away from him, her eyes flashing in temper. 'I don't know why the hell I let Ben talk me into coming!'

'You did it because there was no alternative,' he said, a flicker of amusement in his hard grey eyes. His hair was very dark and waved back from his brow, his mouth might be sensuous if he ever smiled in a certain way. Which wasn't likely because they had disliked each other on sight. 'What happened to him?'

'He hurt his ankle. He had to parachute in because there were no flares. You let him down.' Her voice was accusing, her look enough to kill at ten paces.

'Because there was a German patrol nearby. The plan was for them to take him elsewhere, but the mist was so bad they couldn't have landed anyway. He would have needed the parachute even if we'd lit the flares.'

'Well, that's your story. You know all I have to say. He wouldn't give me a message. You have to come and see him for yourself if you want to find out what it is.'

'I might come but when I'm ready,' the man said. 'Tell me where you are based and I'll think about it.'

'The hell you will!' Hetty snapped. 'If you come, you come now – and you'll be blind-folded.'

'No, I don't think so. I may be seeing you, mademoiselle. You and I have some unfinished business.' He got up and strolled off whistling.

Hetty stared after him in frustration. Should she run after him? Tell him where he could find her?

No, she was damned if she would! She didn't trust him. If he was so clever let him find out for himself!

She got up and walked away without turning her head. Bernard was waiting for her at the edge of the village. He frowned as he saw she was alone.

'What happened? Did you make contact? Why hasn't he come back with you?'

'He is a pig,' Hetty muttered. 'I am glad he didn't come. Ben will have to make contact some other way.'

She got in the car, feeling furious as Bernard started the motor. It wasn't her fault that she'd messed up an important mission. How were they to know someone else planned to infiltrate what they thought of as their territory? She took a compact from her pocket and glanced at her reflection, averting her eyes from the road only for a moment, and was shocked as Bernard suddenly trod hard on the brake. She gave a little scream as she saw two men blocking the narrow lane. They were both carrying guns and pointing them at the car – at her. And one of them was the pig.

'I make the rules, mademoiselle,' he told her as he dragged open the car door. 'Get in the back with my friend and behave yourself. Or I might just decide to teach you a few manners.' He pulled Hetty out, pushing open the back door and gesturing to his companion to get in with her. Then he turned to Bernard. 'I hope you have more sense than your friend here. Take me to the man I need to see or both of you will end up with a bullet in the brain. I don't mess with amateurs.'

'Yes, monsieur, certainly,' Bernard said. 'But there is no need to treat Mademoiselle 'Etty so roughly. She is a brave and good woman – even if she does lose her temper easily sometimes.'

'Bernard!' Hetty muttered. 'Keep your mouth shut. He knows my name now.'

'And your friend's.' The pig turned and grinned at her. Hetty had been right, his mouth was sensuous when he smiled. 'But I have known them for a while, mademoiselle, and yes, you are brave, if a little foolish. If I had not suspected a traitor in our midst I should have made contact with you weeks ago.'

'A traitor?' Hetty glared at him. 'We know how to deal with them!'

'Believe me, he is no longer in a position to betray us.'

The man sitting next to Hetty laughed and she shivered as she saw the look in his eyes. Yes, these two would know how to deal with traitors.

'You could have come when I asked you. I wouldn't betray you.'

'That remains to be seen,' the pig answered her smugly. 'Since I know your name, I shall tell you mine. I am Stefan Lefarge.'

Hetty frowned as the name rang bells. 'Lefarge ... Your grandparents own the inn, don't they?'

'My grandfather was killed some months ago, by a German who was stealing wine,' Stefan said and a nerve twitched in his cheek. 'My grandmother died a week later of her grief. My father owns the place now but he has no heart to run it alone. Perhaps after the war...' He shrugged his shoulders.

'I am very sorry. They were lovely people.'

'Yes,' he said. 'That is true. My father wanted to kill the soldier who murdered Grandpère, but I told him there is a better way. We want to be rid of them completely, mademoiselle, not just kill a few here and there for revenge. If we are to help the British defeat them we must act together. Personal feelings do not enter here.'

His quiet words struck home. Hetty went pink and remained silent. He was right, she knew it in her heart, just as Ben had been right when he told her she was in the wrong. Killing Germans in blind revenge wasn't helping anyone, not even her since her first black rage had evaporated.

'All we want to do is help.'

'And I'm sure you can be very helpful,' Stefan said. His smile did strange things to her stomach, making her swallow hard. He was an arrogant devil and not particularly handsome, but there was something about him that appealed to her. 'But in future we work together – yes?'

Hetty nodded. She didn't trust herself to speak for the moment. All her instincts were screaming at her not to trust this man. He was too sure of himself, too arrogant. And yet what he said made sense.

'That is good, mademoiselle. We shall see what your brother has to tell us, but before that I would like to hear your story. I know that you are not French, though don't worry, a German wouldn't – and you've told me you have an English brother. So how do you happen to be working for the French resistance?'

Hetty hesitated and then lifted her head proudly.

'I ran off to Paris to live with an artist when I was seventeen,' she said. 'When he betrayed me for the fifth time I left him but loved France too much to go home. And when the Germans arrived I left Paris – and ended up at the château.'

'Ah, now I see,' he said and laughed softly. 'That explains a great deal, mademoiselle.'

'I hoped it would,' she said. She was drawn to him against her will. 'Is there any more you need to know about me, Monsieur Lefarge?'

'Oh no,' he murmured. 'I think that will do very well for the moment.'

Hetty didn't answer but inside she felt as if she were laughing for the first time in months. He was still an arrogant pig, of course, but there was something compelling about him. She would have to be careful not to let him under her skin, but there was no reason why they shouldn't be civil to one another for the sake of their work.

* * *

Georgie had been reading a long letter from Jessie Kendle. It wasn't often that Jessie wrote letters, she preferred to telephone, but it was clear that she had a lot on her mind and needed to unburden herself. Harry hadn't been well again, and they'd had a man from the War Office round to see if Kendlebury was suitable for use as a convalescent home for wounded officers.

After some hours of poking his nose in everywhere he said we were too large, Jessie had written with a mixture of frustration and relief. *I was so pleased, and that was awful of me, but you know what I mean. They would have wanted us to move out and I just couldn't cope with all that.*

One good thing has happened recently. Walter told his father that he wants to help him with the business when he leaves college. He's been doing a course in design and he's come up with some really good ideas, but he also has other plans for his design work – and it's rather clever. Of course nothing can happen until after the war. I do wish it was over but Harry says he thinks we've got a lot more to put up with yet.

Georgie sighed as she turned to her other letter, which she'd opened before Jessie's. It was a coincidence that it should have arrived by the same post. It seemed it was her turn to be inspected by a man from the ministry and for the same purpose. Arthur would turn in his grave at the thought, but she wasn't sure how she felt about things. The house was too big for her on her own, and yet it was her duty to preserve it for Geoffrey. If it was her choice she might have sold it, even though she loved both the house and the garden. But she wouldn't want to live here with Ben; there were too many memories of the past and with Geoffrey at school she found it lonely at times.

God she did miss Ben! Some days the ache inside her was so painful that she felt ill. In fact she had been feeling a bit under the weather altogether of late. It must be this awful winter.

She got up and went to look out of the window. The garden was looking a bit sorry for itself because the weather had been too bad to do much out there of late. She must try to do a bit to it when she was feeling better.

Arthur would hate it if the military took over the house for a convalescent home. He had always been so proud of it, of the fact that it had been in his family for generations. She could almost see the look of displeasure on his face.

'I'm sorry,' she said out loud. 'I'm sorry I disappointed you, but it isn't my fault if they want the house.'

Now she was talking to herself! Georgie smiled wryly. That was what loneliness did to you. It was a good thing she was going to spend Christmas with her mother. And after that she might go and visit Annabel or Jessie. Annabel was feeling down herself because Beth wasn't coming home for Christmas.

'You can get us out of London, Beth,' Arnold told her as he took her cases and stowed them in the boot of his car. 'I have some work to do and I want to get it finished so that we can both enjoy our holiday.'

'I'll drive all the way if you like,' Beth offered with a smile. 'I always enjoy driving.'

'I'll take over after we stop for lunch,' he said. 'I'd hoped to have this damned thing done before we left but it's been one meeting after another. I thought we might have to cancel altogether at one point, but I put my foot down in the end. *They* tend to take you for granted if you let them and I'm due for a break.'

'You work very hard,' Beth agreed as she got into the driving seat. 'Off we go then...' Arnold nodded to her, his head bent over his work as he sat in the back seat. She was a little amused, knowing it would be a wonder if he even remembered to stop for lunch.

But she was glad of his company or she would be when they reached Drew's home, which she knew was a rather large and important house set in one of the best areas of Hampshire. Drew's family was wealthy, and though that hadn't seemed to matter when he was with her, she suddenly felt very intimidated. His parents were bound to think he might have done better for himself. After all, she wasn't particularly pretty, even though

207

Drew had said she was lovely, and her mother had been an actress – and the victim of a murder.

Beth had always felt there was something slightly shady about her mother's death that Annabel hadn't told her. She'd suffered torments about it at her private school, from one rather unpleasant girl in particular, and in the end she'd been glad to leave and live with her grandmother. Her life had been uncomplicated and mostly happy after that. However, having been to an exclusive school had made her aware of the difference between *them* and her. And she was feeling even more conscious of the divide than usual as she prepared to meet her parents-in-law. She just knew they wouldn't like her.

To Beth's surprise Arnold did remember to stop for lunch. It turned out that he'd telephoned ahead and made arrangements at a rather nice coaching inn about two-thirds of the way there.

'This used to be marvellous before the war,' he told her as they went inside. 'I dare say they won't be quite up to their old standard, but it should be all right. They told me they had a rather special game pie on the menu and recommended we try that – that's if you like game?'

'Yes, Annabel has it quite often at the hotel,' Beth said and smiled at him. 'It was good of you to go to all this trouble, Arnold.'

'I wanted to make it a bit special for you. You deserve it, Beth. I think you've been wonderful to keep going. I was sure you would have got fed up and gone home by now, and I should have been sorry to lose you.'

'Only because you hate breaking new secretaries in,' she said and laughed teasingly. Of late there had been a feeling of warm companionship between them.

'Oh, secretaries are two a penny,' Arnold said. 'But there's only one Beth.'

She blushed at the compliment, surprised that he had made it. Arnold usually kept his thoughts to himself and got on with his work, because he didn't have time for chatter. But they were on holiday and this was the first time she'd seen him as relaxed as he was now.

True to his word, Arnold took the wheel when they left the inn. The meal had been much better than Beth had expected and there was even a sherry trifle for afters, which seemed almost decadent after the strict rations of recent months.

'How did they manage that, do you suppose?' Beth asked when they left. 'Real cream too!'

'They have their ways,' he replied. 'But I have a feeling it was only for special customers. It wasn't on the menu.'

'Using your muscle as an important man from the Government?' Beth teased.

'No, as a son-in-law of the owner actually,' he replied. 'Montgomery is a decent old boy and he told me when I rang that he would lay something on for us.'

'Your wife's father?' Beth stared at him, her heart thumping.

'Yes. I suppose Drew told you my history?'

'Just a little,' she acknowledged. 'I – it was sad. I'm sorry.'

'Don't be, Beth. It was a long time ago. I grieved and I'm over it, as Tilda's father is at last, I'm glad to say. We've helped each other through and remained good friends. He asked to meet you sometime and I told him to come and see us at Brigsham House over Christmas. I think he may.'

'I should like to meet him,' Beth said. 'Will Mrs Bryant mind you inviting him?'

'Lady Bryant?' Arnold frowned as he saw her eyes widen. 'Surely someone told you? Well, that's a bit stupid of them – to just spring it on you out of the blue. I would have mentioned it before but I assumed you knew. Drew's father is a baronet, you see. Sir Edward Bryant.'

'Oh...' Beth swallowed hard, her panic growing by leaps and bounds. 'When she writes to me, she signs her letters Sonia Bryant. Drew's father spoke to me once on the phone but he told me to call him Ted. I had no idea ... thank you for telling me. I should have felt such a fool if I'd called her Mrs when she's a lady...'

'They are the fools for not making things clear,' Arnold growled. 'Drew should have taken you home at some point, told you about his family. I can't understand why he didn't make things easier for you, Beth. It's hard enough to meet your in-laws for the first time without having to do it on your own.'

'I suppose he meant to do it but things just caught up with us,' Beth said defensively. The few hours they'd managed to spend together had been too precious to share. Besides, Beth had resisted the idea and so it wasn't all Drew's fault. 'I dare say I'll survive – as long as you're there too.'

'Sonia and Ted are nice people,' Arnold told her. 'She will expect you to call her Sonia, I'm sure. But I'm there if you need me. I shan't let them eat you alive, scout's honour!'

Beth laughed. 'I don't believe you were ever in the scouts.'

'Yes, I was, a team leader,' he said and grinned at her. 'Precocious little beggar, I promise you.'

'You've made me feel so much better,' she said. 'I'm not sure I could have done this without you.'

'Oh, I'm sure you would,' he replied. 'But I wanted to come.' After that they drove in silence for most of the time.

The house when she first saw it took Beth's breath away. It was as large as Kendlebury but it didn't have the soft, worn, welcoming feel of Jessie and Harry's home. It looked pristine, the grounds kept as neat as a new pin, not one weed in sight in the rose beds, and it made Beth shiver. She knew at once that she couldn't have her child here no matter what her in-laws said about Drew's child being born at home.

211

Inside the house seemed cold and uninviting despite all its treasures, and there were plenty of those. Sir Edward hadn't given an inch to the war. The threat of a few bombs wasn't going to make him hide his family pictures in a dark vault somewhere, as he later told her in a booming voice that made her eardrums ring. And the antique furniture was the very finest from the Chippendale and Adam eras, beautifully polished and free of blemish. Beth wondered how anyone ever dared to sit on the chairs.

Her host was a genial man with a habit of speaking very loudly as if he was afraid that people wouldn't hear him otherwise, but Beth sensed that he was kind and inclined to be friendly. Lady Bryant was a small, thin woman with elegant clothes and immaculate hair. She wasn't beautiful but she had good bone structure and held herself well. She smiled and greeted Beth warmly, but there was a reserve that the girl sensed immediately.

'Arnold, my dearest boy,' Sonia Bryant said as she turned to him, having given Beth the once over. In Beth's mind she had been found lacking, though Lady Bryant hadn't shown it; it was just a gut feeling. 'It is much too long since we've seen you. It was so good of you to bring dear Beth to us for Christmas, but I am going to scold you for keeping her in London all this time. She really should be with us now, preparing for the birth of Drew's child.'

'Can't possibly spare her just yet,' Arnold

replied and looked at Beth. 'She's far too valuable an asset, Sonia. Besides, Beth doesn't want a lot of fuss. She's as strong as an ox and she'll do the thing on her own without help from any of us.'

'Arnold!' Lady Bryant looked at him in horror. 'That's the last thing I expected to hear from you. Beth needs taking care of properly. I want you to help me persuade her to come here to us.'

'I rather think Beth will make up her own mind.'

'It's very kind of you, Sonia,' Beth said drawing courage from his staunch support. 'I shall think about it when the time comes, but Annabel wants me to go and stay with her for a while before the baby is born and when I'm ready to leave London I probably shall.'

'Well, as long as she takes care of herself,' Sonia said and looked at Arnold rather than her disappointing daughter-in-law.

Beth could see her answer had displeased Drew's mother but she wasn't going to give in. She was feeling a bit annoyed with Drew for not telling her more about his home and leaving her to visit alone. If it hadn't been for Arnold she would have felt completely out of her depth.

'Have you had a card from Drew?' Sonia was saying. 'We got one a week ago, but of course it was posted in England. I think he must have done all his cards before he went abroad. I had a birthday card with the same postmark. He left them with friends to post.'

213

'Oh, I had one from overseas,' Beth told her. 'But there was a present that came from a jeweller. I think he must have asked for that to be sent at Christmas before he left.'

Catching Arnold's eye at that moment, Beth guessed who had been given the job of sending the cards in Drew's absence. Had he also arranged for the gift of her pearl ear-rings? She decided against asking now, but would do so when they were alone.

'Well, come and sit down,' Drew's mother was saying. 'We'll all have a nice glass of sherry – at least, I'm not sure. Do you drink sherry, Beth?'

'I'll have a very small glass,' Beth told her. 'I like it medium dry please, Ted, but not much because of the baby.'

'Do the little blighter good,' Ted Bryant replied as he handed her a glass that held far more than she wanted or could possibly drink. 'Give him a bit of red blood, what?'

'I'm sure you're right,' Arnold said and then gave Beth a rather wicked grin, which made her wonder just what was in his mind. He leaned towards Beth as his host turned away. 'Don't worry, I'll finish it for you. Ted's sherry is some of the best in the country.'

Beth smiled at him. She was so lucky he'd come with her. Otherwise she would be way over her head and drowning.

Christmas had been every bit the ordeal she'd imagined, Beth thought as she dutifully kiss-ed her mother-in-law on the cheek. Although everyone had been kind and generous, giving her lovely presents to take home, she had felt awkward and out of place. The one bright spot had been when Freddie Montgomery had popped in for drinks before lunch on Boxing Day. He was a perfect poppet and she wasn't surprised that Arnold cared for him as much as he did.

'What a lovely young lady you are,' he said when he kissed her cheek. 'I wanted to meet the marvel Arnold has been telling me about for months and I'm glad I have. You must get Arnold to bring you to my house for dinner one evening – after the big event if you like. You'll be feeling more the thing then.'

He had brought Beth a pretty rattle for the baby. It was made of solid silver and she thought Victorian, and she loved it immediately.

'Saw it at an auction the other day and couldn't resist it,' he'd told her. 'Always buying things I've no use for – but then I remembered you and thought it was just the ticket.'

'It's beautiful. I shall treasure it.'

Her reply had pleased him. Beth thought that, if he had been her father-in-law, she wouldn't have minded staying at his house.

However, he was there only for an hour and she felt the contrast even more after he left. Compared to his warmth, Sonia Bryant was icy despite her smiles and friendly gestures. Beth knew she didn't really like her and she made up her mind that she wasn't going to have the baby in this house.

'Now, you must promise you will come to us soon,' Sonia cooed over Beth as she prepared to leave. 'You will have a lovely room and the use of the nursery. And I know it would please Drew.'

'I think I should like to be with my mother for the birth,' Beth said and as soon as she'd said the words she knew it was what she wanted.

'Can't blame the girl for that,' Ted boomed at her. 'Come to us afterwards. Don't press her, Sonia, stands to reason a girl would want her mother at a time like that.'

'But she doesn't have a mother,' Sonia said and then looked awkward. 'I meant...'

'Annabel is my mother,' Beth said and the truth of it struck her with force. She had wanted to escape from Annabel's fussing, but now she realized that Annabel fussed over her because she really cared. 'She took me on when my mother died and she's been a wonderful mother to me. I shall go home to her in a few weeks. After the baby is born I'll bring her or him on a visit, but my home is with Annabel until Drew comes back.'

Beth felt better now that she had stood up to Sonia and made her position clear. And a part of that feeling better was due to getting her thoughts about Annabel straight in her head. Yes, she had enjoyed her freedom, and she might want it again one day, but for the moment she would welcome some of Annabel's loving care.

'Well, you know you are always welcome here.'

Beth smiled but didn't reply as she went out to the car. Arnold opened the passenger-side door for her and helped her in, tending to her as solicitously as if he were her husband instead of her boss. It was almost as if he knew she was feeling a bit fragile and wanted to protect her. She smiled and thanked him, but he merely nodded and went back to shake hands with their hosts.

They drove most of the way back in silence, stopping for a picnic that Sonia had pressed on them. It was beautifully prepared and enjoyable, especially with Arnold sitting beside her. The rain began as they neared London.

'It's just as well,' Arnold told her. 'The frost will go now and it may feel a bit warmer. Better for our airmen too.'

'Yes.' Beth smiled at him gratefully. 'I want to thank you for everything, Arnold. I shall never be able to repay you for your kindness these past few days.'

'Stuff and nonsense,' he said. 'Wait until I get you back to your desk, young woman. I've got three reports in my head that have to be dictated and typed up and I needed them yesterday!'

Back to normal, Beth thought; how good that felt to her. She would miss working with Arnold when the time came for her to leave. In fact, a little voice in her head told her she was going to miss him far more than she ought.

★ ★ ★

Georgie let herself in the front door and collected the letters from the table in the hall where Mrs Townsend had left them for her. The house smelled of polish and lavender, and as she went into the front parlour she saw a fire had been lit earlier. It was beginning to die down now, but a good stir with the poker and a nice dry log would soon have it going again.

She went into the kitchen and put the kettle on. Her wonderful housekeeper had done some baking for her and she picked up a plain bun and took it through to the parlour, munching as she went. It was good to be home again, though she'd enjoyed Christmas with her mother.

Priscilla had cheered her up and her practical manner had helped Georgie to sort things out in her mind. There was no point in wishing for the moon. Nothing could change the fact that she'd spent nine years married to a man she wasn't in love with or that the man she did love was probably somewhere in France risking his life for the country he loved. Another thing she was certain of was that she having Ben's child. She hadn't been sure before she left to spend Christmas with her mother, but she was now, because she'd visited a doctor and had had it confirmed.

That last little holiday with Ben had given her a special present to remember him by, Georgie thought with a wry smile. It didn't matter whether she was happy or sorry, it was a fact and, like everything else, would have to be faced up to when the time came. It wouldn't be easy explaining to Geoffrey. She owed no explanations to anyone else.

Sitting down by the fire, which had sparked into life after some careful ministrations, Georgie saw the official letter in her pile and her heart thumped. She could have done without this to greet her on her return. The inspection would take place tomorrow! Damn them, Georgie thought. She had almost put off her return for another few days and now she half wished she had – and yet that would merely delay the inevitable. She knew in her heart that her house was going to be just what they were looking for. Arthur had spent a small fortune getting the plumbing up to date only a year or so before he died, and it was in good repair. There were enough bedrooms to make it viable as a small convalescent home without being a vast rambling place like Kendlebury.

That meant she was going to have to find somewhere else to live for the rest of the war, and who knew how long that would be? Would she have to store all her things? Most of the furniture was solid, sturdy stuff, made of oak and almost indestructible. She would pack anything she valued, naturally, and the rest could stay if they wanted it.

Both her mother and Jessie had offered her a home if she needed it, and she rather thought she might stay with Jessie. In a way it was a blessing. She'd been lonely before the visit to her mother, and besides, she knew Jessie could do with some help. She was struggling to keep Kendlebury going against all the odds and with Harry unwell...

Yes, that was the sensible way to think, Georgie decided. There was no point in being miserable about something that was out of her hands. She would stay with Jessie and tell everyone about the baby when she had to – but she wouldn't tell them who the father was, not yet. Not until Ben came home. He had promised to leave Helen, and perhaps now he would realize there was no reason to wait any longer. Georgie was smiling as she began to read the rest of her letters.

'I'm sorry, Mrs Bridges. I'm sure it's not what you want to hear but I have to tell you that your house is exactly what we are looking for. I shall be recommending that we use it for the purpose you were advised of in my letter,' Philip Rathmere told her the next morning after a brief tour of the house.

'I was expecting you to say that.' Georgie replied. 'I can't say I'm surprised. When will you want to take it over?'

'If my report is accepted – about two months, I imagine – but I shall keep you informed. We shan't just turn up on your doorstep and evict you, I promise.'

Georgie smiled. 'I never thought you would. What do I do about the furniture? Do you want to move everything?'

'That's really up to you,' Philip Rathmere

said. 'Some people want to take everything with them or store it. If you prefer to leave the heavy stuff we will compensate you for any damage done. You will, of course, receive compensation for the use of the house.'

'Yes, your letter was clear.' Georgie wrinkled her brow. 'If it's all right with you, I think I shall store what few valuables we have and take my personal things; the rest is solid and won't hurt much whatever your men do.'

'Most of them are too ill to cause much trouble. We really do need quiet, comfortable houses for them to stay until they can face the world again.'

'Then they obviously need the house more than I do. I'll arrange to move as soon as I get your confirmation.'

'Thank you.' He looked relieved. 'You've taken it better than most. Some ladies get very upset at the idea of their home being invaded.'

'What must be,' Georgie said and shrugged. She supposed he must hear a great deal of complaints in the course of his work, but he wouldn't from her. 'Do you do much of this, Mr Rathmere?'

'I'm in charge of finding and supervising property all over the country for the War Office. We need all kinds of property for all kinds of purposes.'

'So your job doesn't finish once you've selected a property?' Georgie was interested. He was a man she felt comfortable with, someone you could talk to and not at all officious as she'd expected him to be before he had arrived.

'Oh no, I shall be keeping an eye on your house – on all of those I've taken over.'

'That must keep you busy?'

'Yes, but I enjoy property. It was my business before the war – renovating old places and putting them to new use.'

'That sounds interesting,' Georgie said. 'I was just about to put the kettle on – would you like a cup of tea?'

'That's very kind. I have a long drive ahead of me when I leave here.'

'So it's settled then,' Annabel said when Georgie phoned her later that day to tell her the news. 'Where will you go – or haven't you thought it through yet?'

'Yes, I have thought about it a lot. My mother offered me a home of course, but Jessie told me I could stay with her and I believe that would suit me better. Jessie needs some help at the moment and it will save me fretting if I'm busy. I can store a lot of my things there too, though I'm not taking all that much. I thought I would leave the heavy furniture. If the worst happens and it gets wrecked I can always buy new. Most of it had been there forever and belonged to Arthur's grandparents. I never particularly liked it, but it was comfortable and it's the personal touches that make a house anyway. All my own stuff will go with me.'

'You've taken this well. I'm not sure I could

be so sanguine if it was my house they'd taken over.'

'That's what the ministry man said. He was rather sweet actually and apologized for wanting the house. But he has his job to do and, after all, it is in a worthwhile cause.'

'As long as it hasn't upset you too much?'

'Oh no. I've got more important things to worry about.'

'Yes, of course. I've had some wonderful news. Beth is coming here soon. She wants to have the baby at home and stay with us until Drew comes back. She sounds better in herself, quite cheerful. I've been worrying about her but Paul said she would make up her own mind and she has.'

'That's lovely. I'm so pleased for you.'

'I'm really excited – and if you're staying with Jessie it will be marvellous. We shall see you often.'

'Yes...' Georgie hesitated. 'I may have some more news but I'll keep that until I see you.'

'Now you've made me curious.'

'I promise I'll tell you soon. I have to go, Annabel. I've got to fetch someone from the hospital.'

Georgie replaced the receiver feeling slightly guilty. She would have to tell Annabel about the baby, of course, but she was hoping Ben would be home before then, because otherwise it might be awkward.

Eight

'We shall miss you, Mrs Bryant,' Beth's landlady said as her husband finished carrying all
the various bits and pieces downstairs. 'You
will bring the baby to see me one day?'

'Yes, of course, Mabel,' Beth said, and then
as the door-knocker sounded, 'That will be
Mr Pearson.' She looked expectantly towards
the door as it opened but instead of seeing
Arnold standing there she glimpsed a youth
in an official uniform. He was delivering a
telegram and like most other wives, sisters
and mothers she had learned to dread seeing
him at her door. 'No...'

'Telegram for Mrs Beth Bryant.'

Beth made no move to take it; she couldn't.
Her head was spinning and she felt faint. This
couldn't be happening! Her landlady
accepted the small orange envelope and sent
the boy off with a sixpence in his hand.

'Do you want me to open it for you?'

Beth shook her head. Her throat was too
tight to speak. She felt sick and her face was
deathly pale. She was still staring at the telegram when the door was opened once more
to admit Arnold. It was as if she'd turned to
stone and she watched Arnold take the

telegram from her landlady's hand and open it. His eyes flew to Beth.

'Missing in action,' he said as he came towards her.

'Oh, Arnold,' Beth whispered as his arms went round her, supporting her. She felt as if she might faint as the ground cut away from under her feet. The scream was building inside her head but somehow it didn't come out. She wouldn't let it, she forced it back, and held her emotions tamped down.

'It's all right, dear Beth,' he murmured against her ear. 'Missing means there's still hope.'

Her eyes sought his in a desperate appeal and he touched her cheek with his fingertips, infinitely gentle, caring.

'Yes.' Her eyes were smarting with tears but she held them back. She had stopped shivering now; the urge to scream was under control. She wasn't going to make a fuss because there was still hope: Arnold said so and she trusted him. 'Yes, there's still hope, isn't there? He will be all right. I'm sure he will.'

She avoided her landlady's pitying gaze as she asked if Beth wanted a cup of tea or a drop of brandy.

'We'll get off if you don't mind,' Arnold answered for her. 'It's good of you to ask but we've a long journey ahead of us and I want to make an early start.'

Beth had recovered enough to thank her for her kindness. She was grateful for the firm pressure of Arnold's hand on her arm steadying her, guiding her to the car and helping her inside.

She felt stunned, as if she were in some kind of a nightmare. This couldn't be happening; it was unreal – a bad dream. In a little while she would wake up and discover it was all the same as before. She felt unnaturally calm, controlled; refusing to believe that the telegram had arrived. Her mind seemed to have gone blank. She sat as if in a daze, staring straight ahead. It was not until some twenty minutes or so later that she was able to look about her. The rain of early morning had abated and there was even a faint glimmer of blue in the sky.

'It looks as if it will be nice later,' she said.

Arnold glanced at her, noting the glazed look and unnatural control but decided to ignore it for the moment. 'Yes, that's what the forecast on the wireless said. I managed to fix us a picnic. We'll stop about halfway but if you need to stop before that just say. We can have a cup of tea whenever you feel the need for a break – answer the call of nature, walk about to ease your back – that sort of thing.'

'You're always so thoughtful,' Beth said. 'I'm not sure how to say thank you. When you came this morning ... but I won't think about it. Missing doesn't mean Drew is...' She choked on the word, unable to go on, and he saw how fragile her control really was. She was holding herself on a thin thread.

'It means there may still be hope,' Arnold said. 'But it may be unwise to hope for too

226

much, my dear.'

'I just want him to come home.'

'Yes, of course. We all hope for that, but we have to be prepared for something less than a perfect result.'

'You mean he could be seriously injured?'

'That is one explanation, yes.'

Beth thought about Drew being badly injured. She knew what that might mean, had heard other girls talk about lost limbs and horrific burns. It couldn't have happened to Drew. She couldn't bear that! He had been so full of life, so happy and loving. Oh, why did this hateful war have to start at all? It wasn't fair, Beth thought, the resentment burning inside her. Why did Drew have to be hurt or killed? She knew it had happened to thousands of others but that didn't make it any easier to accept. Anger was taking over from the shock now. They'd had no right to send him out there to be killed. No right! She hated the war and everyone connected with it, because they had robbed her of her happiness. She loved Drew so much and she wanted him to come home. She wasn't sure she could go on if he didn't. But she wouldn't think about that. He had to come home. He just had to!

'She has been very quiet most of the way here, very calm,' Arnold told Paul when the two women had gone upstairs to look at the room that had been prepared for Beth's homecoming. 'But I'm not sure that's a good

227

thing. She's holding it all inside.'

'She'll cry when she's ready,' Paul told him. 'She was always very intense and private as a child. It was a good thing you got her home. She'll be all right with Annabel to look after her.'

Arnold looked a little self-conscious. 'You know I'll always help in any way I can?'

He felt the guilt prick him. He had wanted to save her pain but perhaps he'd been wrong to give Beth hope. A telegram like that one was usually bad news. A letter from Drew's commanding officer would in all probability follow in a few weeks time. But by then Beth's child should be born and she would be stronger, more able to stand up to the pain of bereavement.

'Are you sure you won't stay overnight?' Paul asked as Arnold prepared to leave. 'I know we have room for you and you would be very welcome.'

'That's very kind. I should like to visit Beth at another time but I have to get back to London – meetings coming up and a new secretary to break in, I'm afraid.'

'Yes, of course. Well, do keep in touch, won't you?'

'Perhaps I could come down one weekend – I'll telephone. You'll let me know how...'

'We should all be pleased to see you. I'll ring you myself after the birth.'

Arnold inclined his head and went out. He didn't trust himself to stay longer. His feelings for Beth had almost overwhelmed him

228

when she wept in his arms, and he knew that she wouldn't want to know. Not yet anyway, perhaps not ever. He was too old for her and her heart was broken. It would be selfish of him to put himself forward when he knew how unhappy she was.

Beth woke in the night with a searing pain in her back, and then another in her stomach. It was like a really bad cramp but much worse than she'd ever experienced. She bit her lip against the cry that came out despite her effort to hold it back. Oh, it hurt! It hurt so much. It had to be the baby, but it was too soon. She had almost a month to go yet! She got out of bed and began to pace the floor of her bedroom. It was too soon. It was just cramp or indigestion or something. It would go away if she waited for a while. The pains didn't stop coming, in fact they got fiercer and more terrible and in the end Beth knew she couldn't wait any longer. She picked up the in-house telephone and rang Annabel's room. She answered after the first few rings.

'Beth – what's wrong, love? Are you ill?'

'I think the baby's coming. It's too soon but the pain has been getting worse for the past hour and I think it must be...'

'Yes, I shouldn't be surprised,' Annabel said. 'I'm coming to you now and Paul will ring the hospital. I had made arrangements to take you in if need be and they will know all about you.'

She put down the receiver and seconds later

she was in the room with Beth. She held out her hand, taking Beth's and giving it a little squeeze.

'Nothing to worry about, dearest. Babies choose their own moment to come and it might be the shock of that wretched telegram. Not that it matters. You're not so early that it will harm the baby.'

'Will it be all right?' Beth looked at her anxiously. 'I don't want to lose my baby...' The note of near hysteria in her voice was the only clue to what she was feeling. Even now she was refusing to give in, refusing to admit her grief or cry. 'I won't, will I, Annabel?'

'No, I'm sure you won't, love,' Annabel said. 'Now we're going to get you into a warm robe and a coat, and some slippers, and then Paul will have the car waiting. By the looks of things you're going to make me a grandmother sooner than we'd thought.'

'Oh, Belle ... Mum,' Beth said and her eyes were bright with the tears she would not shed. 'I'm so glad I came home to be with you. You love me and there's no one else to care.'

'Of course we love you – all of us,' Annabel said. 'And all your friends. We're all here for you, darling. You're not alone while you have us and you never will be.'

Beth's bottom lip was quivering. The tears began to trickle down her cheeks as Annabel put an arm about her shoulders and led her from the room, but she brushed them away. She was determined not to cry. If she cried it would mean Drew was dead and he wasn't dead; he couldn't be because she loved him too much.

'She had the most awful time,' Annabel told Georgie when she rang to give her the news that Beth had a daughter. 'But she was terribly brave. She cried when they showed her Elaine, of course, but I was glad because until the birth she'd hardly wept at all – and she needed to.'

'It's so unfortunate that the news should come now,' Georgie said. 'It would be bad enough at any time, but so close to the birth was unfortunate. I'm not surprised the shock brought it on early. Poor Beth. I'm so sorry she has to face all this. She's too young to be a widow.'

'She isn't the only one,' Annabel said. 'But I hate to think of her having to bring up the baby alone. Beth needs support and love. I know she wants to be independent, but she needs looking after. We've always loved her and made her one of our family, but I think there is a certain insecurity because of what happened to Alice.'

'I'm sure you're right. I've always thought she felt it more than she showed.'

'She's carried it inside her all these years – and losing Drew will bring it all back to her.'

'Well, as long as she and the baby are all right – no complications with the child because of the premature birth?'

'No, none that will have a lasting effect. The

doctors were a bit worried and Elaine is being monitored and given special feeding, but otherwise I think she's fine. She has all her bits and pieces and she's beautiful. I think we've been lucky, Georgie.'

'That's all right then,' Georgie said. 'I suppose in a way she's lucky to have the baby to remember him by, but she told me once she wasn't happy having it without Drew being here. Still, she may have changed her mind now.'

'She seemed very happy to hold Elaine. I think most mothers feel a bond once the baby is born, even if they are a bit reluctant beforehand.'

'Yes, I think you are right.' Georgie heard the kettle whistling. 'I had better go, Annabel. Thank you for ringing. If you think she's ready to hear it, tell Beth I'm thinking of her. I'll come and see her when I move to Kendlebury next week.'

'You've been given a date then?'

'Yes, this morning. I have three weeks to move but I thought I might as well go straight away.'

'I won't keep you then, because you must be busy packing. I shall look forward to seeing you.'

'Now it has come to it I can't wait,' Georgie said. 'It had got a bit lonely here on my own. But I'll talk to you when I see you.'

Hanging up, Georgie went into the kitchen and made the tea. She looked at the box of cooking utensils on the table. A lot of them were old but she was used to them and she wouldn't want to lose them; it was silly little things like that that had been making her feel a bit low – and Annabel's call hadn't helped much. Oh, she was pleased to know that Beth had a daughter and that they were both doing well, but the news that Drew had been reported missing was very upsetting. It made her worry more about Ben. She had been thinking about him more and more of late, even though she was packing to leave her home of the past eleven years. Her memories of Arthur and her marriage were mixed, some good, some bad, but they no longer had the power to hurt her. She had tried to be a good wife and if she'd failed there was nothing she could do to put matters right.

It was the future that counted now. She just prayed that Ben would come home soon and that when he did he would find the strength to tell Helen that he wanted a divorce.

'You should tell Helen that you want a divorce,' Hetty said as she offered her brother a glass of cognac. They were in the sitting room that Hetty thought of as her own, preparing for an important sabotage attack on a German patrol. Ben had just surprised her by telling her he was thinking of getting a divorce after the war. 'If you're in love with someone else you should do something about it, Ben, not waste the rest of your life in regret. Do it as soon as you get back, don't wait for the end of the war.'

'Yes, of course you are right,' he said and sipped his drink. 'This is good stuff, Hetty.'

'Adele's finest,' Hetty said. 'She reserves it for special occasions.'

'Thought I needed some Dutch courage, did she?' Ben grinned at her. 'She's a wonderful woman, Hetty. In some ways she reminds me of Mother and yet she is so different.'

'If she was like Mother I wouldn't have been here,' Hetty said with a wry grimace. 'I could never understand why you married Helen – now *she* is just like our dear Mama.'

'You never did like Helen. Annabel told me I ought not to marry her. I was a damned fool.'

'Well, that's water under the bridge now,' Hetty said. 'Life is all about learning from your mistakes and going on. I've made mistakes as well, but I've survived – and I intend to survive tonight too.'

'I don't like the idea of your coming with us tonight, Hetty. It's too dangerous. I'm not denying what you've done. Stefan says you're one of his best men – now that you take orders from him instead of giving them.'

Hetty's eyes flashed. 'I've had no choice for the moment, but he shouldn't count his chickens before they come home to roost. He's still on trial.'

Even as she said the words she knew she was protesting for no good reason. In the weeks since she'd joined forces with Stefan she had been delighted with the success of their joint missions, and she had come to respect him. That didn't mean he wasn't an arrogant pig or that she liked him, but she did respect him. He was brave, quick and clever, all the things he needed to be to be a good leader. The sparks flew between them on occasion when he was too harsh, but most of the time they understood each other.

This time they were after a special convoy. It was carrying ammunition and supplies, but also something that both Ben and Stefan considered far more important – a German general who could be very useful if they could take him alive. That was why they had divided the group into two again. Stefan's group was to take the prisoner and Hetty's men to create a diversion by attacking the rear of the convoy and going for the ammunition truck.

'Wait until you see the cars pass,' Stefan told her. 'Then you detonate the explosives we've planted – but make sure you let the General's car go through first. Remember we want him alive. We need the convoy split into two by that explosion, that's the only way we stand a chance of getting him out of there. He's no good to us dead.'

'He'll be in the third car, right?' Hetty looked at him, her eyes narrowed. She wanted to be sure of getting it right. 'How can you be sure of that? He might be further back in the convoy and caught in the blast from our explosives. What happens then?'

'We've been working on this for months,' Stefan said. 'I can't tell you, Hetty...' He laughed as he saw her eyes spark. 'It isn't that

I don't trust you, believe me, but a lot hangs on this tonight. It isn't quite what you might think and it's very important.'

'Ben knows what it's all about, doesn't he?'

'Yes, he's known from the start. It's why he came out here – or one of the main reasons. As I told you, it's important.'

'He won't tell me either. I think you're both rotten, but I'll do what you've asked anyway, and I shan't make a mess of things.'

'I'm sure you won't.' Stefan grinned at her. 'If I thought you might I wouldn't have you with us – but keep an eye on Ben, Hetty. He hasn't had much experience of operations. He's one of the best at transmitting and he has a wonderful memory for codes, but he isn't confident with explosives, that's why I've taken that end of it. My men will set things up. All you have to do is set it off at the right moment, then attack and create a diversion so I can get our General away.'

Hetty knew Stefan was right. She could see that Ben was nervous. This was the first time he'd been involved in anything like this, though he'd helped in a lot of other ways. He was good with the transmitter and got his messages through with the minimum of fuss and quickly, which was important, because if the Germans locked on to a frequency often enough they would eventually discover the source. All the codes Ben used were in his head. He wrote nothing down, remembering everything accurately and never making a mistake, but she knew he wasn't as quick or clever with his hands. She'd watched him practising with wiring the remote detonator and she'd seen him fumble over it.

'Why don't you let me do the detonating tonight?' she said as Ben finished his cognac. 'I've done it before. Bernard taught me.'

'You're better with a gun than I am,' Ben replied. 'I can do it, Hetty. Trust me. I shan't let you down.'

'All right, if you want.' Hetty smiled re-assuringly at him as he put his glass down. 'Time to go – the others will be waiting. Good luck, Ben.'

'We shall need it,' he said and gave her a nervous grin. 'They say the devil looks after his own – well, let's hope he's on our side tonight.'

The convoy was on its way. They could see the lights of the motorbikes out front, three of them heading it up. Anything too obvious would have attracted their attention, but the explosive device was hidden beneath a pile of horse manure and it was unlikely the outriders would investigate that, Hetty thought with a smile. It was a nice touch and one that had amused Stefan when she came up with it.

'Give the bastards some of their own back, eh, *chérie*?'

She smiled in the darkness as she recalled her answer and the look in his eyes. Why was it that she felt so attracted to Stefan? He wasn't the type of man she dare trust. She

237

didn't want to get involved with him on a personal level, but he made her heart race whenever he looked at her that way. It wasn't fair. She must not like him too much or he would let her down the way Henri had; she had learned too well that men could not be trusted once they had what they wanted. She had better keep her mind on the job.

'They're coming,' Hetty whispered as she saw the lights of the convoy, her pulse jumping with a mixture of excitement and fear. This was important. It had to be right. 'Get ready, Ben.'

He didn't answer her. Glancing at him, she saw beads of sweat on his forehead and knew he was terrified. It was his first time on this kind of operation, of course, but she felt angry with him. If he felt this way he shouldn't have come.

'Do you want me to do it?' she asked quietly as the motorbikes went whizzing by without seeming to notice the ordure on the road. He shook his head, giving her a grin of bravado. 'Remember, the first three cars to go through, then detonate when the first lorry is going over the explosives.'

Ben nodded but didn't answer, his tongue moving over his bottom lip in a nervous gesture. Hetty counted the cars: one, two, three, and then the first of the lorries, which was the one carrying the ammunition according to Stefan. She made a gesture to Ben as the lorry approached. He had the handle raised, poised to plunge it, but she could see his hand was shaking. The lorry was in exactly the right spot.

'Now,' she hissed, but looking at Ben she saw that he had frozen. He couldn't bring himself to press the plunger down. She acted swiftly; rolling over the ground between them, Hetty placed her hands over his and forced them down. The explosion went off but caught only the tail end of the lorry, which was enough to send it skewing off the road to end drunkenly in a ditch, and to ignite a fire in the rear compartment, but it didn't explode. 'Damn! Come on, we attack now!' she yelled at the others waiting in the darkness behind her.

Soldiers were jumping out of the back of the lorry. It had been carrying men not ammunition. Stefan had got that part of his information wrong! Hetty registered the fact as she started firing at the soldiers below. Some of them in the truck they'd hit were staggering about as if blinded by smoke or shock, but some of them were already firing in their direction. She aimed her fire at a group of them and saw one of them stagger away with a wound in his chest. She kept on firing until she had to stop and reload her rifle. The other trucks had screeched to a halt and more men were pouring out, rushing to the defence of their colleagues. It looked as if there was a whole division of them!

In the midst of the fierce gun battle that ensued, Hetty knew that they had no chance of winning this fight. All they could do was to hold the Germans back for a while and hope it gave Stefan time to get his quarry away. She could hear firing coming from the front end of the convoy and the German soldiers had heard it too. There was shouting, running and she saw that some of them were diverting to the front of the convoy.

Most of the soldiers had begun to recover from their first blind panic and were trying to trace the source of the gunfire. They were settling down now, shouting orders instead of running around like headless chickens. One of them had brought up a small truck, and doing a neat turn in the centre of the road, he swung the back round to face in their direction and then someone opened up with a rapid-fire machine gun.

'We'd better get out of here,' Hetty said to Louis. 'Tell the men to fire and run, and disperse into the woods. Split up because they're not going to leave that convoy for long in case it's a trick. Get going, one or two at a time.'

'What about you?'

'I'll follow in a minute,' Hetty told him. She was waiting for a signal, and seeing the flare burst over the heads of the startled soldiers below, she smiled. It meant that Stefan had got what he wanted, and had the added bonus of making the Germans wonder if they were about to be attacked from the air. She saw several of them looking up and knew that this was her moment. 'Come on, Ben, let's get out of here.'

'Not sure I can,' Ben's muffled voice answered her. 'You'd better go. Give me your gun and I'll cover you.'

'What's wrong? You've got to move, Ben. In a moment they'll come looking for us.'

'I've been hit,' he said.

'Where?' she demanded, moving towards him anxiously. He looked very pale and there was blood on his sleeve. 'It's just a flesh wound. You'll be all right. Come on, I'll help you.'

He was kneeling on the ground and when she went to haul him to his feet, she saw that there was more blood oozing from a wound to his side. He groaned as she put his arm around her shoulder, lifting him so that she was taking his weight.

'You've got to try,' she muttered fiercely. 'I can't manage you unless you try. I know it's bloody painful but if I leave you here you're dead.'

Ben muttered something but she knew he was putting effort into helping her, and they began to walk as quickly as he could manage into the trees. They were moving so slowly that Hetty knew they were vulnerable.

'Leave me and go on,' Ben gasped. 'I'm holding you back, Hetty. I don't want you to die for me – for my foolishness. I let you down...'

'It wasn't just you,' Hetty muttered furiously. He was right, of course, but he was her brother and she couldn't abandon him, couldn't let him take all the blame himself.

'Stefan is always so bloody sure he's right and he got it wrong. There was no ammunition in that truck, just men. If it had blown as it ought – even with the timing being late – we would have had them at our mercy.'

'Maybe I got it wrong,' Ben muttered and stifled a groan. 'I gave him the information. It came through HQ. It wasn't Stefan's fault. You mustn't blame him for this.'

Hetty cursed but made no further comment. It was taking all her strength to support Ben. She didn't know these woods as well as those surrounding the château, but if they could just evade the Germans they might find somewhere to hide. The sounds of firing were easing behind them. She knew that she and Ben had been the last to leave the scene of the attack. The Germans must be taking stock, deciding whether or not to come after them. She heard shouting, as if someone had taken charge and was ordering the men to regroup. Once they had realized their precious General was missing they might decide to go looking for him rather than scour the woods for her and her men.

They must be aware by now that it had been a two-pronged attack, and they would be wondering what to do next. Hetty thought about what she would do in their shoes, and decided she would probably split her forces. Some of them would go in pursuit of the captured General, others stay with the convoy, and a small party would be sent out to look for her and her men. A small party wouldn't be able to search woods like these thoroughly at night, which meant she might be safe for a few hours. In the morning they would probably come back with more men to look for them – or simply to take revenge on anyone they could find who might know something. That was the bit that always played havoc with Hetty's conscience. She had brushed it aside when Ben challenged her on it, but of course she felt it when innocent women, children and old men were taken out and shot as a reprisal. She knew Stefan felt it too but it didn't stop him doing what he had to do, and it wouldn't stop her either.

Ben was getting heavier all the time, the effort required to nurse him along becoming more of a strain. She felt him stumble and knew she wasn't going to get him much further; he was nearly out on his feet. He hadn't complained much but she knew how he must be suffering. She'd seen others with wounds like his and she knew they would be lucky to pull him through, but she was determined not to abandon him.

'Don't give up on me, Ben,' she pleaded. 'We'll stop soon, I promise.'

'Can't...' Ben muttered and sagged suddenly. She couldn't hold him as he fell and had to let him go. 'Sorry...'

Hetty looked about her. A light drizzle had just started to fall. She didn't fancy being out all night in this, especially if it got worse, and it wouldn't do Ben any good. Oh, damn!

What was she going to do now? She'd told Louis and the others to disperse and go home. They wouldn't start to worry about her for some hours – and by then it might be too late. She decided to leave Ben where he was and to take a look a bit further on, to see what was beyond the clearing. She bent over him, giving him a little shake to make him aware of her.

'I'm leaving you but only for a few minutes. I want to see if there's anywhere that we can shelter.'

'Leave me here – go home.'

'Don't be a damned fool, Ben. I'm not leaving you. But we need somewhere to shelter or someone to fetch help.'

He didn't answer and she left him lying there. She could see something half hidden in a clump of overgrown bushes just beyond the clearing. If it was what she hoped it was she might have found somewhere to rest, for a while at least.

Hetty had been lucky to find the hut, but she knew there were a lot like this one in the woods: used by charcoal burners and woodsmen, they were deserted for much of the time, many left to rot when their purpose was done. This one looked as if it might still be in use at times. There was evidence that it was kept in reasonable repair and there was a pile of sacking in one corner, which had made a rough bed for Ben.

She'd had a terrible time getting him in

here. He'd been barely conscious and she'd decided to tie him round the waist with a bit of rope she'd found in the hut and fasten the other end about her own waist. And then she'd dragged him, bit by bit, over the damp ground. By the time she got him there she was thankful that he'd passed out.

He was moaning, half conscious, seeming to be in a fever. She wished she had something to give him, if only a little water, but she didn't even have a cup or tin can to catch some of the rain, which was sheeting down now. She thought it might help them. The Germans would probably decide to abandon the search and return in the morning. And that was Hetty's dilemma. Did she leave Ben here and go to get help or wait and hope that someone came looking? The trouble was, that someone might be German soldiers.

'Georgie ... sorry...' Ben was mumbling something. Hetty knelt down on the earthen floor, bending over him to stroke his forehead. 'I wanted you ... loved you ... but it was no good ... no good...'

'It's all right, Ben dearest,' Hetty whispered, her throat tight with emotion. She and Ben hadn't seen each other much over the recent years but she'd always cared about him and it was tearing her apart to know there was so little she could do. 'I'm going to get help.'

'No...' His fingers curled about her wrist and his eyes were open, staring at her. 'You have to tell her – tell her I loved her. I always loved her. I'm sorry I let her down again. I meant us to be together this time. I was going to tell Helen...'

'Yes, I'll tell her,' Hetty whispered, the tears burning behind her eyes as she struggled to stop them falling. She felt so helpless. 'Who do you mean, Ben?'

'Georgie...'

'Georgie Bridges?' Hetty was surprised. She'd never suspected anything between them. Perhaps Annabel knew more but she'd never mentioned it. 'But you'll get better. You'll tell her yourself.' Ben's eyes were closed. His colour wasn't good. Hetty knew the rough bandage she'd made was leaking; he was still bleeding. 'I'm going to get help...'

She got to her feet and then froze as she heard the sounds outside the hut. Someone was there! It must be a part of the German patrol looking for them. She snatched up her gun and turned to face the door as it opened. She would take a few of them with her before she died!

'You can put that damned thing down, Hetty,' Stefan's voice said and she felt faint with relief. 'What the hell did you think you were up to? You left a trail a mile wide to this place.'

'I couldn't help it,' she said, too weary and anxious to argue. 'Ben couldn't walk. I had to drag him the last part. He's unconscious and failing. I was about to go for help.'

'Just as well I came looking for you then, isn't it?' Stefan said. He handed her his gun as he went to kneel at Ben's side. After a brief

246

examination he looked up at her. 'I'm not hopeful but we'll take him to my place and see what we can do. I'll take him over my shoulder, Hetty. It isn't that far to the farm. You were heading in the right direction. Another twenty minutes and you might have found it.'

'I couldn't have got him that far.'

'No, I don't suppose you could,' he said. 'You messed up this time, Hetty. We got our target away but too many of our people were killed.'

'And you blame me for that?' She glared at him. 'You said that bloody truck was carrying explosives. Besides...' She glanced at Ben and decided to keep her denial to herself. 'It isn't important now. I'm sorry if some of your people got killed, mine did too.'

Stefan raised his brows but didn't say anything, merely bending to take Ben up in his arms and lift him on to his shoulder.

'Let's get out of here before they come looking. If I could find you, so can they.'

Hetty was sitting by her brother's bed watching his tortured breathing when Stefan entered the low-ceilinged room. It was typical of a French farmhouse in that the furniture was old, heavy and rather ugly, but the bedding was pristine white and smelled of lavender. Fires and the dirt of centuries had blackened the beams, but the white painted walls were immaculate.

She turned to look at Stefan as he lounged

against the door arch, his eyes intent on her.

'Any change?'

'Not since the doctor gave him something to make him sleep. He hasn't made a murmur.' She caught back a sob as she saw how pale Ben was, his breathing shallow and uneven. 'The doctor didn't hold out much hope, did he?'

'He might stand a chance if he was in hospital, but if he was taken in here the Germans would whisk him off before you could blink and he wouldn't survive more than a few hours.'

'He doesn't stand much chance now, does he?' She heard the bitterness in her own voice, felt the pain deep inside her. It was such a stupid waste. Ben had never been meant for this kind of thing. He was gentle, generous and sweet, but he had balked at spilling blood and now he was paying the price for his hesitation.

'No – but at least he can die in peace here. He won't be tortured for the names of his companions.'

'You selfish pig,' Hetty said, her eyes stinging with tears. There was a tearing pain inside her, a burning need to lash out at someone – and he had broad shoulders. He could take it. 'That's all you care about really, isn't it? Your precious resistance, protecting your men and your work. You don't give a damn that my brother is dying. They threw him in at the deep end before he could swim and now he's paying the price.'

248

'He brought valuable information with him.' Stefan's expression was unreadable as he looked at her. 'You blame me for that? Don't you think he was old enough to know what he was doing? If he wasn't up to it, Hetty, he should have stayed behind at the château and waited. I offered him that choice but he turned me down, said there was a first time for everyone.'

Ben had said more or less the same thing to her, but that didn't make it any easier to bear.

'I hate you,' she said. 'You're made of ice – no feelings at all.'

'Is that so? Perhaps one day I'll show you how wrong you are, Hetty.'

'What is that supposed to mean?'

Stefan raised his brows and then smiled oddly, but went out without enlarging on his comment.

Hetty grabbed a spare pillow from beside the bed and threw it at him as he closed the door. He was too damned sure of himself and she wanted to hit him, she wanted to hit him so hard that he would know how it felt to hurt as she did. And yet even in her distress she knew that was being unfair. This farm had belonged to his grandmother, coming to her through her own father, and she had left it to Stefan. Nothing had been changed as far as she could see. The old people's clothes were still in the closets. It was true there was a war on and Stefan hadn't had much time to make changes, but she thought he'd kept it the way it was for a reason.

Not that many changes were necessary in her opinion. The plumbing could do with being brought into the twentieth century, of course, and perhaps some of the furniture was a bit too ugly, but otherwise it was a beautiful house. The kind of house she had dreamed of living in when she was a girl – a house with roses growing up the walls, a husband, and several children playing in the garden.

She'd imagined a house in England in those days, but her dreams had changed when she fell in love with a charming Frenchman. These days she had no dreams left, only a hope that France would soon be free of the invader.

'Hetty...' The faint whisper caught her attention. She got up and went closer to the bed, bending over her brother. 'Water...'

'Yes, of course, just a little at a time.' She fetched water from the pitcher on the old-fashioned washstand, slipping her arm beneath his shoulders to lift him so that he could drink. He took two sips and then fell back, his eyes closing. 'You should sleep. You will be better soon.'

'Don't lie, Hetty. You were never very good at it.'

'Don't talk, rest.'

'Not much time left,' he said, his breath rasping harshly. 'Mother and Helen are all right, and the children. Don't need to worry about them, but there's something for you and for her ... but it's secret. Helen shouldn't know ... might try to stop it. You'll find it ... key in my desk at the apartment ... something I want her to have...'

'You mean Georgie?' Hetty looked down at him, seeing the exhaustion, how much it was costing him to talk. His brow was beaded with sweat and he was finding it difficult to breathe. 'Should have married her ... loved her all the time.'

'Yes, you told me you'd made a mistake, but you didn't say...' Ben made a horrible gurgling sound, his eyes rolled upwards and then his breath just seemed to run out. As she watched, a trickle of blood ran from the corner of his mouth. One minute he was looking at her, trying to tell her something and then he was gone. Just like that. It was so sudden, so final, she could hardly believe it and she gave a little sob of despair, flinging herself on his body as the sobs broke from her. 'No, Ben ... Oh, Ben, don't go ... don't leave me. I need you, Ben. You always cared about me even when you thought I was wrong.'

'Don't cry, *chérie*.' Stefan's voice offered comfort in the midst of her grief. She felt his strong arms surround her, his body against hers, holding her as she sobbed. And then she was turning in his arms, clasped to him in an embrace of passion that had sprung from nowhere. 'Yes, that's what he would want. Ben would want you to live and love, my darling. He was a man of passion himself, though perhaps he was afraid of giving it rein – but you're not like that; you've never held back, have you, Hetty?'

She shook her head, staring up at him wordlessly. Her body was one mass of need, her ability to think completely lost as she let him gather her into his arms and carry her from the room. When he laid her on the large bed that smelled faintly of him she thought that he meant to leave her and she made a protest, catching at his hand.

'No, no, my little one,' Stefan said, his voice soft and caressing. 'I shan't leave you to weep alone. I'll stay with you, hold you...' His eyes gazed down into hers, dark and hot with passion. 'Love you if you want?'

'Yes...' Hetty heard the pleading note in her voice and was half shamed by her need, and yet she could not stop herself crying out, 'Everyone leaves me. Everyone I love hurts me or leaves me...'

'I shan't hurt you,' he said as he bent over her, his lips sweet with promise as they lingered on hers. Hetty felt that she ought not to be making love when her brother had just died and yet the pain, the aching need inside her was so great that she let herself be swept away on a tide of passion. 'You are so beautiful, *chérie* ... so beautiful. I have wanted you from the first moment I saw you.'

He was helping her out of her clothes, shedding his own to lie beside them on the stained wood floorboards. His eyes seemed to devour her flesh, hungry for the sight of her. She feasted her eyes on the strong, muscled arms that reached out for her, sending shivers of anticipation running through her body. His mouth was warm and demanding, his hands gentle and yet firm as they sought out all the secret places of her sex, arousing her to a need so painful and urgent that she no longer had the ability to think at all. She felt the heat of him burning her, the firmness of his thighs and chest as he drew her against him. His loving was taking her to places she had never been, making her writhe with pleasure, making her scream and dig her nails into his shoulders as he covered her body with his own.

His mouth was warm on her breasts, his teeth teasing and nibbling at her nipples, causing a ripple of sensation to run through her; he suckled at her breasts, making her ache with pleasure, her back arching as he continued to lavish her with his tongue and lips.

The clever, bold, slightly ruthless spirit she had admired in him was there now beneath the tenderness of his loving. It made him an excellent lover, as he was an excellent leader, and she felt something deep inside her surrender to him.

'You are lovely, *chérie*,' he murmured as they lay entwined, satiated by a loving so fierce and satisfying that Hetty felt drained of all emotion. She lay quiet in his arms, her pain eased for the moment. 'I want you for my woman. Come live with me. Be mine. Together we are invincible.'

'You are so sure of yourself,' she murmured against his shoulder. 'I should disappoint you.'

'You could never disappoint me,' he told her, and stroked her hair as she buried her face in the warm dampness of his shoulder. 'Go to sleep now, little one. There are things that must be done. We must bury Ben, but there is no need for you to worry. A priest will say the words that matter, and one day, after the war, we will put up a plaque to him in the church of his own faith.'

'Yes,' Hetty said. She felt the pain curdle inside her but it was not so desperate as it had been. Ben was dead; weeping would not bring him back. 'Yes, after the war...'

Hetty turned over and went to sleep after Stefan had left her. She would think about Ben another time.

The rain had stopped when Hetty woke the next morning. She found that a jug of water and a woman's dress had been brought to the room while she slept. The water was cool but she thought it refreshing as she washed herself and then put on the dress; it was simple, probably old, and yet the colour was still bright. At least it was clean and her clothes had been covered in Ben's blood. No doubt Stefan had disposed of them. Any trace of stained clothes or a body would have brought the Germans down on them hard.

Hetty went downstairs to the kitchen. A young woman of perhaps twenty or so was washing dishes at the sink. She was fair-haired and pretty but as she turned to Hetty her face was sullen with dislike.

'There is bread and cold bacon if you want it,' she said. 'You slept too long. The others have eaten and I have something more important to do than feed you.'

Hetty was startled by her hostility.

'I don't know your name?'

'It's Fleur – but I don't see why you should want to know it.'

'I thought that perhaps you brought the water. I wanted to thank you.'

'Stefan brought it to you himself. He said you were tired and must not be disturbed.'

'That was thoughtful of him.'

'He is too good for you,' Fleur said, her eyes snapping with anger. 'He is fascinated by you now because you wear a man's clothes and do things no self-respecting woman would do – but he will tire of you. I know him! I know that he will hate you one day and then he will come back to...' She broke off abruptly, on the verge of tears. 'Why did you have to come here? You don't belong here!'

'No, you are right, I don't,' Hetty said, feeling cold and dead inside. Fleur reminded her of herself as a young girl in love with a man who had betrayed her. Stefan should be ashamed of himself for using and then hurting this child. 'And I'm just about to leave. Goodbye, Fleur. I'm sorry if I've done anything to hurt you.'

She walked out of the farmhouse, her back

straight with pride. Last night she had lost her head because Stefan had come to her when she needed comfort. It hadn't meant anything to either of them. Obviously, he had someone in his life already and Hetty was just an exciting moment, an amusement. He lived on excitement, was always at his best in the midst of an attack. Fleur was right: he would tire of her one day and then he would look elsewhere for his pleasure. She could not, dare not trust him. He would let her down as Henri had before him. It would be foolish to let him under her skin. She must get back to the château. The Comtesse would be worried about her.

Hetty knew something had changed the moment she walked in. Bernard had been talking to one of the maids, but when he saw her he broke off and came towards her, a look of excitement in his eyes, happy to see her safe.

'Mademoiselle 'Etty – good news!'

'Is there?' She wondered if she would ever feel that anything was worth getting excited about again. 'What is it, Bernard?'

'Monsieur de Faubourg is home. He has been badly wounded in battle – an arm is lost and he has been in hospital – but they have let him come home at last.'

'Pierre is here?' Hetty felt a rush of surprise. 'That is good news, Bernard, but I don't understand – why wasn't he arrested by the Germans if he was wounded in the fighting just before the end?'

'The hospital was run by the Sisters of Mercy, mademoiselle. They kept him hidden behind locked doors as they have other wounded soldiers of France. He was fortunate to be found by them after he had been left for dead.'

'Then we must thank God for it,' Hetty said and gave him a forced smile. Of course it was good news, but it didn't ease the ache inside her. 'I am hungry, Bernard. Do you think I could have something to eat?'

'We were worried about you when you did not return all night, but a messenger came to say you were safe.'

'Did the messenger tell you anything else?'

'I understand your brother was wounded, mademoiselle. Is he also safe?'

'He is where they can't touch him any more,' Hetty said and her eyelids flickered for a moment as she felt a return of the stabbing grief. 'He died last night, Bernard. Someone buried him soon after because they could not allow the Germans to find him.'

'Forgive me, mademoiselle.' Bernard looked stricken. 'I had no idea...'

'How could you?' She smiled wearily. 'There is no need to feel upset. I am truly glad that Pierre is home. I shall go to my room. If someone could bring me something to eat in a little while?'

'Yes, of course.'

Hetty was aware of his eyes following her from the room, but she did not want to grieve in front of him. Ben was dead and she had been foolish enough to seek comfort from a man she did not dare trust. It would take her a while to regain her usual sangfroid but she would do it – and she would do it alone.

Nine

'Harry looks a little better,' Georgie said as she kissed her aunt's cheek. 'At least now that I'm here I can take some of the tiresome jobs from you and that will give you more time to relax with your family.'

'You mustn't think I asked you here just for that,' Jessie said. 'But I must admit I shall be grateful for some help. It would be easier if Jonathan was home, but this wretched war spoiled all our plans.'

'Didn't you tell me that Walter wants to help out with the business?'

'Yes, he does, but he may not be able to if his papers come through. He says he will go into the airforce like Jonathan, but I do wish it could all be over so that he needn't.'

'That doesn't look like happening. This new blitz on London and the South East is wearing people down; the papers seem full of gloom every day.'

'Yes, well, moaning about it won't help and I suppose we are lucky not to be in France or Poland or somewhere like that.'

'Yes, very lucky,' Georgie said and felt a sinking sensation in her stomach. Nearly three months had passed and she hadn't heard a word from Ben. 'Weren't you going to tell me something – about the annexe being off limits?'

'Oh, yes. You remember I wrote to you that the man from the ministry told me we were too big for a convalescent home?' Georgie nodded. 'Well, he needed an office and somewhere to stay. We arranged for him to have the annexe and put a bed in there so he's completely private when he's here. Not that he is here often. He seems to travel a lot.'

'So what happened to your tearooms?'

'One of our workshop tenants gave notice a few months ago, so Harry had his men do some work in there and we're using that for the time being. It isn't quite as pleasant as the annexe, but people don't seem to mind. We don't get anywhere near as many visitors as before the war, of course.'

'But you're managing to keep going?'

'The main business ticks over slowly, but the money I got from publishing those cookery books just before the war has helped a lot. They were a huge success and I'll probably get round to sorting out some more of my aunt's recipes one day. I wanted to share the money with her, but she wouldn't hear of it. Says she's got plenty for her needs and it's all going to be mine one day anyway.'

'I can pay rent if that helps.'

'Not if you want me to speak to you again!'

'I should have known you would say that. Well, I'll just have to do my bit about the place, but there is one thing you should know,

Jessie. You're the first one I've told – I'm having a baby.' Georgie laughed as she saw her aunt's look of shock. 'Close your mouth, dearest, you look like a fish out of water. It does happen, you know – even to women of my age.'

'You're not old. I was only a year or so younger when I married Harry. I'm just surprised. I didn't know there was anyone special in your life.'

'I'm not sure that there is,' Georgie said. 'It wasn't just a fling, but there are complications. It may work out one day or it may not.'

'Is he married?'

'Yes, but that is only half the problem. I can't tell you any more, because it's to do with the war and not something he's allowed to talk about.'

'Yes, of course. I understand.' Jessie wrinkled her brow. At nearly fifty she was still an attractive woman with only one small streak of grey in her hair just above her left eyebrow, which looked almost as if she'd had it put there by a clever hairdresser. 'You haven't told Geoffrey yet?'

'No. I've been waiting for the right time. I shall have to tell him soon, of course, but it rather depends on what happens next. I haven't told the baby's father either, but I think I know what he'll say.'

'Yes. I see that it is awkward for you.'

'You aren't regretting inviting me to stay?'

'Need you ask, my dear?' Jessie smiled at her affectionately. 'A new baby is always welcome and I'm looking forward to having your company. Shall you tell Annabel?'

'Yes, when I visit later in the week. I'm looking forward to seeing Beth's daughter, Elaine. Annabel says she's beautiful – but then she would naturally think so.'

'Yes, she dotes on Beth and is over the moon with Elaine, but to be fair, she is really lovely. I think she looks a bit like Alice, because she has her colouring rather than her mother's at the moment. That can change, of course, babies' hair often gets darker as they grow, doesn't it?'

'Yes, I believe so,' Jessie said. 'Well, I must start work. I have someone coming to pick up a piece of furniture this morning and Harry had to go into Torquay. He has someone to drive him but I worry when he's away, especially since he had that heart attack.'

'Yes, that's only natural. You get on with whatever you need to do and I'll potter about – I could look through those accounts you had a problem with,' Georgie said. 'And then I'll wander down to the shop and have a talk to the girls...'

It had been easy enough to keep the secret of her child's father from Jessie, she thought as she made her way to the study. But evading Annabel's questions was going to be more difficult. If only she could hear something from Ben, at least to say he might be coming home soon.

After spending a little time in the kitchen

talking with Jessie's staff, most of whom had worked for her for years, Georgie strolled down to the shop to see what they were selling these days. There was less variety than before the war, but the shelves were still sufficiently well stocked to attract customers. After buying a box of coloured pencils, with a picture of Kendlebury on the box, to send to Geoffrey, she left the shop and began to walk back to the house. As she neared the annexe she saw that a man was coming out and smiled as she stopped to speak to him. Jessie had said he wasn't often here, but this was obviously one of the times he'd chosen to visit.

'Good afternoon, Mr Rathmere,' she said. 'I was surprised when Jessie told me you had an office here.'

'Good lord, it's Mrs Bridges,' he said and offered his hand. 'How nice to see you here. Is Jessie Kendle a friend of yours?'

'Actually she's an aunt by marriage,' Georgie said. 'She asked me to come and stay with her until I make up my mind what I want to do now that you've put me out of my home.'

'Oh dear...' He looked concerned. 'Are you feeling very upset?'

'No, not at all,' Georgie confessed. 'Actually I'd been feeling lonely for a while and I'm enjoying the prospect of a long visit.'

'You relieve my mind,' he said. 'I do feel for the people I have to tell they must give up their homes, you know – but it's my job.'

'Yes, of course it is,' Georgie reassured him.

263

He was rather a nice man really and she quite liked him. 'I was just going to have some tea – why don't you come and join me?'

'I...' He hesitated and then nodded, looking pleased. 'Yes, why don't I? I was going to drive into Torquay but I can do that later.'

'I need to get a message to my family,' Hetty said to Stefan. 'I suppose you've passed the news about Ben back to London, but I want to tell my sister in my own way.'

'They won't let you say how or where he died,' Stefan said and frowned. 'You know you can't do that, Hetty. If it fell into the wrong hands it could lead back to us and then...'

'That's all you ever think about, isn't it?' she said, her eyes flashing with anger. 'You don't care that my sister is worrying about Ben – or that his lover is probably going out of her mind because there's no news.'

'I'm telling you that you can't send a letter,' Stefan said, his expression grim and unbending. 'I can't allow it, Hetty.'

'Damn you!' she flashed at him, her temper rising. 'I don't have to do everything you say.'

'Yes you do, as far as this is concerned anyway. I can't force you in other things, but when it's a matter of the group's safety, you will do as you're told.'

'Sometimes I hate you!'

'Do you?' He smiled and she felt the desire hit her stomach like a punchbag. 'Not always, eh, *chérie*? There was one night when you

264

loved me.'

'No! I needed someone and you were there,' she retorted, head up, expression proud. 'That's all it was, Stefan.'

'You mean because something better has come along?' His lip curled with scorn. 'Pierre told me he had asked you to marry him. You like the idea of a château better than an old farmhouse – is that it?'

'Damn you!' Hetty raised her hand to strike him, but he caught her wrist, holding her with ease as she struggled in frustration. 'That's why I hate you, Stefan! You're arrogant, too sure of yourself and...'

She got no further for he pulled her roughly into his arms, his mouth devouring hers in a hungry kiss. She felt her whole body melting in the heat of the passion that flared between them and knew that she had never felt quite like this when anyone else kissed her. She'd been a naïve child when she fell in love with Henri, and her feelings for Pierre were luke-warm beside what she felt for Stefan. Making love with Pierre had been pleasant when it happened, but it wasn't like being caught up in the conflagration of the passion Stefan's touch aroused in her. She was panting, nervous as he let her go, struggling to hide her feelings.

'You had no right to do that,' she said. She didn't want to feel like this about him! He would just use her and then cast her aside. 'Just because I needed you the night Ben died...'

'Maybe I don't have your permission,' Stefan muttered grimly. 'But your response, the look in your eyes, gave me the right, Hetty. Deny it all you want, but you belong with me.'

'No! I don't want you.'

'Marry him then,' Stefan spat the words at her. 'Make him and yourself miserable, because that's how it will be, *chérie*. You want me as much as I want you. We fit together and no matter how you deny it you will never be able to forget.'

'I respect you as the leader of our group,' Hetty said. 'But that is all you will ever be to me, Stefan.'

'Have it your own way. I don't ask twice.'

Hetty watched as he turned and strode away through the woods. It was tearing her heart out to let him go, but she couldn't just walk away from Pierre and the Comtesse; they both needed her. Holding back the tears, she returned to the house, entering by a side door. She had hoped to slip up to her room unnoticed but she met Pierre as he was coming downstairs. Her heart wrung with pity as she saw the uncertainty in him. His left arm still gave him pain in the stump above the amputation, and he was finding it difficult to manage with the use of only one good arm. She remembered him as he'd been before he went away and regretted the change. Damn this war! And damn Stefan for refusing to help her.

'You are upset, Hetty,' Pierre said and only

then did she notice belatedly that she had tears on her cheeks. 'Is something the matter?'

'Stefan was here,' she said. 'I asked him to help me get a letter to my family. He refused, said it was too dangerous for the group.'

'He is right, I suppose,' Pierre said. 'But there are other ways, my darling. I have my own contacts and using them will not involve Stefan or our own people. You must be careful what you write, of course, but your sister will be able to read between the lines.'

'Would you really do that for me, Pierre?' Hetty's face lit up. 'I know it would mean a lot to Annabel if she could hear from me and not just through official channels.'

'You know I would do much more to please you,' Pierre said and reached out to stroke her cheek with his fingertips. 'I am no longer a complete man, Hetty, but my feelings haven't changed. It was thinking of you waiting for me that kept me going while I was in hospital...'

'Oh, Pierre...' Hetty whispered. 'I never promised to marry you. I care for you, you know I do – but...'

'You are afraid to say yes because you think I might let you down?' Pierre's eyebrows rose. 'But you must know I would never do that. I want to love you and look after you, to make up for all the hurtful things of the past.'

'Let me think about it for a while,' Hetty said and reached out to take his hand, pressing it to her lips to kiss it. 'You're wonderful,

Pierre, and I do care for you – but I'm just not sure about marriage.'

Georgie looked at the letter in her hand. It had been posted in London and she recognized the writing as being Ben's. Yet there was something about it that made her hold back from opening it. She didn't know why but she was sure that if Ben had been able to post it himself he would have telephoned her instead.

Ben didn't often write letters. He preferred postcards and the telephone. She turned it over in her hand, looking at it for several minutes before slipping it into her pocket. She would read it later, just before she went to bed.

'What's wrong?' Beth asked as she came in from the garden and saw Annabel replace the phone receiver, her face deathly white. 'Is it Drew – have you heard something?'

'Not about Drew,' Annabel said and moved to sit down. 'I'm sorry, Beth, but I feel a bit odd, my legs have gone suddenly. Would you mind getting me a glass of water? I've had some bad news.'

Beth brought her the water, watching her anxiously. It wasn't like Annabel to react like this. Something awful must have happened.

'That was my mother on the telephone. Helen had a letter this morning. Ben has been killed in action.'

'Was he abroad?' Beth asked, puzzled.

'Where? In the desert or France or somewhere else? I didn't know he'd been sent abroad. I thought he was in Scotland training or something?'

'They didn't tell Helen how he was killed. Apparently, the letter just said he'd been in action and was being recommended for a bravery award.'

'Oh...' Beth felt sick and her own knees went wobbly. She sat down on the chair opposite Annabel. 'I'm so sorry. I didn't even know he was in any danger. I feel awful not knowing.' She hadn't thought of much but Drew and the baby since Christmas and now she realized she must have seemed self-centred and selfish. 'I wish I'd known. I was fond of Ben.'

'Yes,' Annabel blinked back the tears. 'We were very close, because of being twins I suppose. He did tell me something, it was all hush-hush and he couldn't be precise, but he said something could happen to him and told me ... well, never mind that.' Annabel looked at her. 'I'm sorry, Beth, this must make it all the worse for you. You must think about Drew all the time.'

'I – I think I've almost accepted it now,' Beth said and swallowed hard. 'I keep hoping they were wrong, but I know it's silly to expect too much. Arnold told me there was hope but he was just being kind.'

'He was afraid for you, with the baby being so close. He is a nice man,' Annabel said. 'He seems to be concerned for you, Beth. It's just a pity he can't visit us more often.'

'That's because he's so busy,' Beth said and sighed. 'I miss all that sometimes. It was fun being a part of his work. Oh, I like being here, with you and Elaine – but it was fun just the same.'

'Yes, I expect it was.' Annabel looked at her thoughtfully. 'You might want to go back to work when Elaine is older. You could probably afford to employ a nanny with the money the lawyers say Drew has left for you in his will.'

Beth pulled a face. 'That's all so horrible. I don't want anything. If there is any money it will be for Elaine.' She sighed. 'Lady Bryant has asked me to go and live with them. I had another letter from her this morning going on about how Drew's child ought to be brought up in her father's home.'

'Well, you did promise to go and visit them, Beth.'

'Yes, I know, but I've been putting it off. I thought that if we had better news...' She sighed. 'But it's not going to happen, is it?'

'I think it would be too much to hope for,' Annabel said. 'You had the letter from Drew's commanding officer, didn't you? I don't think he would have sent that if he'd thought there was hope.'

'It would have been better if I'd known for sure,' Beth said. 'If it had been confirmed instead of just presumed killed.' She smothered a sob. 'I keep thinking he might be out there somewhere, hurt ... asking for me.'

'Oh, my dearest.' Annabel gathered her into her arms, comforting her as the tears ran down her own cheeks. 'I'm sure that isn't so. I think you just have to accept that Drew isn't coming back.'

'Yes...' Beth pulled back and touched her cheek. 'It's just like you to comfort me when you have your own sadness to cope with. I know how hard this is for you, Annabel.'

'Yes, it is hard,' Annabel admitted. 'It hurts a lot, but I know there's nothing I can do and I feel ... I feel proud of Ben for doing what he believed in. I wish he hadn't been killed and I'm going to miss him an awful lot, but I know he always felt he hadn't done much with his life. At least he died trying to help his country.'

'Yes, that's something to cling to,' Beth agreed. 'I try to think like that when I can, but it isn't easy.'

'It's worse for you, because Drew was your husband.'

'We had so little time together,' Beth said, her eyelashes wet. The tears came less frequently now but the sadness sometimes overwhelmed her. 'That's what makes it so hard.'

Beth was missing Drew and she hurt every time she thought about him being wounded or frightened, but in her heart she knew that she was also missing someone else, and that made her feel guilty.

Georgie folded the letter and put it into her writing case. She had read it three times already, but she knew she would read it many times in the coming years ... long, lonely years that she would have to spend without Ben. She wanted to scream and shout, to rail against the unfairness of a world that could take everything from her with just one stroke, but she knew that would not take away the pain.

Ben was dead. He had written the letter in the full knowledge that it might happen, and he had told her of his love, his hope for the future, and his regret for the wasted years.

I love you, Georgie. It was always you. I wish that I'd had the courage to do something about it long ago.

'Oh, Ben,' she whispered as the tears caught at her throat. 'Why? Why did it have to be you? Why did you volunteer for that stupid course? Why couldn't you just stay at home – safe in a boring desk job?' Because he was Ben, her mind told her. Because he'd been bored with his life and restless, because he felt that he'd wasted too much time. Georgie smiled through her tears. It was damned funny really when you thought about it. Ben had finally found the courage to change things and because of it he was dead. Helen would have been told officially, of course. That meant Annabel would know. Should Georgie tell her about the letter? She thought it might help to talk about it and yet she knew that she didn't have the right. Ben was married to Helen. He hadn't spoken to her. It wouldn't be right for Georgie to lay claim to him now that he was dead. She would have to bear her grief in secret. And she could never tell Annabel that the child she was carrying was Ben's. It wouldn't be fair to anyone.

It was a lovely morning in early summer, the sun warm despite a few patchy clouds. Georgie had decided to work in the garden for a while. She needed to do some hard, physical work and some of the flower beds were looking a bit neglected and required attention. She armed herself with a trowel and trug, pulled on old gloves and went out to the front of the house.

Harry was manoeuvring his wheelchair towards the workshops and she waved to him, thinking that he was looking a little frail of late. He wasn't much older than Jessie, but his accident just after the death of his young son, some years earlier, had caused a lot of problems and his health had never been the same. He and Jessie were so happy together and it was a damned shame that their happiness should be threatened by his ill health.

Georgie could hear a blackbird trilling in the tree above her head as she worked, a feeling of peace stealing over her. At least for a short while she was able to keep her grief at bay. She had cried night after night for the past week or so, but during the day she was forced to behave as normally as possible, because she couldn't tell anyone how

273

she felt.

'Will you say one for me while you are down there?'

Georgie glanced up, shading her eyes. She saw that it was Philip Rathmere and wasn't sure whether to be pleased or sorry. She liked him but he was such a sympathetic person that she was afraid she might end up in tears if they sat and talked. And yet perhaps that was just what she needed.

'I'm not sure prayers do any good,' she said, a touch of bitterness in her voice. 'They certainly haven't helped me...' She rose to her feet, finding to her concern that tears had already started to trickle down her cheeks. 'Oh, I'm so sorry. It's stupid of me...'

'Something has distressed you,' he said and looked upset. 'Is there anything I can do to help?'

'Would you mind listening?' Georgie said. 'You see, I've had some terrible news and there is no one I can talk to about it. It's rather awkward and I can't tell my friends.'

'That is unpleasant for you,' he said, his eyes soft with sympathy. 'Why don't I make you some tea in the annexe? We can be private there and I have my own kettle.'

'It's awful of me to ask,' she said. 'But I really do need a shoulder to cry on and you have broad ones.'

'Then make use of me,' he said and smiled at her. 'After all, that is what friends are for – isn't it?'

★ ★ ★

'You should marry Pierre,' Adele, Comtesse de Faubourg, said to Hetty as they were picking summer fruits in the garden together. Hetty had been eating the raspberries and had juice smeared around her mouth. 'You know that he loves you. Why do you not say yes? Do you not care for him?'

'You know that I care for both of you,' Hetty said. 'Pierre is my friend and I have become a part of your family, Adele. But I am not sure that I should make Pierre happy as his wife. He needs more than affection.'

'But you were lovers before he went away. He did not tell me, but I knew.' Adele's eyes narrowed. 'Is it that you cannot bear the arm?'

'No, of course not,' Hetty denied swiftly. 'I do not even think of it.'

'Then is there someone else you wish to marry?'

'No...' Hetty turned away to pick more fruit. Adele's wise old eyes saw too clearly and she did not want her to guess that she was close to the truth. Her feelings for Stefan had not gone away. They met only infrequently these days, for Pierre had taken Hetty's place as the leader of the group from the château and it was only when Stefan came on business that she glimpsed him. He usually ignored her, seeming cold and uninterested in her. His indifference hurt Hetty, but she knew that she had brought it on herself. 'No, there is no one else I wish to marry.'

'I think we have picked enough fruit. The

275

sun is hot. I shall go to my room and rest for a while,' the Comtesse said, changing the subject.

'I shall take the fruit to the kitchen. It is best used while it is fresh.'

Hetty watched as Adele made her way towards the house. She had aged these past months and had begun to look frail and tired, though her spirit was as fierce as ever.

Surprised to find her eyes stinging with tears, Hetty realized that she loved the Comtesse. The bond between them was almost like that of mother and daughter – and she was fond of Pierre. She knew he loved her. Looking around her, feeling the peace and tranquillity of the old garden, Hetty sighed. She would be a fool to throw all this away for a man she could not trust, a man who would tire of her and then transfer his affections to someone else. Stefan was arrogant and set on having his way. If she let down her guard, he would hurt her as Henri had hurt her.

Pierre had sent her letter to Annabel. She'd been told it had reached her sister and been given a message that could only have come from Annabel. Stefan might have done that if he'd chosen, but he'd refused. It was always his work that came first – as it had been with Henri. She was merely a woman, a plaything.

As her steps turned towards the back of the château she saw Stefan leaving the kitchen. Her heart did a rapid somersault and she halted, expecting that he would at least acknowledge her. Instead, he turned away, deliberately ignoring her.

Hetty drew a sharp breath, feeling as if he had slapped her face, but she stuck her head in the air and walked on. Why should she care what he chose to do? He was nothing to her!

She gave the baskets of soft fruit to Bernard and waited but he merely smiled and said the fruit harvest had been good this year. Clearly she was not to be told what was happening. Stefan had cut her out completely. She was no longer of any importance to his group. He chose to talk only to Pierre, and Pierre had taken Ben's place as their wireless operator. It was only right that Pierre should assume command over their men, Hetty admitted that freely. She and Bernard had begun their small resistance, but Pierre was master here. Now that he was home the people naturally looked to him for guidance. She missed being a part of the group but Pierre wanted her to remain behind in safety.

'It is too dangerous now,' he'd told her when she asked to be included. 'The Germans are increasing their patrols. They are determined to stamp out any resistance. I would be happier if you stayed here with Grandmère. To please me, Hetty? She needs you.'

She'd given in because there wasn't much else she could do. Besides, it might be too painful to work side by side with Stefan.

She left the kitchen intending to go up to her room and change her dress, but she chanced to meet Pierre coming down. He was looking much better now, as though he had regained much of his confidence and strength and was learning to cope with the loss of his arm.

'Have you been in the sun?' he said smiling at her. 'You've got freckles on your nose, Hetty.'

'Oh, damn,' she said and laughed. 'Adele warned me to wear my hat but it slipped off when I was picking the raspberries and I didn't bother to put it on again.'

'It doesn't matter. I like your freckles,' Pierre said. 'Come and talk to me for a while, Hetty.'

'Yes, if you want.'

They went into a quiet cool room that looked out on to the front gardens. Pierre poured himself a small cognac but Hetty shook her head as he offered her the same.

'I wanted to tell you how grateful I am for all you've done for us, Hetty.'

'I haven't done anything. Adele has given me a home and I've lived here, that's all.'

She knew that she had gained as much as she had given. Living in the château had been pleasant, though she wasn't sure she would want it to continue after the war. Being Adele's friend and companion was one thing, but to be the mistress here and Pierre's wife was a big commitment.

Pierre smiled and shook his head. 'You've done much more. Grandmère relies on you so much – and you ran the resistance group until I came back. No one has forgotten that. Stefan said you were one of his best people.'

'I was never his!'

Pierre smiled slightly. 'He meant to pay you a compliment. He wanted to know if you were with us tonight.'

'And am I?' Hetty raised her head hopefully.

'I would prefer that you stay with Grandmère. If I should be killed she would be alone.'

'Don't say such things!'

'It is a risk we all take. This is important, Hetty. You have not forgotten what I told you about the solicitors in London?'

'No, of course not. But you mustn't think of being killed or it will happen.'

'Would you mind very much, Hetty?'

'You know I would.'

'Then marry me soon, darling. You know I love you.'

'Yes.' Hetty moved towards him impulsively. She had a sudden sense of impending disaster and she was afraid for him. 'Yes, Pierre. I shall marry you. We'll arrange it as soon as you like.'

'Thank you. I was afraid you would say no.'

'You know I care for you?'

'Yes, I do know,' he said. 'You are not in love with me but you care for me. Is it enough, Hetty?'

'We shall make it enough.'

Pierre reached out to touch her cheek. 'I have dreamed of making love to you again, but for a long time I was not strong enough. I did not want to fail you.'

'Are you strong enough now?' Her smile was enticing, inviting his response.

'I think so but we shall wait until this thing is over. Stefan was here just now. I have to meet him in an hour from now. That is not sufficient time. I want to please you, to show you that the arm makes no difference. I can still make you happy, my love.'

'Yes, I am sure you can.' She gazed up at him as she moved closer, reaching up to kiss him on the mouth. 'Besides, I have two arms and I know how to make us both happy – remember?'

'Oh yes,' Pierre said huskily. 'I remember. I wondered if you had forgotten?'

'I forget nothing.'

Her kiss was sweet and lingering. Pierre's arm held her pressed against him and she felt the shudder of desire run through him.

'You have not been so alive in months, Hetty?'

'I have been grieving for my brother,' she said. 'But this afternoon in the sunshine I realized that we must think of the future. We cannot go on looking back – I cannot.'

It would be a challenge, being Pierre's wife, but she would meet it as she had all the other challenges she had known – and he was going into danger. She wanted him to have something to come back for.

'Good! I am glad that you feel better.' His fingers trailed her cheek lovingly. 'I have things to do, Hetty. I shall see you very soon – but you will not forget the lawyer?'

She placed a finger to his lips. 'Did I not tell you? I forget nothing. When you return, we shall tell Adele of our plans.'

'She will be so happy. It is what she longs for – my marriage and an heir for the family.'

'I am not sure I can give you a child, Pierre.' Hetty's eyes clouded. 'If that is your reason for...'

He silenced her with a kiss. '*That* is my reason. The child will come or not as it pleases.' He looked at her in silence. 'No matter what happens, always remember that I cared for you and Adele.'

Hetty nodded but her doubts surfaced once more. One of the reasons she had held back from giving her promise to marry was her fear that she would not be able to give Pierre the son she knew both he and his grandmother would expect.

But she had given her word now and if Pierre returned she would keep it. If he returned? Hetty shivered. She mustn't let the fear creep in or the waiting would be unbearable. It would be much easier if she'd been allowed to go with them, but she had to do what Pierre asked of her and she knew Adele suffered when her grandson was involved in a dangerous mission.

It was past midnight when Hetty at last persuaded the Comtesse that there was no point in them keeping an all night vigil.

281

'We cannot know how long it will take,' Hetty told her. 'Pierre said he would return when he could – that might be hours or even days.'

'Yes, I know.' Adele's hands were blue-veined and knotted with arthritis. She suffered considerable pain but never spoke of it, the only sign a grimace when she found it awkward to lift one of the beautiful old wine glasses. 'You are right, Hetty. I shall go to bed. You should go too.'

'Would you like some warm milk to help you sleep?'

'Pah!' Adele pulled a face. 'Milk is for babies. I have some cognac in my room. It will help me sleep if I need it.'

'The doctor said it was not good for you, Adele.'

'He is an old woman,' Adele muttered. 'I shall outlive him and his mewling sister!'

Hetty smiled as her friend went off to bed. Adele seemed to delight in defying both her doctor and his well-meaning sister, who visited them occasionally. She waited another hour before going upstairs. Undressing, she sat brushing her hair by the light of the moon, her window open to its silvery glow. That moon worried her. It was too bright! Dark nights were best for what Stefan and Pierre were about. She wished she was with them! Waiting made her nervous.

She remembered how nervous Ben had been the night he was killed. He had felt the shame of his failure, but it hadn't been his fault alone. The ammunition truck had been moved further down into the convoy – a sudden change of plan, an accident or a mistake on her brother's part? No one would ever know. It was just unfortunate that it had led to Ben's death. She'd made up her mind not to brood over that. There was nothing she could do – except wait.

The next two days were difficult to bear. Hetty could see the anxiety in Bernard's face as he went about his duties. Like her, he had been forced to stay behind but his grandson had been one of those picked for the mission.

On the evening of the second day, Bernard went down to the village. When he returned his face was grey with fear.

'No one knows what happened,' he said. 'They think the Germans suspected something. It is said that the men faced huge odds; some were killed, some got away; they think some were taken prisoner. I can tell you no more than that, mademoiselle.'

'Have the Germans been to the village? Have there been reprisals?'

'Not here – in Stefan's village, so I heard.'

'Then they know that he was involved?'

'The reprisals have fallen there so they say – three men and a young woman were shot the following morning.'

'A young woman?'

'They found her at Stefan's farm.'

'Fleur...' Hetty felt her stomach turn. 'She loved him...'

Tears burned behind her eyes but she held them back. She wouldn't cry yet. Not for Fleur; not for Pierre and not for Stefan.

The worst news came late that night. Bernard came to fetch Hetty from her bed and she went down to the kitchen in her dressing robe. Louis was sitting at the table. He had been eating bread and cheese and drinking red wine. Around his head was a bandage that had bloodstains on it.

'Mademoiselle 'Etty,' he said and his eyes looked hollowed in his pale face. 'Forgive me. I had to be careful that I was not followed or I would have been here sooner.'

'What happened, Louis?'

'They were waiting for us. They must have broken our codes again. We had no chance against so many.'

Hetty's stomach churned. She had been expecting this, but it still made her feel sick.

'How many killed?'

'At least ten,' Louis said. 'Another four or five were surrounded. I think they wanted prisoners. Monsieur de Faubourg was one and Stefan another.'

'Then they will come here,' Hetty said. 'If they have Pierre they will know who he is and they will come to take their revenge on us. You must not stay, Louis. If you are taken they will kill you.'

'He is going to his uncle in the south,' Bernard said. 'He can rest for an hour or two, then he must leave.'

'Do you have money?'

Louis shook his head.

'I'll get some for you. Pack him some food, Bernard – and change that bandage. The sooner you are away from here the better, Louis. For your own sake.'

'I have time enough. Monsieur de Faubourg will not betray us. He would sooner die.'

'Yes.' Hetty was white-faced and shivering. 'But someone else may. I'll fetch that money.'

Her grief would come later. For now she had to think about what to do when the Germans came looking for more conspirators. Once they knew who Pierre was, they were sure to pay the château a visit.

Ten

'I thought I should come and tell you,' the young officer said. 'No doubt you had a telegram but they never tell you anything much and I was there. I saw Drew die. The ironic thing was that we were on a ship coming home ... better not say where from. But it was a U-boat that sunk us.'

'How did Drew die?' Beth's voice shook. She curled her nails into her hands. She had long ago accepted that her husband was dead, but she still found the confirmation painful. 'You are quite sure that he couldn't have survived?'

'Yes, quite sure. He was a good friend. I should have got him out of there somehow if I'd thought ... quite sure, Mrs Bryant.'

'Thank you. I've been worrying ... wondering if he suffered terribly or if he was still alive and in pain somewhere.'

'It was very quick. He was dead before the ship went down.'

'Thank you. That makes me feel better somehow.' She gave him a grateful smile. 'I've known he was dead for months, but they didn't give me any details and I couldn't quite accept it. Now I shall be able to settle my mind.'

'I know the kind of thing – just missing in action?' Beth nodded and he grimaced. 'I do know how that feels. It happened to my mother in the last war. She kept on hoping Dad might turn up for years.'

'What happened to you after ... if you don't mind my asking?'

'I was lucky, got picked up by a fishing vessel and taken to an island. Can't tell you where I'm afraid. Apparently, I was off my head for weeks, and then it took me ages to sort myself out. In the end I got someone to take me to ... a larger island where I was able to get a working passage on a merchant ship coming home. When I got home I went through all the usual checks, visited my family and then came here.'

'I'm so grateful, Captain Dawson,' Beth said and then to her horror she started to cry. 'I'm sorry ... didn't mean to...'

'It was my fault.' Jack Dawson looked at her helplessly and then put his arms around her in a hesitant, shy manner. 'Forgive me...'

'Oh no,' Beth said and drew away, accepting the large, clean handkerchief he offered. 'It wasn't your fault at all. It was so kind of you to come. I am very grateful. Take no notice of my tears. I think it's relief really – knowing that it's final. And knowing what happened, that he didn't suffer too much.'

'Drew never knew a thing. We'd been talking – about you actually. He was looking forward to seeing you – and the baby.'

'He must have got my letters then. I wasn't sure.'

'We all had a batch when they picked us up ... not allowed to say much about that. We'd had a bit of a rough time, but we were coming home and we were happy.'

'Yes.' Her bottom lip trembled but she clamped down on her feelings, lifting her chin. 'Will you stay for lunch? Annabel has a treat for us today – bacon and eggs.'

'That sounds like my kind of food,' he said. 'Thank you. I'd like to stay very much. They've given me a month's leave and to tell you the truth I don't know what to do with myself.'

'You're not married?'

'Haven't met the right one yet – but I'm still hoping.'

'Oh, I'm sure you will,' Beth said feeling suddenly shy. 'Come and meet my daughter.'

'So Beth has accepted it at last then,' Georgie said. She was sitting with Annabel in the shade of an apple tree, drinking tea and eating the fatless sponge she had made that morning and brought along with her. 'Well, that's a good thing, I suppose?'

'Yes, I'm sure it is. She seems better now, beginning to get over her grief and take an interest in life again. I mean she has always looked after Elaine, but outside of that she just wasn't interested – now she seems to be. She even made herself a pretty new dress this week.'

'Are you getting over your own grief?' Georgie looked at her. It had been hard to bear offering Annabel sympathy over Ben's death these past months without breaking down herself, but somehow she had managed it.

'Yes, though I don't think it will ever quite go away. We were twins and even though I didn't see him as often as I would have liked these past years, he rang me all the time.'

'Yes, he was good about telephoning,' Georgie said and avoided Annabel's penetrating gaze. Sometimes she thought Annabel had guessed her secret and she was tempted to tell her – but she felt she didn't have the right.

'How long it is now?' Annabel asked, glancing pointedly at Georgie's bulge. 'About a month?'

'Yes, more or less.'

'You know exactly, don't you?'

'What makes you say that?'

'I know you, Georgie. You don't sleep around. You must have cared very much for whoever it was.'

'I can't tell you, Annabel.'

'Because he was married?'

'Yes, something like that?'

Annabel sighed. 'Why won't you tell me? Surely you know you can trust me?'

'Yes, of course I do – but someone else could be hurt if it ever came out accidentally.'

'Someone I know?' Annabel's eyes widened as she guessed. Of course! She ought to have worked it out before. 'Why didn't you tell me about you and Ben? You must have known I would be on your side. Oh, Georgie, how you must have been suffering! I've been going on and on about what I feel and you ... Oh, my dear, I am so sorry.'

'It hasn't been easy,' Georgie admitted. 'I've wanted to say but I didn't have the right.' Georgie sighed as she saw the look on Annabel's face. 'Yes, I know Helen never loved him. Ben was going to ask her for a divorce when he came home – but what's the point in talking about it now? It would only hurt his children. I don't want to do that. Geoffrey thinks it was a brave soldier I met in London and that's near enough. I was terrified of telling him, but Philip made me see that the longer I left it the worse it would be.'

'Philip Rathmere? He's the man who took over your house for the War Office, isn't he? I saw him at Jessie's once. A very ordinary-looking man I thought, but pleasant she says.'

'He is ordinary, but kind and interesting too. I've been able to tell him about Ben and he has helped me through this – I don't know what I would have done without him to be honest.'

'That sounds promising?' Annabel raised her brows.

'Now don't start hatching your eggs before they're laid,' Georgie said and grimaced. 'I like Philip. He's pleasant to talk to and we have tea together sometimes. He tells me about his plans for after the war and I tell him what I've been doing, and that's about it.'

'What are his plans?'

'He develops old houses; finds specialist builders to restore them – either for their owners or to sell. It's all very informative and interesting, Annabel. You would enjoy talking to him.'

'Bring him to dinner.'

'You're matchmaking!'

'So what? You're my best friend. I want you to be happy.' She reached over to touch her hand. 'Ben wouldn't want you to waste your life, dearest. This Philip sounds just what you need.'

'Oh, does he?' Georgie pulled a wry face at her. 'Don't try to manage me, Annabel. I've been thinking I ought to stop seeing him before I get too interested. He wouldn't want to take on the children of two other men – even if he wanted me. And I'm not at all sure that he does. We're just friends. I don't suppose we would have met again if he hadn't asked Jessie to let him have his office at Kendlebury.'

'It's fate then, isn't it? You like him, Georgie. I can tell. Don't cut off your nose to spite your face. Ben wouldn't have wanted that; he was one of the most unselfish men I know.'

'Yes.' Georgie smiled. Telling Annabel had eased the pain a little. 'Perhaps he was too much that way. I can't be sure he would have actually asked Helen for a divorce.'

'I think he would...' Annabel frowned. 'You

knew I had a letter about Ben from Hetty? Well, she said something about it but couldn't give details. I suppose she had to be careful in case it fell into the wrong hands. It was all rather vague. She just said she was with Ben at the end and asked me to look in his desk at his apartment. I found a letter addressed to her but I haven't opened it. I'm hoping she will do that herself one day.'

Georgie didn't ask if there had been a letter for her. She had Ben's last letter put away safely and she knew it word for word. She hadn't stopped thinking of him for one minute since it came, but she knew that Annabel was right. One day she would have to leave her grief behind and move on, though she was a long way short of that as yet. Being able to talk about Ben to Annabel at last was making it a lot easier to heal her grief.

'It was curious that he and Hetty should meet over there, wasn't it?'

'Yes, though it may have been arranged. Perhaps Hetty will tell us one day.' Annabel sighed. 'I worry about her out there. 'You hear such terrible stories. I wish she would come home. If they could get a letter through she could surely get home if she wanted.'

'You know Hetty,' Georgie said. 'I believe she must be very brave, Annabel. I used to think she was just reckless and careless, but now ... if she was with Ben at the end...'

'It means she was very involved with whatever he was doing.' Annabel's eyes were

292

shadowed. 'She is reckless and sometimes careless, but like Ben she would sacrifice herself for others. It really is so frustrating not to know what she is doing. Paul says I worry too much but I can't help it. She is my sister and now I've lost Ben...'

'You are like a mother hen with her chicks,' Georgie said and smiled affectionately at her. 'Beth and Hetty – and me sometimes. Stop worrying, Belle, we're old enough to look after ourselves.'

'Stop fussing over me, Hetty,' the Comtesse said, a note of irritation in her voice. 'I am perfectly able to look after myself and I am sure that you have more than enough to do elsewhere.'

Since the night of Pierre's capture, the people of the château had looked to Hetty to tell them what to do. She had been accepted as the woman Monsieur de Faubourg had intended to marry and the Comtesse was too frail to run things now. Hetty smiled at her. She would do well enough sitting in her favourite room at the front of the house. The windows were open wide because it was so hot and she had a jug of iced water and some sweet biscuits on the table beside her.

'If you are sure there is nothing more I shall speak to Bernard. They have been picking the last of the soft fruit today. It is not firm enough for bottling but will make very good conserve.'

'Go away,' Adele said and waved her hand

at her. 'I'm not a fool and I know you have more on your mind than strawberry preserve.'

Hetty left her sitting there, lost in her memories of a happier time. It was true that she had something more than preserves on her mind. More than three weeks had passed since Pierre and Stefan were captured. She had waited in trepidation each day for the visit that would surely come. The Germans must have discovered Pierre's identity by now – why hadn't they taken their revenge?

She blocked out the thoughts of what both Pierre and Stefan must be enduring. They would be tortured to make them reveal the names of their friends and Hetty knew that the methods the Germans used were ruthless.

Bernard met her before she reached the kitchen.

'We must talk privately, mademoiselle.'

'You have heard something?' Her heart caught with fright as she saw his expression.

Bernard had been in contact with the remnants of Stefan's group, who were hiding out, afraid to go to their homes. They had been trying to discover what they could about the men who had been taken prisoner, but as Hetty looked into the older man's eyes she went cold all over. The sickness rose in her throat. She fought it down as she led the way into what had become her own sitting room.

'Is it Pierre?'

'Yes, mademoiselle. The news came a few minutes ago. They tried to break him with beatings and the burning cigarettes against his flesh but he told them nothing. One of them must have gone too far. He died four days after he was taken.'

'Four days...' Hetty felt the scalding tears behind her eyes. Pierre had been dead all this time and she hadn't known it. She sat down abruptly as her legs went weak. 'Adele will be devastated. She is so frail. I hardly know how to tell her.'

'It is as well she has you, mademoiselle.'

'Yes, she has me.' Hetty raised her head, banishing the tears. 'Have you news of Stefan?'

'They say he killed his guards and escaped the same night he was taken. The Germans went to his home and searched but he was not there. The house was deserted. He will not come here I think. He would be seen and he might be betrayed.'

'Yes, that is so.' Hetty looked at him thoughtfully. 'They have not found the traitor?'

'No – but they will.'

Gazing into his eyes, Hetty shivered. She could guess the fate of the man or woman who had betrayed Pierre and Stefan.

'What shall we do now, mademoiselle?'

Now that Pierre was dead she was in command once more. At the beginning Hetty had been on fire with hatred for the Germans. That fire had burned itself out, leaving sadness and resignation.

'What we can, Bernard,' she said at last. 'I

must think of the Comtesse. If some of our men want to join with Stefan's...' She shrugged. 'For the moment we must be careful. Pierre did not talk but someone else may. In time perhaps we may regroup and carry on as best we can.'

'It is not the same without Louis and the others.'

'No,' Hetty agreed. 'It is not the same.'

It could never be the same.

She left him with a sad smile. Ben and Pierre were dead as were others she had known and respected. Louis and Stefan had been forced to disappear. She was not sure she could summon the will to begin all over again.

Besides, Pierre had wanted her to look after Adele. She would do that, Hetty decided, and when the war was over she would visit the lawyers in London. But for now she had to find the right words to tell the Comtesse that her grandson was dead and with him her dream of the future.

Hetty awoke in the night, her face wet with tears. There was a deep aching need inside her, a need she feared would never be satisfied. She longed for Stefan, feared for his life. Where was he now? Was he being hunted by the Germans, afraid for his life?

But no, Stefan would not be afraid. A feeling of peace came over her as she knew that he would find a way to carry on, would join a new group, would go on fighting to the last.

Somehow that comforted her despite the aching need inside her. She turned over and went back to sleep.

Hetty approached the farmhouse with care. It looked deserted but she couldn't be sure. She had wondered if the Germans would have burned it down, but it was still there, timeless and weathered, blending into its surroundings as if it had stood there far longer than the past two hundred years.

The front door was open and she could see that debris had blown in, leaves and dirt scattered all over the once pristine wooden floors. She saw at once that the Germans had done their best to wreck it, destroying anything that was easily breakable in their search for Stefan. Several chairs and tables had been overturned and smashed, and most of the china was littered all over the large tiled kitchen floor, broken into hundreds of pieces.

The wanton destruction brought a lump to Hetty's throat. She had liked the order and the cleanliness of the house, the warmth of its welcome, and she felt a return of her anger, the apathy of the past few weeks slipping away.

Damn them! Hetty's head went up, her face harsh with pride. She had been feeling defeated, unable to face the huge challenge of beginning the resistance again on her own, but now she felt the strength and determination flow back into her. She would do what she could to make them pay, even if only in small ways. She had done it before and she could do it again.

And she would put this house back to what it had been – no, she would make it better, Hetty decided as she fetched a broom and began to sweep up the broken china. Why not? Stefan could not come here until the war was over, but there was nothing to stop her spending time here.

A flicker of excitement ran through her as she thought of what she might do. Some of the furniture was useless, only good enough for the bonfire, but she knew there were things stored in the attic at the château. She would ask Adele if she could have them, and she knew the answer already. She would bring the heavy things here in a truck and she would paint the walls, clean the whole house from top to toe, and make new curtains from material that she could buy in the market.

It would give her a purpose, something besides her plans for revenge on the Germans – something positive to come out of all this. One day if Stefan came back ... but she wouldn't think about that. There could never be anything but a fleeting relationship between them, but for the moment the house was hers, to do with as she pleased. She would make it into the kind of house she had always longed to live in. A little smile hovered on her lips and she began to hum a tune to herself as she set tables and chairs to rights. Oh, yes, this was going to be wonderful by the time she had finished.

'She is quite delightful,' Philip said as he bent over the pram. 'And she has grown so quickly.'

'Sarah was a few days old when you last saw her,' Georgie said and looked amused. 'Babies grow rather a lot in six months, you know.'

'Yes, I suppose so,' he replied and laughed in a self-conscious way. 'Being a crusty old bachelor you wouldn't expect me to know.'

'You are neither crusty nor old,' Georgie said and wrinkled her brow. There were moments when he reminded her of Arthur, except that he was younger and not so set in his ways. She had missed him these past months, more than she had expected. He had become a good friend before her daughter's birth, but since then she'd heard nothing from him. 'We thought you had deserted us. Jessie wondered if you had been ill?'

'No, nothing like that,' he replied but she thought she detected something odd in his manner. 'Merely pressure of work. I should have written.'

'A Christmas card would have done,' Georgie said. 'Just to let us know you were all right.'

'Yes, you are perfectly correct,' he agreed. 'I should have sent cards. In fact I should have visited and brought presents for the children. I wanted to but...' He broke off, going slightly pink about his neck. 'Well, to be honest I wasn't certain it was a good idea.'

'What on earth do you mean? Surely we are

friends?'

'Yes – and that's the trouble,' Philip said looking awkward. 'I've wanted to make it more than friendship, Georgie, and I was afraid of making a nuisance of myself. I know you were in love with Sarah's father and you wouldn't want to be bothered with an ordinary chap like me. Not after knowing someone like that.'

Georgie stared at him in silence for some seconds as she tried to gather her thoughts. She had thought that their friendship might develop one day but this was too swift for her. She wasn't ready for another relationship just yet.

'You've rather taken my breath away, Philip. I thought we were friends and might perhaps be more one day – but when you stayed away...' She hesitated and then decided to be honest. 'Two children are rather a lot to ask anyone to take on. I wasn't sure you would be interested – even if you liked me enough to want a relationship.'

'It's you I'm interested in,' Philip said and smiled awkwardly. 'The children are a part of you – as I see it you come as a package.'

'I'm not sure I like the sound of that!'

He laughed as he saw the hint of mischief in her eyes.

'I'm no good with words, never have been – but do you think you might learn to put up with me? I think we might get on very well, Georgie. I'm not a wonderful catch but I've enough put by and I intend to do better after the war. There will be a lot of property in need of renovation – and once people get on their feet again they will need somewhere to live.'

'I think we might suit,' Georgie said carefully. She didn't want to make a second mistake. Her grief for Ben had become muted but she wasn't ready to move on just yet. On the other hand she didn't want to throw away Philip's friendship. 'We could start by getting to know one another. I married too quickly the first time, Philip. I need time to be sure.'

'Yes, of course. I'm the last one to rush into things but I am awfully fond of you.'

'I'm fond of you too,' Georgie admitted, but wondered if it was enough. She had been fond of Arthur. 'Let's go back to where we were and let things develop shall we? I want to talk to you about my house.'

'Have they wrecked it or something?' he asked, looking anxious. 'Don't worry, I'll have it put right for you when this is all over.'

'The way things are going that looks like being a long time.'

'It does look black for the Allies at the moment,' Philip agreed. 'But we'll beat them in the end. Seriously, have you heard something that worries you about the house?'

'No, not at all,' Georgie said. 'I wondered if you could tell me what to do with it when I get it back. It is a beautiful house and I want Geoffrey to have it one day, of course. It has been in his father's family for generations so I can't sell but I don't want to live there.'

'You could let it to a family, though that would bring in only a small income and it isn't always easy to get long-standing tenants out when you want your house back. Let me think about it. I'm sure I can come up with something.'

'Oh good,' Georgie said. 'How long are you staying at Kendlebury this time, Philip?'

'For three weeks at least, perhaps more.' He raised his brows. 'Why? Not tired of me already?'

'Geoffrey will be coming home for the holidays soon. I would like you to meet him properly – not just to say hello. I would like you to get to know him. After all, he is a part of the package.'

'Am I on trial, Georgie?'

'Let's say we're all going to be friends, shall we?'

'Yes, we'll see how it goes,' he agreed and then glanced at the pram as Sarah began to cry. 'Is she hungry or does she just want to be picked up?'

'Try picking her up and see what happens. I think it's time we went in and had tea.'

Sarah had stopped crying and blew a raspberry as he lifted her into his arms. She did a cross between a burp and a cough and bubbled a sticky wetness over his jacket.

'There, you see, she approves of me,' Philip said, manfully ignoring the wet patch on his coat. 'She's smiling.'

Georgie thought it was probably the wind but didn't contradict him.

302

'Let's go and have our tea, shall we?'

She smiled and led the way inside, leaving the pram in the passage as she walked into the big warm kitchen. If Philip wanted to get to know her, he might as well start out the right way.

'Are you seeing Captain Dawson this weekend?' Annabel asked as Beth came in that afternoon. She had been shopping in Torquay and her arms were full of parcels.

'No, I don't think so,' Beth said. 'He did say he had a leave coming up but I think he is going home this time. Did he telephone while I was out?'

'No, not as far as I know. Arnold called. He said he might come down on Friday night and asked if you would be here.'

'Yes, of course. I should like to see him. It's ages since he was here. He hasn't visited since last summer.'

'No,' Annabel agreed. She wondered what was going on in Beth's mind; her expression gave nothing away. 'It's been a while, Beth. I suppose he is just too busy to get away. It is a long journey from London.'

'Yes, I know.' Beth dumped her parcels on the kitchen table. 'Most of this is for you. I was lucky and got some extra sugar. Has Elaine been good?'

'She is always good.'

Beth smiled. Annabel would say that even if the child had screamed the whole time she was out.

'Is she having her nap? I'll pop up and see her. I bought her a teddy bear. It was sitting there looking forlorn on the shelf and I couldn't resist it.'

Beth was thoughtful as she ran upstairs. She'd begun to believe that Arnold would never come to visit, that he had forgotten her. Jack Dawson had asked her to think about marrying him, but Beth had asked for time to consider. She was over her grief now. It still hurt to remember Drew and she was still angry when she thought of all she'd lost, but she knew she had to move on. She was young and she didn't want to be alone for the rest of her life. Jack Dawson was nice; she wasn't in love with him but she wasn't sure she would ever love anyone else as she had loved Drew. That didn't mean she had to be alone, did it? A lot of girls she knew had married for reasons other than love. She knew Annabel approved of Jack. He seemed to care for her, but Beth wasn't sure, and that was why he was going home this weekend. She needed time to think things over. And Arnold was coming to visit. Beth had almost forgotten how much she'd enjoyed working with him. Her time in London seemed like another life. She was vaguely disturbed by the idea of seeing Arnold again. He had been so good to her when she was having Elaine, but then he'd gone back to London and apart from one visit in the summer and cards at Christmas, he appeared to have forgotten her.

* * *

'You look really well, Beth,' Arnold said as he handed her flowers and a huge pink toy dog. 'Living in the country must suit you.'

'Yes, perhaps. I've put on weight. I'm not sure that's a good thing.'

It was so good to see him! Beth couldn't help smiling. She felt better than she had in months.

'You were a mere scrap of a girl when you came to work for me,' Arnold said. 'I think you look lovely the way you are.'

'Thank you,' Beth said and made a mental note to stop eating Annabel's cakes and pastries. 'You look tired. I think you've been working too hard.'

'Things don't get any easier,' Arnold said and sighed. 'You're right, I am tired and I needed a break. That's why I decided to come down for the weekend to see you and Elaine.'

'Well, you know we love to see you,' Beth said. She had forgotten how much she enjoyed being with Arnold and seeing him look so tired touched something inside her. She had a foolish desire to reach out and stroke his hair, to kiss him ... Her cheeks went pink just thinking about it. Thank goodness he couldn't read her mind. He would think she was mad! 'I've been remembering how much fun it was working with you.'

'You wouldn't find it much fun these days.' Arnold pulled a face. 'My last secretary left in tears because she said I was a bad-tempered bear. I've got a man now and he is so slow taking dictation that I find it easier to write it

305

all out in longhand and let him type it up for me – and the last driver I had nearly got us killed. Went right past an open gas main with at least three men waving red flags at her. I do miss you, Beth.'

'Perhaps I could find a nurse for Elaine and come back to work for you,' Beth said, a wistful note in her voice.

'I would have you like a shot, but it's against the rules,' Arnold said and glanced at the child, who was waving a chubby fist at him. 'Besides, you can't neglect this little one. Children come first.'

'Yes, I know,' Beth laughed. 'I was just thinking how much I miss seeing you, that's all.'

'Do you really?' Arnold looked surprised. 'I thought you would have forgotten all about me.'

'We all thought you had forgotten us.'

There was a faint challenge in her eyes.

'What did you think, Beth?' His steady gaze met hers and her heart started to hammer against her ribs. He was a very attractive man. Why had she never noticed before – or had she, deep down inside? Was that why she had enjoyed being with him so much, because she was attracted to him as more than just a friend? 'Are you sure you had time to think about me at all? I understood you had a new boyfriend.'

'You mean Drew's friend,' Beth said and frowned. 'Jack has visited me several times. I like him and he tells me things about Drew –

but I'm not in love with him. I suppose I could marry him one day, because I don't want to be alone for the rest of my life – but I'm not sure it's a good idea to marry just so that Elaine has a father.'

Beth wasn't sure why she'd said that, about marrying Jack, because the moment she did she knew it wasn't true. She was never going to marry Jack. It would be the biggest mistake of her life, because she didn't feel excited when she was with him – the way she felt now looking at Arnold, alive and tingling, almost breathless.

'Would you really marry for that reason?'

Beth met his searching look, warmth spreading through her body as she saw something that she had never expected to find in those steady eyes, her mouth a little dry, pulse racing.

'I might if I liked and respected someone,' she said, a secret smile touching the corners of her mouth as she began to know herself, know her own heart and what she wanted from life. Her confidence was growing with every moment she spent with him. 'Especially if I enjoyed being with him, found it exciting to talk about his work and to help him as much as I could – if I missed him when he didn't visit me for months on end.'

Arnold's eyes twinkled with the mischief she had missed so much.

'Are you trying to proposition me, Beth?'

That was just what she was doing, and it was exactly what she wanted. She seemed to have changed all at once, to have sloughed off the old uncertainty and emerged from the chrysalis with bright and shining wings. What had happened to the shy, tongue-tied girl she had been when she first went to London? Somewhere along the way she had got lost and there was a different person in her place – a woman, not a girl.

'I might be. Would I stand a chance if I did?'

'Well, you just might. You see, I'm looking for a secretary who doesn't mind working at odd hours at home, a pretty, intelligent woman who could drive me about sometimes and make me laugh when I'm feeling tired and harassed.'

'What if she had a child who sometimes cries at night?'

'I dare say I could put up with that,' Arnold said. 'Do you think this woman could take dictation and nurse a baby at the same time?'

'No, but she might manage to do it when the baby was asleep.'

'What about love?'

'I'm not sure if I'll ever feel the same way as I did about Drew,' Beth admitted truthfully. 'But then, I don't want to. I want a happy marriage based on affection and respect – and a genuine liking, a strong feeling of attraction and pleasure in that person's company. I want someone who will look after me but not smother me, someone who will share my interests and let me share his on an equal footing, someone that won't treat me as a child but as his partner. Is that stupid of me, Arnold? Should I be looking for something different?'

'I think that sounds a very good basis for marriage,' he said. 'I've had a first love too, Beth, and what I feel for you is different, but that doesn't make it any less worth having. I have been thinking about this for months but I was afraid to speak because I know I'm a bit old for you and I wasn't sure how you would feel about marrying again.'

'I want a normal married life, and more children,' Beth said. 'I don't want Elaine to be an only child the way I was – but that isn't my only reason for wanting to marry you, Arnold. Even when I was married to Drew I loved working with you. I find talking to you interesting and it makes me feel alive when I'm with you. I've been stagnating here in the country and I want to come back to London and be with you.'

'Are you quite sure, my dearest girl?' Arnold held out his hands to her. 'I don't want to take advantage of you. Perhaps you should wait for a while, make sure that you know what you're doing?'

But Beth did know. She had never been more sure of anything in her life. Suddenly it was clear to her, an open book, the book of life, just waiting for her to write on the clean blank pages of her future – a future she had already begun to plan in her mind.

'I have to visit Drew's parents, and I have to do it alone, Arnold. Then I'm going to come up to London for a visit. I'll stay in a hotel or something, or with you if you'll have me. If we both feel the same way in say – three months – we'll announce it to our friends and get married in the summer. Besides, Jack asked me to marry him so I can't marry someone else the week after. It would seem unkind. I shall tell him no when I see him, and then we'll make our plans – if that's what you want too?' She laughed, realizing that she was taking a great deal for granted.

'An excellent idea,' Arnold said, surprised but pleased at the change in her. He had fallen in love with a girl who needed taking care of, but he was going to enjoy getting to know the woman who had blossomed in her place. 'I shall need time to get my affairs in order. My apartment is fine for me and for you to stay for a few nights, but it wouldn't do for a family. We need a house and I shall want to get it ready. July seems a good time. After all, if I've waited this long, I can wait a bit longer.'

'Oh, Arnold,' Beth said and hugged him impulsively. She was surprised and then pleased when his arms tightened about her. Gazing up into his eyes she saw passion and hunger, and an answering thrill of need went through her. 'It won't be long before I come up to stay. I'm going to visit Lady Bryant next week and make my peace with them. I should have gone ages ago, but I kept putting it off. I think I've grown up at last, Arnold. I shan't be afraid of them this time.'

'Don't grow up too much,' he said. 'I love

you just as you are.' He bent his head and kissed her.

'Beth has gone to stay with Drew's family,' Annabel said when Georgie came to visit the next week. 'Something has happened to change her – and I think it has to do with Arnold's visit. She has been walking around looking like the cat that got the cream ever since.'

'Arnold?' Georgie smiled. 'You thought it was likely to be that friend of Drew's didn't you?'

'Yes and no,' Annabel said. 'I liked him but perhaps he was a little young for Beth.'

'But he's older than she is!'

'That means nothing as you very well know. Beth has always been mature for her age, and my one fear with Drew was that in time she would grow out of him. I liked him and I know she loved him, but I never did think he was quite right for her. She was still a girl then, but she isn't any more. She is a very confident young woman and I couldn't be more pleased about it.'

'But you were thrilled when she married Drew!' Georgie pointed out. 'Why – if you didn't think he was right for her?'

'Because I wanted her to be happy. That's all I want now – but if she has chosen Arnold I shall be pleased. I think he will take care of her.'

'And then you will have one less chick to fuss over.'

'Speaking of which...' Annabel fixed her with a look. 'How are things going with the man in your life?'

'Oh, Geoffrey is happy to be back at school. He enjoyed his holiday, but he gets on well...' Georgie smiled as Annabel pulled a face at her. 'You will just have to be patient for a bit longer. I made up my mind too quickly last time and I want this to be right.'

'You've been so much happier since Philip came back into your life,' Annabel said and gave her a look full of affection. 'Take as much time as you like, Georgie, but I have no doubt that everything will work out fine for you. You need someone to look after and Sarah needs a father figure.'

'So that just leaves you one chick to fuss over, doesn't it? What a pity she isn't here.'

'If you look at me like that I shan't give you any of my special strawberry preserve to take home,' Annabel threatened. 'We had a wonderful crop last summer and I have enough left to give some away – so I thought you might like a jar or two? But if you're going to mock me I might think again.'

'Peace,' Georgie said and laughed. 'Yes, I would like some of your preserve. I've been asked to make some sponges for the Women's Institute annual fête and the preserve will be marvellous as fillings.'

'You're always so busy,' Annabel said. 'You make me feel lazy.'

'I've been used to it,' Georgie said. 'But next week I've been invited to a special dance in London. Philip is taking me. Jessie has offered to look after Sarah so I shall have nothing at all to do for two whole days.'

'You are in danger of having your whole moral fibre destroyed by such indulgence,' Annabel said. 'Good gracious. What are we coming to next?'

Eleven

Hetty looked around the big kitchen with satisfaction. It was very different now to the way she had found it all those months ago, just after the Germans had done their best to wreck it. The walls were freshly whitewashed, the dresser stripped of layers of paint down to a lovely wood finish and the shelves set with blue and white china. It was back to its former glory, but it had her stamp on it, her mark, reflecting her taste, her artist's eye in the colours and style.

The china had been a special gift to her from Adele.

'You may take whatever you need from the attics or the outhouses,' she had told Hetty when she mentioned her intention of restoring the house. 'But this china was one of my wedding presents and is precious to me. I want you to have it, Hetty. You have been like a daughter to me and I have no one else left that I care for. There is a distant cousin on my mother's side but no one important. I do not know what will happen to the house when I am gone.'

'I think Pierre has made arrangements with a lawyer in England.'

314

Adele nodded, waving her hand wearily. 'It no longer matters – but I want you to have that china, and anything else you need.'

Hetty had brought the china here a week earlier and set it on the shelves, and the furniture was a mixture of what had been here and small pieces she had chosen with care from the château attics. She had made new curtains for the windows here and in the front parlour, and covered the old cushions with new bright material. The cooking pots were heavy and good quality and she had merely restored them to their original position over the fire.

The destruction in the rest of the house had not been as ruthless as here but she had made a few changes, putting things that she found ugly out in the sheds and bringing in new pieces that she liked. Some things she had bought in the market, and those particularly pleased her.

She had made the house into a home that she would like to live in, Hetty realized, but of course it didn't belong to her. It would be good for Stefan to find it like this when he came back though, she thought and then sighed.

She had heard that he was still working for the resistance in another part of the country, and it was unlikely they would meet until the war ended. Perhaps they would never meet again.

She ought to get back to the château. Adele claimed she did not need her but she became restive if Hetty was gone too long.

As she came out of the house she saw a man looking at it and for a moment her heart caught with fright. Was it a German? Was it Stefan? And then he came towards her and she saw that it was Louis.

'You are back,' she said, going to meet him gladly. He seemed to have grown up in the past months, to look older, more serious. 'Have you seen your grandfather?'

'Yes...' Louis nodded gloomily. 'He threw me out of the house.'

'But why? The Germans never came looking for you. I think you could come back now if you chose.'

'I do not want to,' Louis said and looked uncertain. 'I was told you were here. I came to tell you something but you may not believe me. Grandpère accused me of lying to him, that's why he threw me out.'

'What did you tell him?' Hetty's spine tingled as she looked into his eyes and read something that puzzled her. It was a kind of shame mixed with anger.

Louis hesitated, then cleared his throat. 'The traitor was Monsieur de Faubourg; that's why they have not come to the château – and he is not dead. That story of his being tortured and dying of a beating was false, meant to deceive us into thinking him a hero. They let him go and he is believed to be in Switzerland.'

'No!' Hetty was stunned, disbelieving. 'That's not true, Louis. It can't be. Pierre

316

hated the Germans. He would never have betrayed his own people. His grandmother would have died of shame.'

She remembered Pierre saying that he would rather die than surrender to the enemy – but then she remembered the way he had looked when he first came back from the hospital, defeated and weary. No, it couldn't be true. Pierre couldn't have sold out to the enemy he hated.

'He told us that the nuns had cared for him when he lost his arm, but that was a lie. He was taken prisoner by the Germans and he made a pact with them – his own safety and the safety of the château in return for Stefan.'

Hetty shook her head in denial, Pierre's smiling face vivid in her mind. How could he have deceived them all so cruelly? It wasn't possible. Surely it wasn't true? And yet the sickness was curling in her stomach, rising in her throat. She didn't want to believe what Louis was telling her, but it had all begun to make perfect sense. Pierre had been so insistent that she must go to the English lawyers, and she had sensed that he believed he was not coming back – a premonition of death, she'd thought. Now she remembered that Pierre had been nervous and it was that nervousness that had communicated itself to her. He had known he wouldn't be coming back. It was planned that way – because he had betrayed his comrades.

For weeks she had lived in dread of a visit from the Germans, sure that they would

317

come to wreak havoc in revenge for what Pierre had tried to do, but they had not come. No reprisals had taken place at the château, only at Stefan's home village. She tasted the bitterness of betrayal on her tongue as she looked at Louis, knowing that he too had felt the horror and bitterness of this, perhaps even more keenly since he had trusted and respected the master of the château.

'How do you know this?'

'My cousin Marie worked at the German hospital as a cleaner. She saw Monsieur de Faubourg brought in, recognized him from a visit to the château before the war – and she heard things. She had wanted to help him escape if she could but what she heard frightened her and she told no one until I started to brag of his brave death – and then she confessed to me. At first I denied her, but then she told me exactly what she'd heard, names, places, dates. They wanted Stefan's group totally wiped out. He had been too successful; he was blamed for everything, even the train we blew up at the start.'

'Yes.' Hetty was thoughtful. 'The Germans were not to know that there were once two groups operating here. It would have suited Pierre to keep it that way. He had his reasons for protecting the château.'

'The cellars,' Louis said. 'Yes, we know of them, mademoiselle, but we are loyal to the family. In times past they have given us work, protected us.'

She nodded, understanding the kind of

loyalty that ran in old, respected families. Bernard and Louis felt themselves to belong at the château. Pierre had relied on that loyalty, which would have been destroyed had he been suspected of collaborating with the Germans. He had planned his own death – and after the war, what then? Monsieur de Faubourg could not return but the lawyers knew what to do.

The treasure would be sold and the money placed in an account in the name of the person named in the documents held by Pierre's lawyers – Pierre under another name perhaps? No doubt it was all properly signed and sealed, the Comtesse as much a dupe of his machinations as everyone else. She had believed in him implicitly and would have signed anything he asked of her, based all her hopes of the future on him. Oh yes, it was all arranged very neatly and Hetty was to be the go-between, to make sure that things went according to plan.

He had used her. His talk of marriage had been for the purpose of securing her loyalty. If she had married him, would she ever have known the truth? Would he have come back for her? She doubted it. Pierre had intended to abandon the château and its responsibilities in favour of the freedom his money would buy him.

'Who else knows of this?'

'Grandpère. I have told no one else. It was hard to believe, mademoiselle. I did not want to believe at first. When my cousin told me I

319

went out into the yard to vomit. I could not face anyone. If I had seen Monsieur de Faubourg I should have killed him.'

Hetty saw the anger and grief in his face, the pain of betrayal. If Pierre ever returned to the château he would face retribution. She understood Louis' bitterness, the frustration of knowing that his grandfather disbelieved him, but there was nothing she could do to ease the hurt.

'Stefan should know. He will tell you what to do.'

'Yes.' Louis met her thoughtful gaze. 'I believed you ought to know the truth, but I am going to join Stefan – and I shall tell him everything.'

'Yes,' Hetty agreed. 'Make sure you tell him *everything*, Louis. Stefan will know what should be done.'

Beth turned and snuggled up to Arnold in the warmth of his bed. She had just woken and the pleasure of feeling him lying beside her was so strong in her that she couldn't resist kissing him even though he was still sleeping.

They had made love for the first time the previous night and it had been good between them, so good that Beth had felt a little guilty. Remembering Drew's embarrassed fondling, she hadn't known what to expect but it had all been so natural and right that she'd responded in a way she never had for Drew.

Amazing as it was, she knew that she was in love with Arnold. It had probably happened after Drew went abroad, but she had never realized. She'd been grateful to him for his kindness and care of her when she was carrying her child, but she hadn't understood what was happening between them. Perhaps it would never have developed if Drew had come back, but Beth wasn't sure. Her feelings for Arnold were stronger, more mature than her youthful infatuation with Drew. She suspected that perhaps first love was often like that, especially for a quiet girl without much experience. Drew had simply swept her off her feet, but the attraction to Arnold had happened more slowly. It was all the sweeter for that. Beth smiled as Arnold opened his eyes and looked at her.

'Good morning, my love,' he murmured huskily. 'Am I right in suspecting that you are intending to have your wicked way with me again? If so, I must tell you that I think you should make an honest man of me. I am not accustomed to finding wanton women in my bed at this hour.'

'Oh Arnold,' Beth said and pressed herself closer. 'Do you know, I could quite enjoy being wanton with you at any hour.'

'You tempt me, lovely lady – but I have work to do. I must love you and leave you.'

'As long as you love me first.'

'If you insist,' he murmured and pulled her hard against him so that she could feel the throbbing heat of his arousal against her thigh. 'Oh Beth, my darling, I've wanted you so much. When will you marry me?'

'In July, as we planned. I cheated Annabel of a wedding last time. I won't disappoint her again – but I may have to stay in town every so often before then. I shall need to buy a few clothes and … I dare say I can think of an excuse to come up.'

Arnold laughed and kissed her.

'Knowing you, I dare say you will.'

It was very warm; this summer was even hotter than the last, Hetty thought as she straightened her back. She had been working in the kitchen garden at the château all afternoon and what she wanted most now was a long soak in a nice cool bath.

'Mademoiselle 'Etty…' A young maid came running up the path towards her. 'Bernard says you must come now!'

'What is wrong?' Hetty's stomach clenched. 'Is it the Comtesse? Is she worse?'

'The Germans are coming here,' Giselle said, her face pale with fright. 'They came from the village to tell us.'

'But why?' Hetty stared at her. So many months had passed peacefully that she had thought they were safe. 'Why should they come now?'

'There was talk of treasure,' Giselle said. 'The Germans want it and they are coming to find it. What will happen to us, mademoiselle?'

The girl was very young and very frightened.

'You will stay in the kitchen with Bernard

and the others, and say nothing,' Hetty told her kindly. 'Give them no reason to notice you, Giselle, and they will not bother you. I shall meet them and talk to them myself.'

She lifted her head, walking slowly into the house. She would not have time for the leisurely bath she had planned, but she would be clean and dressed suitably when they came.

'I shall come with you to meet them,' Adele said when Hetty went to her, room and told her what was about to happen. 'We shall face them together.'

'There is no need for you to tire yourself, Adele.' Hetty looked at her, concerned. She was failing day by day, her strength leaving her little by little. Soon she would need help to wash and dress and to feed herself. It was a sad time for those who loved her and remembered what she had been. 'Stay here. If I have my way they will not harm us.'

'What are you going to do?'

'I shall give them what they want.'

'The treasure...' Adele was silent for a moment, and then she nodded wearily. 'Yes, you must give it to them. It is not worth the lives of our people. Let them take it and go. Perhaps then they may leave us in peace.'

'I shall do my best, Adele. Just rest and leave them to me.'

'Yes, perhaps you are right.'

Hetty bent to kiss her withered cheek. When General von Steinbeck had come to the château things had been so different.

Adele had been strong then. She had had her grandson to give her hope. Now she believed him dead, and with him had died her hope, taking her strength and leaving her only memories.

Hetty had kept Louis's revelations to herself. No good would come of destroying Adele's pride. She believed that Pierre had died a hero, let her go to her grave believing it. If Hetty could do nothing more, she would do that for her. Leaving Adele to rest, albeit uneasily, Hetty went down to wait for their visitors.

They did not arrive quietly as General von Steinbeck had but in full force: a convoy of trucks, soldiers and two officers in an armoured car. Immediately, the tranquil old courtyard was filled with noise: shouting, running feet, the backfiring of a car, and the noise of heavy vehicles sending the doves rustling into the trees as the peace was shattered. And then they burst into the house, their heavy feet trampling over the beautiful marble tiles, clattering, harsh and out of place, shattering the peace of the ancient house; rifles at the ready, their strident voices were demanding, shouting as if expecting to be met with resistance.

Instead, Hetty stood alone at the foot of the imposing staircase. She had banished everyone else to the kitchen, telling them to keep out of the way and respond meekly to any orders they might be given. She didn't allow so much as a muscle to flinch as the guns were trained on her, a slender, proud figure, defiant yet unresisting. Inside, her stomach might be tying itself into knots, her palms damp with sweat, but outwardly she showed not a flicker of emotion.

'You would be unwise to kill me just yet,' she said. 'You might not find what you seek.'

An officer came through his men. He was young, eager, his eyes bright with greed.

'You know why we are here?'

'You have heard that we have a fortune hidden in the cellars?'

'I know it exists. I was there...' A second officer, older than the first, pushed his way past the others. 'And who are you, mademoiselle?'

'Marguerite. The Comtesse de Faubourg's niece.'

'Where is the Comtesse?'

'She is ill and resting in her room. I have come to meet you instead.'

'Are there no others here – no more family?'

'Only servants. I beg you not to harm them. They have done nothing to deserve this ... intrusion.'

'We have orders to search for and confiscate the treasure. It belongs to Germany as the spoils of war.'

'I thought France was at peace with your country?' Hetty's eyes glittered as she looked at him, her anger simmering. A part of her wanted to fly at him, to rent his face with her nails and spit her defiance, but the saner, wiser part of her mind cautioned her to be careful.

'Hold your tongue, bitch,' the younger officer said. 'Otherwise I shall teach you to respect your betters.'

'Leave her alone, Hans. We don't have time for this.' The older man unbuttoned the gun holster at his waist. 'Show us where the treasure is stored or I might be forced to use this.'

'I shall show you the cellars,' Hetty said. 'I do not know what you may find there. Only Monsieur de Faubourg knew the secret – and you killed him, didn't you?'

Something in the officer's eyes glittered and she knew that Louis had been right to believe everything his cousin had told him. This man knew of the bargain made with Pierre, but he also knew of the treasure and he wanted it, not for his country as he claimed but for himself. That was why most of the German soldiers had been left outside.

'Lie to me and it will go hard with you.'

'Please follow me. The entrance is in the old part of the château. We do not use it. I should warn you that it would be unwise to shout or use your guns there; the ceiling is unsafe and might come crashing down.'

'Be careful, bitch. You had better not lie to us!'

Hetty's eyes flashed blue-green fire but she held her tongue. She saw no point in antagonizing them any more than need be. Besides, why should she protect a fortune for a man who had betrayed them? Let them take it and good riddance!

Hetty's anger kept her fear at bay as she walked just ahead of the officers and the small group of men they had chosen to accompany them. Let them do their worst. She had no choice but to obey. Hopefully, when they saw Pierre's hoard of art and antiques, their greed would take over and they would forget about her. They would take what they wanted and go, leaving them to continue their lives in peace.

Hetty led them down the steps to the first cellar, as Pierre had taken her when she came to the château so many months ago. It contained only old crates and vats long discarded and covered in dust. Rats scuttled as they approached, disappearing into their hiding places. She could hear the officers muttering in disgust but smiled inwardly; they would soon change their tune.

She found the rusty iron lever that controlled the mechanism; one sharp tug set the wall sliding back with a grinding noise that made her clench her teeth. Beyond the wall that slowly opened was a passage that led to a series of caves. Champagne had once been stored there because they were cool and dry, but now they contained Pierre's treasure – the treasure he had thought it worthwhile betraying his own people to keep safe.

'I have been no further,' Hetty lied. 'What you will find is unknown to me.'

'Go ahead of us!' The younger officer pointed his pistol at her as if he feared a trap.

She felt a shiver of fear as she stepped into the passage. He was a man who hated women, she could see the contempt in his eyes, feel his bitterness. It was cold and frightening to be here with these men, particularly the younger of the two, and she wondered if the caves might become her tomb.

Her heart beating wildly, Hetty led them to the first cave. She remembered that it had been filled with crates, which Pierre had told her contained valuable pictures. Nothing remained. Hetty was puzzled. She couldn't have made a mistake; the crates had been here – so what had happened to them? She'd believed that Pierre had meant to return after the war, but perhaps he had been too impatient. Whatever had been done had been done in secret and she had known nothing of it.

She walked on to the second cave, which had contained more crates containing antique bronzes and precious artefacts, including Sevres porcelain and silver candlesticks. Again there was nothing to be seen except a few pieces of broken wood.

In the third cave there were two crates remaining. The officers gestured to the soldiers, who broke them open with iron crowbars. One contained items of silver, the other pictures, though they seemed to be watercolours and not the valuable oils Pierre had told her were in the first cave.

'This is all?' the younger officer grunted,

clearly disappointed. His finger moved on the trigger of his gun, clearly threatening, his eyes filled with malice. She knew that he would have killed her with less compunction than she might a fly, but his mind was still on the treasure he believed hidden somewhere in the château. 'You've hidden it somewhere else, bitch. Tell me or I'll make you wish you'd never been born!'

'There may have been more once,' Hetty said. Her stomach clenched as his eyes narrowed and she knew that she could die at any moment. 'But the family has fallen on hard times. You have only to look at the state of the rooms through which we passed. I have no knowledge of anything beyond what you see.'

'Take these,' the older officer instructed the soldiers. 'Then we'll search the rest of the house. Strip it of anything worth having.'

'Please – you cannot take everything. How shall we live?'

'Why should we care? You can starve and good riddance!'

Hetty's eyes stung with unshed tears. She had hoped to save the château from the wanton destruction she'd seen at Stefan's farm but she knew these men were ruthless. They were not satisfied with two small crates. They would take everything.

The older officer turned, directing his men to carry the crates out to the waiting lorries. He noticed that the younger man was lingering and looked at him, a sudden leer on his

329

thick lips.

'All right, Hans, she's yours now if you want her – but don't be too long about it. There isn't much time. I shan't wait if you aren't there when I'm ready to leave.'

'She won't take much time,' the younger man said, his expression derisory as he looked at Hetty. She shivered as she saw the way his eyes gleamed, knew him for the man he was and knew what was in his mind, the pleasure he would take from humiliating and hurting her. He was going to kill her but he was going to have his sport first. 'So, bitch, I get to have you to myself after all.'

Hetty listened to the sounds of the soldiers' feet dying away. Her heart was racing and she felt sick. He was gloating, anticipating his triumph over her. She took a step backwards as he reached out for her. She wasn't going to give in without a fight; she would fight tooth and nail even if it cost her more pain. Looking about her for a weapon, she saw that one of the soldiers had left his crowbar. If she could just get to that she might have a chance. But he had seen the direction of her gaze and moved deliberately between her and the weapon.

'Oh no, I don't think so,' he said grinning at her. 'I'm going to teach you a little lesson, bitch. It's time you learned your lesson...'

'You couldn't teach me anything,' Hetty said, anger making her forget to be afraid. She laughed in his face, head up, eyes flashing with pride. 'I've known real men – and you are but a poor excuse for one.'

The insult stung, as she'd known it would. He rushed at her, catching her arm as she tried to dodge past him and swinging her round. With his other hand he slapped her so hard across the face that her ears rang. She spat in his face and brought the heel of her court shoe down hard against his ankle. Dragging one arm free, she raked at his face with her nails, bringing blood to the surface. He swore but didn't let her go. Instead, he hit her again and again across the face and she tasted blood on her mouth. Then he forced her up against the wall and started to grope at her skirt. Struggling, Hetty was vaguely aware that there was someone behind him. Had one of the soldiers come back to help him out? Would they take turns in raping her? There was nothing she could do to stop them.

Suddenly she saw the face of the man behind him, saw his arm go back and the iron bar come crashing down on the back of the German's head. Blood spurted all over the place, some of it splashing into Hetty's face. She saw the grotesque image of death as the officer fell away from her, the startled look in his eyes moments before he died on the ground at her feet.

'Are you all right, mademoiselle?' Louis asked. 'I'm sorry but I could not come before – there were too many of them.'

Hetty wiped the back of her hand across her face, wondering how much of the blood was hers and how much the German's.

'You were in time,' she said. 'How did you get here? You took a risk, Louis.'

'Stefan sent me to take care of you,' he told her. 'These caves are not the only secrets of the château, mademoiselle. There are some that even Monsieur de Faubourg did not know. Come, I shall take you away from here. They are going mad up there, tearing the place apart. I heard them say they intended to fire it when they are finished.'

'Set fire to it?' Hetty was startled. 'What about the Comtesse – Bernard and the others?'

'They are all safe. Stefan took them away while the soldiers were busy with you. German soldiers are like puppets; their masters told them to wait outside until summoned and so they waited.' He spat on the dead German lying on the ground. 'Stefan told me to come for you and get you away.'

'Thank you.' She smiled at him and then glanced at the German officer. 'What about him?'

'Leave him here. If they come looking for him they are welcome. We shall be long gone.'

'Where are we going?'

Louis shook his head. 'You will see for yourself soon enough, mademoiselle. Let's go before they come looking for him...'

It was peaceful in the farmhouse bedroom where Adele lay dying. Hetty looked down at her, her heart wrung with pity. It had been too much for her – the initial news of Pierre's death had taken the hope from her life and the destruction of the château had drained the last of her strength. Tears caught at Hetty's throat as she reached out to stroke Adele's fine hair back from her forehead. She had learned to love the old woman and she would miss her, miss her indomitable spirit, her kindness and her company.

'You should rest, mademoiselle,' Louis said from the doorway. 'There is nothing you can do for her now.'

'Nothing except sit with her,' Hetty said. 'It is little enough, Louis, but I will keep a vigil while she lives.'

'You should eat and drink. I will watch over her for a little.'

'Yes, perhaps I should eat something,' Hetty agreed. 'You will call me if she wakes?'

'Yes, of course.'

Hetty went out, feeling sad. It was hard to lose her friend like this after she had tried to protect and care for her. Anger raged in her as she thought of what had happened at the château. Louis had been back to see what had been done after the Germans had gone and he'd told her that it was a wreck, partly destroyed by fire and stripped of everything of any value. It would take a great deal of money to repair the shell and there was none, nor any to care; it would moulder away, left to the rats and birds to use as they would.

Going into the kitchen, Hetty paused as she saw someone making up the fire in the range, her heart pounding. He turned as she waited on the threshold as if sensing her there, his slate grey eyes steady, not accusing but not smiling either, his hair longer than it had been, spiralled into curls that had been tangled by the wind.

'How is she?'

'Dying,' Hetty replied, moving towards him. Her emotions were as tangled as his dark hair. She was wary of him, not trusting and yet longing to touch him, to be touched by him. 'It can't be long now.'

'I suppose not. I understand she has been failing for a while. If she had to die it was a pity it didn't happen before they came so that she never knew – but it can't be helped.'

'They destroyed everything, her dreams, her home, her memories. Why did they do that now? I expected them for months but they did not come – and now this. Why?'

'They have been ordered to pull back towards Paris,' Stefan said. 'Apparently, they are abandoning this area. I think we've made it too uncomfortable for them. The Allies have begun to beat them on several fronts, Hetty: at El Alamein, Tripoli and Stalingrad; the "dambusters" devastated the Ruhr, and they are getting a beating in Russia. The Germans have had many reverses this past year or so and they need more soldiers at the front; they can't spare the men to patrol as they used to so they are consolidating – that's my information, though I can't promise you it is true in all respects. I have made mistakes, as on the night Ben was killed.'

'Ben told me he gave you the information. He may have made the mistake.'

'I blamed you for what happened that night, but Louis told me what you did. I have never apologized for that, Hetty.'

She shrugged her shoulders. 'It hardly matters any more.'

'What will you do now? Will you stay in France?'

'No, I don't think so,' she said, avoiding his penetrating gaze. 'I shall try to get home.'

'I can arrange that for you, Hetty.'

'Thank you. I thought perhaps you might.'

He moved towards the chair where his coat, satchel and a rifle lay, bending to pick them up. He slung the rifle over his shoulder.

'I should leave. I never stay long in one place.'

'You said the Germans were leaving the area?'

'I shall find somewhere else to give them hell,' he said and grinned at her in his old manner, making her heart turn over. 'The war isn't won yet, Hetty. It may be turning our way but we still have work to do. I shall only come home for good when the last German has been driven from French soil – or until they put me in my grave.'

'Good luck,' Hetty said. Her throat was hot with emotion but she kept the tears inside. This was goodbye. She would never see him again. 'And thank you.'

'For what?'

'Sending Louis to rescue me.'

'That was owed,' he said. 'I have to thank you for my house. Why did you do it, Hetty?'

'It is a beautiful old house. I loved it when I stayed here – and it gave me something to do, something to relieve my grief over Ben. It was a healing process for me, that's all.'

He nodded, his eyes lingering on her face for a moment. She tried to read his expression but failed.

'I sent Louis to fetch you and you gave me back my home. I think that makes us even.'

'Yes, I suppose it does.'

He nodded, smiled at her and went out. Hetty stared after him, the tears trickling down her cheeks. Why hadn't she tried to stop him, to make friends with him? She turned as Louis came clattering down the stairs.

'The Comtesse is awake and asking for you, mademoiselle.'

'Thank you.' Hetty brushed the tears from her eyes and went up to the bedroom. Adele held out her hand to her and she reached to take it, smiling gently. 'How are you feeling?'

'Very tired. I want to sleep and I shall soon – but first I wanted to say goodbye to you, my dear one. You have been like a daughter to me. It was God's blessing to me when Pierre brought you to the château.'

'And you have been a mother to me,' Hetty said. 'Thank you for loving me, Adele.'

'How could I help loving you? Surely everyone who knows you must love you?'

Hetty shook her head and bent to kiss

336

Adele's cheek. As she straightened up she saw that the Comtesse had closed her eyes and as she watched she saw the colour drain from her cheeks. Her breath issued in a harsh rattle and then it was over.

'Oh, Adele,' Hetty said, the tears she had tried to hold back pouring down her cheeks. She was crying for the hurt that Adele had suffered in her last hours, for the loss of a friend – of all the friends who had died – and for herself. 'You said that everyone must love me, but they don't ... they don't. Stefan doesn't love me. He never did...'

'I am sorry that you go,' Louis said. 'But it is right that you should return to your family. You have done your share for us and I thank you from the bottom of my heart.' He kissed her on both sides of her face formally and then laughed and hugged her. 'Take care, Mademoiselle 'Etty, and come back to us one day.'

'I shall if I can,' she promised and smiled at him. 'Tell me, Louis – what happened to the treasure?'

Louis shrugged expressively. 'Who knows, mademoiselle – but I do not think it should give you cause for tears. Perhaps there is someone who knows more but I cannot say.'

'Ah yes, I thought as much.' Hetty laughed. 'Keep your secrets, Louis. I don't want to know. I'm glad it has gone. After all his scheming, Pierre deserves to lose it.' She surmised that he must have laid his contingency

337

plans before he was wounded, perhaps even before the war. Why she would never know, but she did know that he had used her for his own purposes just as he'd used the Comtesse and everyone else.

They saw the plane circling in the sky, preparing to land and then Louis gave her a little push and she was running across the open strip, being pulled into the small aircraft and welcomed by a smiling young Englishman.

'Welcome aboard, Miss Tarleton,' he said and gave her a respectful salute. 'It is a privilege and an honour to meet you.'

'Good gracious – why on earth is that?'

Hetty was genuinely surprised.

He grinned at her. 'They will have my guts for garters if I spoil the surprise but I think you'll find there's quite a welcoming party waiting for you at the other end. We know how to treat heroines at home, Miss Tarleton.'

'I think there must be some mistake,' Hetty said. 'I haven't done anything very remarkable.'

'I believe you will find there are quite a few people who think differently back home.'

'I can't imagine why,' Hetty said and she couldn't. Why on earth should anyone think her a heroine?

'Thank goodness that is all over!' Hetty said when at last she was in the chauffeur-driven car with Annabel and heading towards home. 'I never expected all that and it was quite

338

unnecessary.'

'We were so excited when we got the call,' Annabel said. 'Apparently, they think the world of you in France. You've been praised very highly and they say you will get a medal – here, and over there too, once the war is over.'

'When it's over,' Hetty said and sighed as she thought of friends who remained behind, still risking their lives, their homes, living beneath the rule of a hated invader. 'I wish I knew when that was likely to be, Belle.'

'Not for a while, I expect,' Annabel agreed. 'But it's heading that way so they tell us. The Germans are suffering some of what they've been handing out to everyone else at last. Paul says give it another year and it will be all over bar the shouting.'

'I hope he is right,' Hetty said fervently. 'I want to go back home as soon as I can.'

'But this is your home and you've only just got back,' Annabel said, a note of disappointment in her voice. 'I was hoping you might settle here – if not with me, at least near me.'

'My home is in France,' Hetty said. 'You know I love you dearly, and I shall visit when I can and you must come to me too – but my home is in France.'

She was thinking of an old farmhouse, the walls freshly whitewashed and the dresser set with china that was finer that would usually belong in a kitchen like that. And she was thinking of the man who owned it and the way he had once made love to her – and the way he had said goodbye.

'I shall live in Paris as I used to, but I may buy a little cottage in the country just outside the city. That's if I can afford it.'

'I think Ben may have left you some money,' Annabel said. 'I have a letter for you and it feels as if there may certificates or something inside it. He was quite anxious that Helen shouldn't get her hands on it so I think it may be worth something.'

'Yes, he did mention it. I had forgotten,' Hetty said and looked thoughtful. She had also forgotten about the message for Georgie but perhaps she would see her soon and then she would tell her that Ben had thought of her as he lay dying.

Hetty read her brother's short letter to her. He hadn't known they would meet in France and he was saying goodbye to her. He had left her five thousand pounds in bonds and there was the same amount for Georgie.

'I've given them to you,' Ben had written. 'It's up to you what you do with them, but I would like Georgie to have the money if she needs it. Otherwise you keep it, Hetty. Annabel is comfortable and I know things have been hard for you, but I have always loved Georgie and she ought to have something.'

If it was Ben's wish that Georgie should have the money, then Hetty would give it to her, of course, though according to Annabel she had already begun to recover from her grief and was thinking of marrying again. But

340

that really had little to do with it; it was what Ben had wanted that mattered.

When Hetty saw Sarah she knew at once that the child was Ben's. She picked her up, cradling her in her arms and smiling as the child reached up to pat her cheeks.

'She is Ben's, isn't she?' she said as Georgie sat silently watching. 'He told me that he was in love with you, you know. He spoke of nothing but you just before he died.'

Tears sprang to Georgie's eyes and Hetty's heart softened towards her as she saw that she did still care. She might be thinking of marrying again, but she hadn't forgotten Ben. She probably never would but she wasn't the kind of woman to live alone, and she had children who needed a father. Hetty understood although she didn't think she would have taken the same solution.

'Did he ... did he suffer much?' Georgie asked, her hands working in her lap. 'Was he in a great deal of pain?'

'No, not too much,' Hetty lied knowing that Georgie couldn't bear the truth. 'It was very quick. He asked me to tell you he had always loved you and then he died.'

Georgie bent her head and wept for a few minutes, then she lifted it and wiped the tears away. She looked quite calm, in control, accepting, as though she had already made the decision to move on.

'Thank you. He wrote me a last letter, but his death has always haunted me. I couldn't help wondering if he suffered terribly at the end.'

'You can stop worrying now,' Hetty told her. 'Ben left you five thousand pounds in certificates. They are some sort of American bond so you may have to wait until after the war to redeem them, but he wanted you to have them.'

'I shall save them for Sarah,' Georgie said. 'It will be nice for her to have something her father left her. You won't tell Helen that she's Ben's child – will you?'

'Wild horses wouldn't drag it out of me,' Hetty said and grimaced. 'I can't stand her and never could. Once Ben married her I knew I could never live under the same roof as her and my mother. I wrote to my mother and asked if she would like to see me but she didn't answer so I imagine I am still not forgiven.'

'Your mother is a very foolish woman!'

'Well, it doesn't bother me,' Hetty said. 'I have Annabel and Paul, and their children – and you and Sarah, and there's Beth. That is surely enough relatives for anyone.' She laughed as she said it but she couldn't help feeling a pang of regret inside as she looked at Sarah. If only she'd had a baby ... Stefan's baby. That was the most ridiculous sentiment! She was an idiot if she let herself dwell on such nonsense. Obviously she wasn't meant to have children but she would find other compensations, when the war was over and she could go home.

'What will you do now?' Georgie asked.

'Stay here for the time being,' Hetty said. 'I want to take up my art again. I might go back to college when the war is over and learn to paint the right way.'

'I think your pictures are wonderful,' Georgie said and she meant it. 'Surely you don't need to learn anything about art?'

'Art is like life, you never stop learning,' Hetty said. 'I'm not nearly good enough, Georgie. Not if I want to earn a living at it and I'm not much good at anything else either.'

'You used to design some pretty dresses for Madame Arnoud. Wouldn't you consider taking up something like that?' Georgie raised her brows as Hetty shrugged her shoulders in a very French way. 'Or you might even meet someone and get married.'

'Married? Me?' Hetty went into a peal of laughter. 'Oh no, I don't think so. If I see a man I like I might have a relationship with him – but marriage isn't for me.'

'You're such an independent person,' Georgie said and smiled. 'There was a time when I thought you were selfish and careless to run off the way you did – but I didn't know you. I feel very proud to know someone who has been as brave as you have, Hetty.'

'Now don't you start,' Hetty moaned. 'What on earth all the fuss is about I just don't know. I wish I could just crawl in a dark hole and hide.'

'But they want to give you a medal and

write stories about you, take your picture for the women's magazines. You are a heroine, my dear, and they want to celebrate that in the newspapers, make a big thing of it.'

'Over my dead body!' Hetty said and felt genuine revulsion. Did they think she was going to smile prettily for the camera and tell them her adventures? They wouldn't like what she had to tell them if she did; about the men she had killed, the way she had hated, and killing blindly in revenge until Ben and then Stefan made her see how useless it was. 'I just wish I could get my hands on whoever told them all this nonsense.'

'But surely that would be whoever you were working with out there – wouldn't it?'

Stefan? Hetty frowned as she considered. When you thought about it, it must have been him – but why had he done it? She had thought he considered her a nuisance, a liability, and now he had told them all she was a heroine.

'I can't imagine why he did it,' she said. 'He doesn't even like me.'

But she loved him, and she knew she would carry this endless, aching need inside her for the rest of her life. She might meet other men who would give her pleasure for a while, but none of them could ever be Stefan. Why did she know that now it was too late?

Twelve

Hetty watched Beth's daughter playing in the sunshine with Sarah. It was a happy family scene. The smaller girl was left far behind as Elaine ran rings round her, but she manfully tried to keep up with her older friend and rival.

How lucky they were to have children, Hetty thought as she saw Beth and Georgie carrying the loaded trays outside to set on a table in the garden. It was the spring of 1945 and it looked as if at last the war was finally coming to an end. It had been over for months, all bar the shouting really, when French troops had led the Allies to the liberation of Paris, but now it was almost finished. The Allies were in Germany and there were rumours that Hitler had committed suicide.

For some time after the liberation of Paris Hetty had thought that she might hear from Stefan, but no letters had come and she had finally lost all hope of seeing him. She had been a fool to expect anything, experience should have taught her that there was no point in looking for the happy ending of storybooks. Why should Stefan bother about an English girl he had once comforted and then sent home when she had served her purpose? Perhaps that wasn't quite fair of her. She had left him and gone back to the château. She had promised to marry Pierre – but that was before she had known he was a traitor. She still felt sick when she remembered that she had kissed him, made love with him – but she hadn't known what he was really like. It just showed that you could never trust a man, even if he did seem charming. She had never been to see his lawyer in London and she didn't intend to. If Pierre wanted his treasure he could look for it himself. She could imagine his disappointment when he found the caves empty, and the welcome he would receive from the village people if he were seen – much like that collaborators in Paris had received after the liberation.

How easily he had deceived them all, not just Hetty but his grandmother, friends, and the men who followed him – some to their deaths. The taste of his betrayal was still bitter and it remained in her mind, like so much more that had happened during that time. No, men were not to be trusted!

Still, she rather liked Arnold Pearson. Beth seemed very happy with him and it was obvious that he doted on her. Georgie had settled for marriage with her man from the ministry, as Annabel always called Philip Rathmere. They had been married for six months and were settled in the area, just a few miles the other side of Torquay in a beautiful old manor house that he was having done up in stages. Hetty found him a bit of a dry stick, but if he suited Georgie that was all that mattered.

Ben had been the love of Georgie's life, of course, but if she felt cheated she wasn't showing it as she laughed in the sunshine with her friends. Hetty felt a kind of envy as she watched them all, Annabel and Paul and their son and daughter; Beth, Arnold, Georgie and the children all happy together in Annabel's glorious garden. Philip was away on business at the moment, looking for more property to buy. He was clearly going to be a rich man one day, far richer than Ben would ever have been.

Hetty looked round at the members of her family. The only ones missing apart from Philip were Harry and Jessie Kendle, who although not strictly family had become a part of Annabel's so that she thought of them that way too. It was a shame that Jessie wasn't here to join in the fun, Hetty thought, but she had so much to do and Harry wasn't always as well as she would like. But fortunately they had both their sons back in one piece and not many families could say that after the war that had devastated Europe and half the world.

Hetty was considering returning to college for a year before going back to France. She had written to Madame Arnoud but so far there had been no reply. Perhaps her friend no longer had any interest in running her business or perhaps she had decided to retire.

347

She must be past sixty, of course.

It would be very different now in Paris, Hetty thought. Most of her old friends would be gone – but she would find new ones. She had had to make a new life for herself after she left Henri and she could do it again. She knew that her heart belonged in France, and she would return there one day.

'Are you listening, Hetty?' Annabel's voice broke into her thoughts. 'Paul was saying we were going to have a big party to celebrate the victory. We shall invite all our friends. I know Mary and Mike will want to come down, and Laura might if she's not too busy – then there are all our friends locally – but we were wondering if there was anyone you wanted to ask?'

'No, I don't think so,' Hetty said. She hardly knew some of Annabel's older friends, people who belonged to that shadowy part of Annabel's life, the part she never spoke of, but it didn't matter. 'Your friends are mine. I shall be quite content to help out with the food.'

'You are not going to hide in the kitchen all night,' Annabel told her. 'What about that nice young officer who came to see you last week? What was his name – David something? Why don't you invite him?'

'I can if you like,' Hetty said with a shrug. 'He was one of the welcoming committee when I came home. He wanted me to go on a lecture tour of some kind, do publicity work for the Government, that's why he came to see me a few times, but there's nothing

348

between us – nothing for you to get excited about, Belle.'

'But he likes you. You can see it when he looks at you, Hetty. If you made an effort...'

'What?' Hetty pulled a wry face. She was aware of a physical attraction but knew there was nothing more. 'Do you think he would ask me to marry him? I don't think so, Belle. He knows all about me – my whole story – and he thinks it would be rather dashing to have an affair with me, something to brag about to his friends.'

'Then don't ask him,' Annabel said looking disappointed.

'No, perhaps that would be best,' Hetty said. 'I'll go and fetch some of those fruit tarts your cook made, Belle – they looked delicious.'

She heard her sister say something to Georgie as she disappeared into the house and knew Annabel was worried because she took no interest in any of the young men who were produced for her benefit. She had tried to tell Annabel that there was no need. She wasn't interested in going out for dinner with any of them, and she could find her own men when she was ready for some fun.

She sighed as she went into the kitchen. She supposed the ache in her heart would go away one day. There would be someone who made her feel excited inside one day...

The victory was official at last and Annabel's party was in full swing. Hetty had been busy helping in the kitchens all day. She liked cooking, especially for a party and sometimes wondered if she ought to have chosen that as a career rather than her painting. Perhaps she might try that when she returned to France, she thought, smiling a little at the idea.

She would quite enjoy running a small café – or a country hotel, that would be even better. She wondered if the five thousand pounds her brother had left her would be enough to buy her a small hotel of her own. Perhaps not but she might be able to find someone to be her partner. It was something worth giving serious thought.

She watched from the doorway as more guests came in and kissed Annabel. Most of them brought an offering of some kind, either wine or food they had made themselves. The war might be over but there was still difficulty about finding enough to feed everyone, though Annabel seemed to manage very well.

It was living in the country, Hetty supposed. Annabel had a lot of friends and they brought her gifts of game and little things from the farm that were smuggled under the counter as it were. It was a game the country folk played and had done throughout the war, pinching a few eggs or a pig here and there that the poor old ministry never knew existed. And of course, Annabel kept her own ducks and hens at the bottom of her very long garden. Over the years she had bought an extra bit of land and that had been devoted to a kitchen garden during the war, though Paul had plans for building extra accommodation there when things got better. He was always interested in expanding his business interests and might be interested in helping her to open a small hotel in France.

Annabel called her over to introduce her to a couple of young men; both of them were handsome and full of talk about themselves and what they were going to do now that the war was over. Hetty listened politely and made an excuse to leave them as soon as she could. Men like that bored her.

What kind of a fool was she? A wry smile touched her mouth; she needed the challenge of danger, a man who could not be led around on a chain, a man who dominated and led rather than trailed behind. She needed Stefan but she had thrown her chances away and she must forget him, take that place at art college, and get on with her life. It was so easy to decide but so much harder to get rid of this emptiness inside her, this longing for a man she would never see again.

She went out into the garden, seeking a little privacy. It was such a lovely night and the moon made it romantic. People called that a lover's moon, didn't they? She stared up at it, making a wish, then laughed at herself. There had been a time when the last thing she had needed was a moon! Oh damn! This wasn't doing her any good; she might as well go back to the party.

'Hetty? Your sister told me you would be here.'

Hetty felt the tingle run down her spine. It couldn't be! How could it be? Turning, she saw him standing there and her heart began to race wildly. Her mouth had gone dry and she couldn't move; she was turned to stone and had to wait as he came up to her. He was smiling, a hint of challenge in his eyes and yet there was also something more ... something uncertain, seeking. This was Stefan as she remembered him, strong, arrogant, proud – and yet there had been a subtle change. Was she imagining it or were there shadows beneath his eyes, signs that like her he spent restless nights when sleep just would not come?

'How are you, Hetty? I hope you didn't mind that I came out to find you?'

'No...' she swallowed hard. 'I'm just surprised. What are you doing here, Stefan?'

'Your brother-in-law invited me,' Stefan said. 'I telephoned earlier in the day and he said you were out but asked me to come this evening. I would have been here earlier but I was delayed.'

'Out? Yes, perhaps I was in the garden picking strawberries,' Hetty admitted after thinking about it. Her heart was hammering wildly as she fought for calm. 'But I meant here in England?'

'I was invited here by the British Government,' Stefan said. 'I have avoided it for as long as I could but they were most insistent. It seems they want to present me with a medal, take some pictures. Nonsense of course, but I wanted to see you so I gave in.'

'You wanted to see me ... why?' Hetty's mouth was dry, her knees trembling. Why was he looking at her like that, in that hungry, yearning way that made her insides turn to water? 'I thought...' She broke off, unable to go on.

'You thought you meant nothing to me?' Stefan's eyes were intent on her face. 'You thought I wanted to use you – like Henri and Pierre?'

'Aren't all men the same?' she asked but her voice was hoarse, merely a whisper.

'In many ways, yes,' he replied and his smile made her heart turn over. 'I shall not pretend that I am not arrogant or that I do not like my own way as often as I can get it – or that I am not inclined to be lazy sometimes.'

'Madame Arnoud told me never to marry a Frenchman because they were too lazy.'

'I am afraid that was good advice. We are spoiled by our women, you see. They do everything for us when we are children and then when we are older they expect us to change.' He shrugged expressively, his eyes meeting hers, challenging and yet pleading with her to understand. 'But there the resemblance to the others you have known stops. I do not want to use you, Hetty. I do not want an affair with you. I want you to marry me; I want you to be my wife.'

'I've decided I'm never going to marry.'

'But I shall change your mind for you – no?' His eyes were intent on her face. 'I think you love me, *chérie*. You will marry me one day.'

'I might,' Hetty said. She had no idea why she was holding back, but something inside her could not give in so easily. 'But then I might not. I will come to France with you. I will live with you – I'll be your partner. We will run a hotel together and live at the farm...'

'So that is why you brought the Comtesse's gift to you to my kitchen,' he said and grinned wickedly. 'You were planning to move in all the time. You were making it your house. When I went back there I saw you at every turn, haunting me, forcing me to remember, to admit that I still wanted you. Everywhere I turned you were there, mocking at me with those green eyes, witch's eyes. You have certainly bewitched me, Hetty. I could even smell your perfume, feel your presence in the house, as though your spirit haunted it as it haunted me. Did you do that on purpose, Hetty – was it your intention to drive me mad until I had to come looking for you?'

'It was a house I knew I could live in,' she admitted, responding to his teasing. 'I might perhaps be able to take the man who lives there as a part of the bargain – if you promise to help with the washing up.'

Stefan pulled a face of horror. 'You ask a great deal, Hetty – it would shame me in front of my friends. You ask *me* to do the washing up?'

It was impossible that a man who had fought and schemed against the enemy and

354

won so many fierce battles should be reduced to a pinafore and the washing suds – and Hetty gave in.

'Perhaps that is too much,' she said laughing now. Suddenly the world was brighter, life was worth living again with all its challenges and disappointments, all its risks. 'You must help with the cooking instead.'

'Ah, now that is something I can do,' he said, a wicked gleam in his eyes as he threw her challenge back at her. 'I shall cook and you will wash up.'

'Over my dead body! We share the cooking – and we'll hire someone else to wash up!'

Stefan's eyes danced with humour. 'I see I have found myself a clever wife. You have found the compromise I think.'

'A clever mistress perhaps.'

'You will marry me one day.'

'What makes you think that?' She threw down the gauntlet, her eyes bright.

'Because you love me and because the children will expect it. They will plead with you to marry their poor papa and you will give in, my darling.'

Hetty's laughter died. 'I do not think I can give you children, Stefan. I have never fallen for a child and there have been two other lovers in my life.'

'But they were not me,' he replied as if the answer were that simple. 'It was not meant that you should bear their children. You were meant for me. You are my woman and I shall give you the child you long for – yes?'

Hetty smiled, her eyes meeting his.

'Give me a child, Stefan, and when the doctor confirms I am pregnant I shall marry you.'

'There! I knew you would give in,' he crowed and grabbed her by the waist pulling her close to him. His kiss was passionate, hungry, demanding but also tender. He let her go and smiled down at her. 'So where is your room, *chérie*?'

'Why?' Hetty gazed up at him, her heart racing.

'Because the sooner I get you into bed, the sooner I can give you a child, my love.'

'You are so certain,' she said. 'Do you have children by other women?'

'Perhaps thousands,' he said and grinned at her. 'But I do not know of them – and perhaps I have saved them all for you.'

Hetty laughed as the joy swept over her. His confidence was impossible to resist and perhaps it would happen because Stefan willed it so. 'If I have you it will be enough,' she whispered. 'But I think we should slip away – go somewhere we can be entirely alone.'

'That is the most sensible thing you have said all night,' Stefan said, and taking her hand they began to run together round the side of the house to the car Stefan had left parked outside.

Annabel stood with Paul at the French window and smiled, watching them go. She looked up at Paul as his brows arched in enquiry.

'That was very clever of you, darling,' she

said. 'Pretending that Hetty was out when you knew all the time she was in the garden. But supposing he had turned your invitation down?'

'Well, I knew there had to be someone. If he had turned me down he wouldn't have been the one, but I had a pretty good hunch when he asked for her,' Paul said. 'There was something in his voice, a kind of longing, a need that I recognized. He was feeling the way I did when you hid yourself from me, Annabel. Besides, a woman like Hetty had to have someone waiting for her somewhere. The French may be a strange lot and we shall probably never understand them – but they can't all be blind.'

Annabel laughed. 'She looked happy didn't she? I wish we could have heard what they were saying.'

'I don't think we need to,' Paul replied. 'Judging from the way he looked at her I think we both know exactly where they are going.'

'You look beautiful,' Annabel said and kissed Hetty. She dabbed at her eyes and then laughed. 'I don't know why I'm crying. It's just that I never thought I would see you married.'

'No? Well, there was a time when I didn't either – but Stefan always gets his way, and a promise is a promise.'

'Did you really tell him you would only marry him if he gave you a baby?'

'Yes, but I might not have stuck to it if things hadn't turned out as they have.' Hetty smiled and placed her hands tenderly on her stomach, which was hardly showing the evidence of her condition. 'It was really because I couldn't believe that things would work out between us. I was afraid that Stefan would tire of me, find someone else, and I thought it wouldn't hurt so much if we weren't married.' But of course it would have hurt just as much, because now that she had given herself to him completely she could never bear to let him go.

'But surely you couldn't think he was like Henri?' Annabel looked amazed. 'You could not find two men as different as those two if you searched for a year, Hetty. I was never very happy about your relationship with Henri, though I knew you were in love with him – but Stefan is completely trustworthy. Both Paul and I like him very much.'

'Yes, he is rather wonderful,' Hetty said. 'I was an idiot not to trust him from the start but there were reasons – but don't tell him I said that, Belle. I don't want him getting too sure of himself. He's bossy enough as it is!'

'But in a nice way,' Annabel said and glanced at her watch. 'If you're ready we ought to be leaving for the church. Otherwise Stefan will think you're not coming after all.'

Hetty laughed. 'Don't be fooled by that charm. If I didn't turn up he'd come and fetch me! Stefan doesn't give an inch when he wants something – and it seems that getting his ring on my finger is priority for the moment.'

'Well, if you promised him...'

'For my sins,' Hetty said and laughed as she saw her sister's expression. 'Of course I want to marry him, Belle. I would be mad not to. I've never been this happy in my life. I have the house I've always dreamed of, a business that I love, a baby on the way – and a man that I adore. What more could I want?'

'I can't think of a single thing,' Annabel said with a smile. 'But I still think we should get a move on or we shall be late.'

Hetty was smiling as she drifted down the aisle in a cloud of white lace and silk. She had told Stefan it ought to be a civil wedding since they'd been living together for six months, but his answer was unequivocal.

'We're having a church wedding so that you can't wiggle out of it in a few months, Hetty. I'm a Catholic and once married I stay married.'

'Supposing I don't want that kind of marriage?'

'Then you'd better say quickly, because I shan't be changing my mind once you've agreed.'

'Well, as a matter of fact I like the sound of it,' Hetty said. 'I converted some years ago, though I haven't told my family that – but living in France it seemed the thing to do. Most of my friends were Catholics and I became interested in the rituals and the

359

churches. I like the richness and the colour.'

Deep down, Hetty liked the sense of commitment the church gave her, the feeling of belonging, of having someone care about what happened to her soul. She thought it came from the insecurity of her childhood, when all her mother had seemed to care about was appearances. It was one of the things that had drawn her to Adele, something they had shared.

The ceremony was longer than others she'd attended as a young woman, and she felt it was more binding. She glanced at Stefan once or twice but he was unsmiling and she wondered what was wrong. She knew him so well now that she could feel that he was on edge. Once she would have thought he had changed his mind about marrying her, but she knew him better than that. No, something else had disturbed him, but it wasn't a question she could ask in the middle of their ceremony.

It wasn't until all the photographs had been taken, the cake cut and the toasts drunk that she had a moment alone with him just before she went up to change out of her dress. He was taking her to the south for their honeymoon, which meant a long drive, so they were going only a part of the way that night and continuing the next day.

'Something is wrong,' she said. 'Don't tell me I'm mistaken, Stefan. I can sense it, feel it – what has happened to disturb you?'

'I didn't want to tell you yet,' he said. 'But

you'll imagine all kinds of things if I don't –
Pierre de Faubourg's body was found in the
grounds of the château this morning. He had
been blindfolded and shot through the head
from the back.'

Hetty made the sign of the cross over her
breast. 'God have mercy. It was an execution?'

'Yes. Everyone knew that he betrayed us. It
was bound to happen if he came back.'

'And of course he did – for a fortune that
was no longer there.'

'The Germans would have taken it if we'd
left it,' Stefan said. 'It went to help others
who had suffered losses during the war – to
the wives of men who died and to the families
of those who will never work again.'

'I told Louis you would know what to do
with it,' Hetty said and kissed him. 'You don't
have to tell me if you don't want – but did you
know about the execution?' Had he wanted
vengeance for the death of Fleur and the
others? His eyes met hers, holding them,
making her look into the clear depths, making
her see. He had explained about Fleur and
her childish crush on him, a love that he had
never returned, or taken advantage of, despite
the girl's attempts to seduce him.

'Do you think I would have ordered it on
the eve of our wedding?'

'No,' she said. 'I don't believe you would.
And that means we can forget about it. Pierre
got what he deserved in natural justice. As far
as I'm concerned the past is gone and

forgotten. I'm only interested in the future – with you.'

Stefan smiled at her. 'I thought you might still feel something for him despite everything.'

'No, I don't. I never loved him. He was charming and kind to me and I found him good company at times – but that's all it ever was, Stefan. I loved Henri when I was a girl and was blind to his faults – but the only man who could ever bring me real contentment is you.'

'You are happy?' he asked, his eyes searching her face. 'I know I pushed you into this wedding but I was afraid you might change your mind.'

'I am more than happy,' Hetty said. 'I am content. You can be wildly happy and yet at the same time not feel satisfied, be insecure and uneasy. With you I feel loved; that's something I haven't known before. I have everything I want of life, Stefan – and as long as we are together I always shall.'

'You could ask me for the moon and I would give it to you if I could,' he told her, his eyes intent on her face. 'I am arrogant and sometimes thoughtless, and I go all out for what I want – but I would do anything for you, Hetty.'

'Why should I wish for the moon when I've got you?' She laughed and pushed him away. 'Stop fretting, Stefan. I know your faults and I love them. It is you I love just as you are. If you were too soft with me I should lead you on a string like a tame bear.'

'That might be interesting, just for a change,' he said and grinned at her. 'Go and change then, my darling. The sooner we are on our way, the sooner I can have my wife to myself...'

Philip saw Georgie standing in the garden gazing up at the moon. It was full and rather beautiful and he hesitated before going out to her. There were moments when his wife liked to be alone, and he thought that this might be one of them, and yet it was a beautiful night and he wanted to share it with her.

Georgie turned as he approached her and he saw she was smiling. He had been afraid she might have been sad, thinking of the past, of people she had loved.

'I saw you and wanted to come and wish the moon down with you,' he said. 'Is that what you were doing, Georgie – wishing on the moon?'

'No, I gave that up long ago,' Georgie said and held out her hand to him. 'But I'm glad you've come, darling. I was just standing here thinking about how I was going to tell you my news.'

'What news?' he asked, a heart-stopping fear making him run cold all over. He was aware that she had been to the doctor that morning, and had been waiting for her to tell him what was wrong. 'Are you ill? Is it serious?'

'Well, it's quite serious,' Georgie said with a

teasing look. 'Because it means you're going to have to work even harder, Philip – in a few months there will be five of us to keep...'

'You're having a baby?' Philip felt the relief sweep over him and let out a Red Indian whoop that shattered the peace of the evening and sent the rooks flying from their roost. 'That's wonderful, darling. Absolutely wonderful.'

'I'm glad you think so,' Georgie said. 'I was a bit worried about telling you, but now it's all right.'

'Is it – really all right?'

'Yes, very much so,' she said and reached up to kiss him softly on the lips. 'This is what I want, Philip. You, the wonderful house you found for us, the children ... and peace. You're happy too, aren't you? You don't feel cheated or let down in any way?'

She held her breath, her fingers crossed behind her back. Once before she had thought everything was fine, but then Arthur had told her she'd cheated him and it had cut away the ground from beneath her feet. She didn't think she could bear it if Philip felt the same way. It wasn't that she was still yearning for Ben, but the memory was precious to her and it would always be there in her heart.

'Good lord!' He stared at her in amazement. 'I feel as if I've reached heaven right here on earth. What in blazes made you ask such a question?'

'A woman's foolish fancy at a peculiar time,' Georgie said and laughed. It was all

364

right at last. She'd found a safe harbour from the storms of life, and it was good between them in every way. 'I expect I shall want pickled onions with strawberry jam on toast very soon.'

'Really?' Philip smiled as she nodded. 'Well, I never. One thing is certain, Georgie darling. Life is never going to be dull with you and the children around.'

'Did it used to be dull?' she asked. 'Poor darling. Well, I can promise you it is never going to be that way again. Shall we go in and have a nice glass of sherry?'